BOOK ONE OF THE SAND TRAVELER DUOLOGY

OCEANS OF SAND

JESSICA FLORY

IMMORTAL WORKS
SALT LAKE CITY

Immortal Works LLC
1505 Glenrose Drive
Salt Lake City, Utah 84104
Tel: (385) 202-0116

Cover Art by Lenore Stutznegger
www.lenorestutz.com

ISBN 978-1-953491-56-5 (Paperback)
ASIN B0C5TXTSXL (Kindle)

For Devin. I love you, always.

For Devin. I love you, always.

1

———

NORAH

The ocean of sand is endless.

Everywhere I look, orange-gray sand waves peak and crash, spraying particles into the air. Soft flecks blow against my shins. The chill of the desert night squeezes my lungs with every breath.

I am a tiny dot in the center of the universe, a small being in infinity.

I glance back at Zadock. He sits at the stern of the boat, steering us by Shaking the waves. Sand swirls through his fingertips. Shaking is his sand gift, and it allows him to control the sand and guide the boat forward. I can't Shake the sand. Without him, I'd be helpless out here.

The moon rises on the eastern horizon, an enormous white orb conquering the sky. Her gravity is what pulls the sand, churns it into waves.

We crest another swell of sand. For a moment, all is still. I smile. Then we plunge down the other side, and my stomach drops. I grip the sides of the boat. Sand splashes over the edge and onto the bench where I'm sitting.

I turn to Zadock. "You doing ok back there?"

"I'm just fine, thank you." He grins. Zadock and I have been best friends our whole lives, but it's only recently that my heart flutters when he smiles. His hair is the color of the desert at dusk, his skin tanned from the sun. Like me, Zadock wears a soft camehl hair coat to keep warm. "Do you still know where we're going?" he says. "I can't see the plateau anymore."

"Of course." I tilt my head to look up at the stars. The moon blocks my view of half the sky, but I still locate several constellations to navigate by. The shower of glittering lights takes my breath away. Clusters of stars give the telltale sign of distant galaxies, and a hazy purple smear streaks across the sky. A nebula, giving birth to more stars.

Zadock follows my gaze. "Wow. It's incredible."

I find the Haridian star in the foot of the Sleeping Fox constellation. I point forward and slightly to our starboard side. "The plateau is that way."

"All right. Thanks, Nors." Zadock smiles and moves his arms in a circular pattern. The sand beneath the boat obeys, adjusting our heading. "I've got to get home soon, or Potah will feed me to the scorpions."

I frown. I wish we could stay out here forever. These stolen moments sailing the sands with Zadock are the best parts of my life.

Out here, I'm not broken.

"Yeah, ok. Let's head back." I lean over the railing and touch the sand. It's a fine powder, and it's still warm from baking in the sun all day. I let it slide through my fingers.

I catch Zadock watching me. "Do you miss him?" he asks.

I pull my hand in. "Yeah."

When my potah died three years ago, everything changed. The light went out of Motah's eyes. The joy went out of our home. And a week later, the unnatural famine that still plagues the villages today began. The plants just started to fail. It was like the desert mourned him, too, and it never stopped.

Potah. It used to be him taking me out to sail. Now, Motah refuses to even look at this boat, let alone allow me to sail it. If she knew we were out here, she would not be happy. Sailing the ocean of sand isn't exactly safe. The sand has a pulling, sucking quality to it. That was how Potah died—he fell off the boat during some rough waves. The sand towed him under, and I never saw him again.

As far as Motah knows, the *Norah* never leaves the boathouse on the edge of our plateau.

Even with the danger, I can't stay away. I love this too much. Potah used to take me on trading voyages to other villages, but Zadock and I can only steal an hour of sailing here and there whenever we can, just for the pleasure of it.

In the distance, our home plateau juts into the skyline, and on top of it, the village of To'Rahn. The black outline is stark against the orange and purple hues mixing in the darkening sky.

And then I see something on the horizon that I don't expect.

"Zadock!" I lean forward. "Is that...?"

Zadock squints and pushes hair out of his eyes. "Nors." His face falls. "That's a sandstorm."

I gasp. It's clearer now. The gray-orange sand is churning into one enormous cloud. The wind will pick up, and the speed of the sand will increase until it stabs like a thousand tiny knives. If we're out here when it hits...

"We've got to get back," I say. "Now."

Zadock pushes his hands forward, propelling the *Norah* toward the plateau, but I can already tell we're not going to make it. The storm is moving too fast. It's going to engulf To'Rahn, and then it's going to hit us.

Sheer panic overwhelms me and drives away any clear thought. Our boat will be overturned, we'll be sucked into the ocean of sand—

"Norah! What do we do?" Zadock cries. The sandstorm rages closer. In an eyeblink, it devours To'Rahn.

There was so little warning. I hope the weather wardens were able to get everyone inside in time. They know when a sandstorm is forming. I checked the schedule before Zadock and I left—this sandstorm was not expected.

I've never been caught out in a sandstorm before, not once during all the times Potah took me out with him.

We've got minutes until it hits us.

"Zadock!" I shout over the wind whistling past my ears. Particles of sand whip through the air, stinging my eyes. The boat has a small hold, a crawlspace beneath the deck for storage. We might be protected down there, but if the boat is overturned, we'd be trapped. *What to do?* "Encase us in sand. The boat should stay afloat, but you have to cover us."

Zadock's gaze flicks from me to the storm, and then he nods. "Ok." Zadock drops his control of the boat, and we pitch and rock. I fall forward and stumble into Zadock, and he catches me in strong arms. My heart leaps into my throat.

Stop it, Norah. You're in a crisis.

I push myself away. We sit cross-legged, facing each other, as close as we can be without touching. Zadock brings up sand around us in a swirling cascade, forming a dome. The darkness is smothering, and the rage of the wind is muffled.

The storm hits.

An enormous force punches the boat. I fall into Zadock's sand wall, but it holds strong. The waves toss us up and down, and my stomach lurches. We're ok. We're alive. As long as Zadock can keep it up.

It hits me that there is just a thin wall of sand between me and death. My heart thunders in my chest, feels like it's pressing into my throat. My breathing speeds up. We're going to die. We're going to be smothered by the sands just like—

Zadock's hand grabs onto my arm, and I choke back a sob. The panic ebbs.

"Norah." His voice is barely audible over the rage of the wind outside our dome. "We're ok."

I nod. I focus on taking deep breaths, one at a time. In and out.

My eyes adjust, and I can make out the outline of Zadock's face. The boat leaps up then slams down, and my stomach rolls. The sand continues to beat at our meager shelter, and my knees bump into Zadock's with the jolting of the waves.

Sandstorms can last hours. Sometimes only minutes. How long can Zadock keep this up?

"Norah. Norah." Zadock's hand runs up and down my arm. I shiver. "I'm here." He pulls me closer to him, and I practically fall into his lap against his chest.

My breathing slows, the pounding in my heart lessens. I bury my face in him, trying to hold back tears. I'm ashamed. I want to be strong.

Zadock's grip tightens around my back. "You're safe. I can hold this up for a long time."

I nod. Zadock holding me like this feels strange and amazing. I can't believe that it's taken me this long to realize how good-looking... how adorable...how perfectly wonderful he is.

Sand dusts my head and arms, and I lean away from Zadock and press my hand against the grit of the wall. It's squishy and soft, and I hurry to pull back before my hand breaks through. The dome is loosening. Zadock is losing his grip on it.

Fear knots in my throat, constricts my chest. "You—you can do this, Zadock. You can hold it." The muscles of his arms quiver around me.

This should be easy for him. He's the strongest Shaker our village has ever known. Why?

My breath catches.

I loosen my grip on his shirt and press away, leaning back until I touch the sand behind me.

Whatever I'm feeling, whatever he's feeling, he cannot feel it right now.

Love weakens sand gifts.

Love can lessen the power of a sand gift in the moment, and too much love overall can make someone lose their sand gift forever.

Is that what's happening? Could Zadock really feel that way about...me?

My heart leaps into my throat again, this time for another reason. But terror soon replaces whatever that was.

"You ok?" Zadock asks.

Despite how warm the air is, I miss his arms around me. "I'm ok. You?"

"Just fine." His voice comes out strained.

I close my eyes, shutting out the stifling blackness. The boat jolts, and a cry escapes my lips. My breath comes in rapid gasps.

"Norah," Zadock says. "It's going to be ok." He touches my cheek.

Tremors go through the sand behind me.

I savor the warmth of his skin against mine even as the wall behind me shifts and cracks.

My voice comes out in a whimper. "Please don't touch me."

He snatches his hand back, and a piece of my heart breaks. The wall of sand behind me resolidifies in an instant.

I long to tell him how I feel, even though that would be disastrous. "I'm sorry, I—"

"No." He clears his throat. "You're right."

I study his face in the dimness. It's hard and determined, focused on holding up the sand.

It hits me how completely I rely on Zadock while we're out here. He steers the ship, he moves the sand, and now, he's protecting me from the sandstorm. I couldn't do this without him.

I can't manipulate the sand. I can't move the boat. If I had been out here by myself when this sandstorm hit, I would've been dead in minutes.

Because I have no sand gift.

And, as far as I know, I'm the only one.

2

NORAH

We're lucky. The sandstorm lasts about fifteen minutes, but it feels like hours. Hours of being tossed around in the *Norah,* worried that the boat would be overturned. Hours of the sand pummeling our dome, of breathing the thick air, of longing to hold Zadock but knowing that it will never happen.

Finally, the shriek of the wind lessens. The ocean of sand calms into a gentle sway. The knots in my stomach loosen.

"Do you think I can take it down now?" Zadock asks.

"I think we're ok."

Zadock lowers his arms, and the dome dissipates little by little. I blink in the sudden light. Even low in the sky, the moon is so large and so close that the night is bright. The deep cold of the desert hits me like a slap, and I shiver.

I bury my face in my hands. I can't stop shaking. I want to stop. I *need* to stop.

"Norah." Zadock puts a hand on my shoulder, his touch light and hesitant. "We're ok. We're safe."

I can only nod as I keep my face hidden behind my fingers. After a moment, I lift my head and meet his eyes. They're a dark blue, but the color is paler than normal in the moonlight. "You did it. You saved us, Zadock."

Zadock half smiles and takes his hand away from my shoulder. A twinge of disappointment pokes me in the gut. "*You* saved us, Nors. I had no idea what to do."

I close my eyes for just a moment and savor the sweetness of being alive. A sandstorm. In the ocean of sand. And somehow, we survived.

"We've got to get back," I say, urgency filling my voice. "We've got to see if everyone's ok." *Please. My motah and little sister. Please say they made it inside in time.* I send the prayer to the moon goddess, Atoille. She's never heard any of my prayers for a sand gift, but I hope she hears this one.

Zadock works his arms to move the sand, propelling us toward the plateau in the distance. "I'm sure they're ok, Nors."

"Yeah," I say, but I chew my lip with dread.

Finally, we reach the plateau, a wall jutting from desert into the sky. To'Rahn, our home. Waves of sand crash and spray into solid rock. Without sand Shaking, we'd never be able to get a boat from the bottom to the top or vice versa.

Zadock creates a column of sand to lift the *Norah* up, higher and higher. The sand is chaos far below, and the sky is quiet far above. I love being held in limbo like this, like I'm between two worlds. Tonight, I can't savor the feeling because I'm sick with worry.

We reach the top of the plateau, and Zadock settles the boat onto the edge. I hop out, scanning the expanse of flat sand that separates the village from the plateau's drop-off, expecting and dreading to see bodies. There's nothing—not here, anyway. Dust blowing in the breeze, a few twisted brown trees and withered cacti. The guard tower that looks out over the ocean of sand is empty, the boathouse deserted.

Zadock guides the boat over the sand and into its slot in the boathouse, a shelter with a few dozen other trading boats, all modest in size. Not like the fleets of ships I've heard that some other plateaus boast. Regardless, trade has all but halted between the desert nations. The famine has stricken us all.

I meet Zadock's eyes, and we take off in a run toward the village. Candles flicker in a few windows, but otherwise, everything is quiet. *They've got to be ok. Please let them be ok.*

I expect Zadock to head to his home in the merchant section of To'Rahn, but he stays with me, and I'm glad.

We pass rows of houses, humble structures built of quartz framework with clay and hardened cactus fibers filling in between. Those who have the sand gift of Forging can transform sand into quartz or crystal, taking its basic molecular structure and altering it. Only the finest homes in To'Rahn are actually made of wood.

We race through dusty streets, particles of sand floating about a foot off the ground, swirling around my feet. The sand is responding to the strong pull of the moon's gravity. I feel it in my footsteps as well. I am lighter, and my strides take me farther.

The moon is in our sky two weeks out of every month, and everything feels the extra tug of her gravity. Sand floats. Footsteps bounce. Then Atoille orbits around the other side of our world. For two weeks, everything feels heavier, and the ocean of sand is calmer. But for now, I'm grateful for anything that can make my feet fly even a bit faster.

People emerge from their homes, blinking in the moonlight. "Is everyone ok?" I call. I get a few nods. So far, no dead, which is a miracle from Atoille. Maybe because the sandstorm happened at dusk when most people were already in their homes.

My breathing is labored, but I can't stop running. Just a few more streets until we make it home.

We pick up the pace around a corner, and then I see it—a black shape lying on the road. A woman steps into her doorway and her hands go to her mouth in shock. "No. No no no no." She rushes to the shredded lump of tissue and bone, falling to her knees in a pool of blood. She screams.

My stomach heaves, and suddenly I can't take any more. The jolting, the jarring, the running. This. I turn to the side and vomit.

Zadock puts a hand on my back, and I spit and wipe my mouth. "C'mon." I stumble into a run again, passing the mourning woman. Zadock stops to help her and give her a bit of comfort, but then he's running again next to me. My family. I have to get to my family.

We turn down another street, hear more screams and cries. My eyes glaze over two more bodies in the street, one of them small. Sickness rises in my throat again, but I choke it down.

How could this have happened? The weather wardens are dedicated to their work of tracking and predicting sandstorms. They've never been wrong, to the point where sandstorms are a mere inconvenience, a foreseen time when everyone has to go into their homes and wait. How could there have been a mistake?

At last, we're at my door, a modest home nearly identical to the others around it, and I burst inside.

"Motah!" I call. "Shrey!" The kitchen is empty. Embers burn in the hearth. An empty stewpot lies on its side on the quartz countertop. Where are they? I rush down the hallway and throw aside the curtain that leads into the bedroom that my little sister and I share.

Relief washes over me. Zadock is right behind me, and I almost crumple backward into his arms. Motah and Shrey are there, huddled together on the floor, Shrey shaking and crying in Motah's arms.

That Motah is holding Shrey in and of itself is a small miracle. Motah has never held me like that. Love weakens sand gifts, even loving your own children.

"You're ok." I sag to the floor, everything drained out of me. "You're ok."

"Norah!" Shrey shrieks and rushes to throw her arms around me. I hold her tight and stroke her blonde curls. Children need love to thrive, up until a certain age, anyway. Shrey's still young, only eight years old. She needs me. She needs me to love her.

Motah looks from Zadock to me, and the worry eases from her

face. "We thought—" She swallows. "We didn't know where you were."

"We were out sail—" Zadock begins. I elbow him in the shin, and he cuts himself off.

"We were in the street," I say, "but Zadock made a dome of sand to protect us. We're ok. We're ok." I whisper it again in Shrey's ears because her cries haven't stopped. She's always been terrified of sandstorms. Potah was the only one who could calm her down.

Motah brushes wisps of dark hair from her face. She touches the turquoise jade necklace Potah brought back for her on one of our trading voyages. She never takes it off. "I'm glad you're all right." Motah turns to Shrey. "That's enough, Shreyen."

I frown and tighten my grip, but Shrey's cries have softened, and she pushes away from me.

Motah moves her gaze to Zadock. "You better see if your family needs you."

Zadock nods and then looks at me. "Are you ok, Nors?"

My heart melts. Atoille help me, what is happening? "Yeah, I'm ok. Thanks, Zadock. Thanks for everything." He saved my life tonight.

Zadock jogs out of our home. Motah lets out a sigh and gets to her feet. She is tall and striking, beautiful and imperious. Capable. Strong. It's no wonder she serves on the village council.

She is everything I want to be. And to her, I am nothing but a crushing disappointment.

Motah extends her hands and helps Shrey and me up. "Come, girls. Let's see what we can do to help."

3

NORAH

I bake under the sun's heat, watching Zadock spar with one of our classmates. Puffs of sand rise when Zadock or his opponent move in the open circle before me. The sand floats in the air, a mist swirling around Zadock's feet. Atoille is visible on the horizon even in daylight, so close I can count her craters. My fifteen classmates and I sit on the edge of the arena.

I was hoping school would be canceled, with everyone dealing with the aftermath of the sandstorm, but we were lucky that the death toll was relatively low. Zadock's family is fine, thank Atoille. A few students are home today, but most of us are here, carrying on as usual.

Our teachers, Ki'Rhen Hainan and Ki'Rhen Dalayn, explained the strange storm away as "unusual weather patterns this time of year." Which is a load of speck, but everyone's scared, and tensions are high anyway because the famine has gone on so long. No one questions them.

Hainan and Dalayn watch the sparring and take notes from the sidelines. The Ki'Rhen are the village religious leaders and teachers, distinct from the council but partners in governing To'Rahn. The notes Hainan and Dalayn record will help the Ki'Rhen and the council decide who will be Anointed with who when we graduate in two weeks. Dalayn's motherly face creases in concentration, and Hainan strokes his long white beard.

My fingers grip the bench. The Anointing. There will be a ceremony, and we'll be placed into partnerships for life. The decisions are made based on sand gift strength, to keep the genetics of the gifts strong. The Anointing is not an actual wedding. It's a promise to wed, where neither party has any say about it, and neither can back out.

Zadock lifts his arms. He plants his feet in a powerful warrior's stance, knees bent, foundation solid. There are four types of sand gifts—Shaking, Absorbing, Extracting, and Forging—and Zadock is the best Shaker our village has seen in generations.

To be Anointed with him... I can't even think it. It won't happen.

Zadock moves his arms, and the sand moves with them, forming a wall to block his opponent's way. To beat his sparring partner, Zadock either has to pin him with sand or incapacitate him in some other way.

Zadock was raised by the Ki'Rhen. His parents chose to give him up when he was born to reduce the risk of them feeling love for him, as many people do. Some choose to raise their own children, like I was raised by my motah and potah. Zadock and I moved in different circles and lived on opposite sides of the village, yet we were drawn to each other as schoolmates, and we've always been inseparable. He made it easier for me. Being different.

Zadock is everything to me, but I can never tell him that.

His sand gift is important to him. It's part of who he is. If he knew how I felt, if there was even a chance that he felt the same way, he could lose it. And the village needs him more than ever. The famine is relentless, and the desert nations are getting desperate. There are whispers that war may be coming.

Last night during the sandstorm, something kept Zadock's gift from working completely, and we could have died because of it. It's foolish, but my heart swells when I think that Zadock might have been feeling something for me.

With the Anointing happening, we don't have a say, anyway. So I keep my feelings inside and do my best to smother them.

Felhar, Zadock's sparring partner, dodges around Zadock's wall. Felhar throws up a screen of dust to blind Zadock, but Zadock takes control of the screen and pushes it away. They continue to circle in the arena, trading blows of sand.

Saeri lets out a low whistle from where she sits beside me. "Speck. Zadock is *good.*"

I nod. "He's been working hard."

"He's so cute, isn't he?" Saeri's cheeks turn pink, though it could just be the heat of the sun. "And strong. Do you think I have a chance at being Anointed with him?" She twists a strand of ebony hair around her finger.

I stiffen. Saeri is the closest friend I have besides Zadock. She's never cared about me being different the way some of our other classmates have. The jealousy that flares up inside me is useless and unfounded.

We can't choose, anyway. It doesn't matter how either of us feels.

"Maybe," I say. Saeri is a strong Shaker as well, so she actually does have a good chance at being paired with him. The thought makes me nauseous.

With a cry, Zadock shoots a spear of sand toward Felhar, hard and fast. A skilled Shaker can sharpen the sand so that it can cut like a knife.

Felhar crosses his arms in an X in front of his chest and puts up a wall in time to block.

Zadock forms a long whip of sand. It lashes forward and tears through Felhar's defenses, smashing the wall to dust.

Felhar stumbles and waves his arms to Shake, but Zadock shoves both hands forward and sends an onslaught of sand right into Felhar's stomach. He lands on his back with a cry.

"All right." Ki'Rhen Dalayn steps forward into the circle, her hands outstretched to stop the sparring. She beams at Zadock with pride. He lowers his arms.

Dalayn's pen slips from her hand, and she absently Shakes the sand to lift it, but the pen only wiggles and hovers an inch off the ground. She sighs and bends down to pick it up.

"Poor Dalayn," Saeri whispers. "She used to be so strong."

I frown. Dalayn was always the Ki'Rhen who showed us the most kindness and—I guess it would be love—as kids. It's sad that it's caught up with her. Every so often, gossip spreads through the village about who is showing too much love, about who may lose their sand gift forever. People obsess over it, driven by the fear that it could happen to them.

My gaze goes to the statue behind our teachers. A crystal woman, about double my height with long, flowing hair, sparkles in the sunlight. She represents Atoille's spirit. Her face looks over the practice arena, one hand outstretched toward us and the other reaching for the sky.

One eye socket glows with a blue gem—the sacred moonstone of Atoille. The other socket, creepily enough, is empty. It's said that the stone was given to our ancestors by Atoille herself, a gift that made sand magic possible. That empty eye gave me nightmares when I was little.

Zadock straightens out of his fighting stance, breathing hard. Saeri grabs the waterskin at her side and hurries over to him. Zadock looks at her with surprise, but he takes the water. My teeth grind together.

Felhar stands and Shakes sand from his clothes, scowling.

"Zadock is the victor." Dalayn smiles and Zadock raises one fist, grinning. His eyes meet mine, and I smile back.

"Zadock and Felhar will continue sparring," Ki'Rhen Dalayn says. "Henli." She nods to another student. "You're on Felhar's team."

My eyes open wide. "They're making him fight a Shaker and a Forger?"

Saeri returns to her seat next to me, looking pleased with herself.

"They're trying to test him. When the To'Morat attack, they'll attack with both."

"We don't know for sure if they'll attack."

Saeri turns to me with a conspiratorial lift of her eyebrows. "Oh, they're going to attack. My potah has been talking about it. The famine has gotten so bad that the To'Morat are pillaging other plateaus and taking their resources to survive. They haven't hit To'Rahn yet, but it's only a matter of time."

I glance back at the Atoille statue and send another silent prayer, yet another plea for the famine to end. If we are attacked, I will be helpless. There will be nothing I can do to defend Shrey or Zadock.

The thought is terrifying.

Henli stands and ties her hair back with a band. She walks forward with her nose in the air and then trips on her way to the fighting arena. Saeri covers a laugh, but Zadock steps forward and helps Henli up with an encouraging word.

Saeri rolls her eyes. "Henli's such a klutz."

"Yeah," I say. "She's also the fastest Forger in our class."

Zadock readies himself. Sand swirls through his fingertips and around his feet. Zadock is strong, but the Ki'Rhen have never pitted him against two at once before.

Felhar and Henli take their places opposite Zadock in the circle. Hainan raises one arm and then lowers it. "And...begin."

Felhar darts forward. He brings up a screen of sand and lashes it toward Zadock. Zadock wrenches the sand out of Felhar's grip and throws it back. At that same instant, Henli places her hands on the ground and Forges.

The sand ripples, glistening and crystallizing. From Henli's fingertips and spreading outward, the ground morphs into a smooth pool of quartz. Weaker Forgers need more time to transform the sand, but for Henli, the reaction is almost instantaneous.

"Wow," Saeri says. "That was quick."

Zadock slips on the slick surface and barely stops himself from falling. Only the sand behind Felhar and Henli is unaffected. Zadock swirls his hands, yanking sand from behind his opponents to create a platform. He leaps onto it and flies above them. Felhar scowls and stretches his arms, trying to take control of Zadock's sand, but Zadock continues to fly. He smiles, his face determined, and I can't help it that my heart leaps with him. Speck. When did the muscles in his arms get so well-defined? Why am I noticing things like this?

"Atoille's ashes," Saeri says. "He is so dreamy."

"Careful, Saeri," I whisper. "You're sparring next. Don't let your feelings get in the way."

She tosses her hair over one shoulder. "Don't worry. I've got it under control. I can appreciate a good-looking boy without feeling any love for him."

Love.

Is that what's wrong with me?

Dalayn made the sacrifice to give the children love, and eventually, her sand gift was permanently reduced. Love is the reason why after school, I'm usually assigned to help care for the Ki'Rhen children. Because I'm the only one with nothing to lose.

Potah's Shaking did get weaker over the years, but he always told Shrey and me that it was worth it. He loved us. He loved me.

Motah, well. She's kept her sand gift strong.

Felhar hurls spears of sand at Zadock, and Henli turns them to quartz. She's good enough that she doesn't have to be touching the sand to affect it. The quartz spears are stronger and faster, but Zadock dodges out of the way. My fingernails grind into the bench.

Ki'Rhen Hainan is an Absorber. He can take energy from the sand and use it to heal, and he's watching from the sidelines. But still.

Felhar creates his own platform of sand and jumps aboard, long blonde hair blowing back in its tail. He sails through the air, trading and deflecting blows of sand with Zadock. Henli turns each of Felhar's sand knives into quartz so Zadock can't take control of them. A Shaker can only move sand.

Sweat glistens on Zadock's face. He's focused, dodging blows and sending some back.

"Go, Zadock," I breathe. "You got this."

A quartz knife tears through the skin on Zadock's shoulder, and he yelps and grips his arm. Blood leaks through his fingers.

I shoot to my feet. "He's hurt!"

Dalayn frowns and stands, but Hainan holds out a hand, and she steps back. Saeri pulls me down.

Felhar flies forward, closing in. Then, with lightning speed, Zadock throws a spear of sand toward Henli. She shrieks and stumbles out of the way.

Now! C'mon, Zadock!

Zadock yanks away the platform of sand that his opponent floats on. Felhar falls, screaming. Right before he hits, a cushion of sand forms to catch him, and I know it's Zadock's doing. Felhar was way too out of control.

Zadock lowers himself to the ground. Felhar climbs off the platform, scowling. Henli turns the quartz arena to sand again before bringing herself to her feet.

"Zadock Penvaren is our victor!" Ki'Rhen Hainan steps into the circle of sand and takes one of Zadock's hands to raise it. Zadock grins and meets my eyes. I smile back.

Students clap, and Saeri cheers. Hainan takes a handful of sand from the ground and places it on Zadock's hurt shoulder. A soft glow emits from the sand. Hainan removes his hands, and the bleeding has stopped, the skin has become whole. The sand is gone, Absorbed by Hainan's healing.

"Thanks, Ki'Rhen Hainan," Zadock says. He clasps hands with Felhar. "Good fight."

Felhar nods, jaw clenched. "You too."

Zadock takes Henli's hand next. "Well done. You made things really tough for me."

She blushes and smiles. All three take seats on the other side of the circle, where the other students who have finished sparring wait.

"We're up, Erno," Saeri says.

The boy sitting next to Saeri gets his fingernail out of his mouth with a jolt.

"Erno and Saeri," Ki'Rhen Hainan says.

Saeri looks back at me with a wave and then strides to the center of the circle. Erno follows her, dragging his feet. He's a Shaker, like Saeri and Zadock, but not nearly as strong. Sand gifts can be honed and skill increased through practice, but there is an inherent strength that won't change. Unless love gets in the way.

Instead of watching Saeri beat Erno to sand shards, I turn my attention to the fire ants marching along the sand at my feet. They are deep orange in color, perfect for blending into the desert sand. At this hour, the ground is scorching hot, hot enough to burn bare skin. But these ants keep walking along. They're among the only creatures who can stand the temperature, but if they stop walking, they'll burn to death. I've always liked watching them.

Out of the corner of my eye, I see an inverted cone shape in the sand about the length of my shoe. The center is filled with bits of quartz and other shiny things. I jolt back.

One of the fire ants marches straight to the edge of the cone, attracted by the glittering quartz.

A scorpion darts out of the sand. It has a clear, white exoskeleton and yellow-pink innards, a sharp stinger on the tail, and two long front pincers. The deathstalker scorpion. I shudder. Without treatment from an Absorber, the poison from a deathstalker sting can kill a man in less than an hour.

The scorpion uses its front pincers to sweep sand toward the top of the cone, and the ant slides down to the scorpion's jaws.

Before I can think too much about it, I scoop up the hot sand with the poor ant inside and shove it to safety. The deathstalker lashes out with its barbed tail, missing me by an inch.

I sit back on the bench, my hands burning from the heat of the sand. I shake them out and blow on my fingers. Ugh, why did I do that? It was just an ant.

"Saeri is the victor!" Dalayn declares, and I look up to see that

Erno is struggling to stand after being half-buried by a mound of sand. Saeri waves her hand, and the sand flies off him. Hainan steps forward to check Erno for burns or other injuries. Saeri turns on her heel and bounces toward the opposite side of the arena, where she sits right next to Zadock. She smiles and starts chatting away.

My jaw clenches.

Ki'Rhen Dalayn glances toward the students who haven't fought yet. I'm next in line. Dalayn gives me a sympathetic smile. "Sorry, Norah," she mouths. I look down and blink moisture from my eyes. She passes over me and moves on to the next pair of students.

The next two to spar are Extractors, so they head off to the side of the arena where weapons are stored on a rack. They grab spears tipped with quartz. Extracting is not as rare as Absorbing but not as common as Shaking or Forging. The energy they take from the sand increases their speed and strength.

I sigh. It gets old, sitting here day after day while everyone else practices with their sand gifts. But I sit and watch because it's what Motah wants me to do. The Ki'Rhen have offered to let me use this time to study something else, but Motah refuses, and her place on the council ensures that her opinion holds weight. She still believes that someday my sand gift will manifest and that I have to prepare by watching everyone practice.

I let out a sigh of exasperation. Though I still pray to Atoille, though I still study the movements of Shakers, Forgers, Absorbers, and Extractors alike, I've long given up hope.

4

ZADOCK

I push food around my plate at the dinner table. My mind wanders
to Norah. How she looked today at school, her dark hair short
and straight, her eyes deep brown and shining. The rare smiles she
seems to reserve just for me. And how Ki'Rhen Hainan spoke of the
Anointing, only two weeks away. *Atoille have mercy.*

"Zadock," Potah says with a smile, "how did your studies go
today?"

Potah already knows the answer to this. He asks the question
because Saeri Rahlen and her family are here eating with us. Saeri
glances at me from across the quartz dinner table. Black hair curls in
waves down her back. Her parents, Hael and Aiyan, sit on either side
of her.

My motah sits next to me, picking at her food with a shaking
hand. Everything about her is delicate. Fingers, features. Dark circles
plague the space beneath her eyes. She hasn't said much the entire—
two months?—it's been since my parents decided to take me back
from the Ki'Rhen. And her hands tremble a lot. I worry about her,
but I'm not sure how to approach this woman who gave me up as a
baby and then only recently decided she wanted me back.

I'm not bitter.

"Fine, Potah." I try to smile for Potah's sake, but something about this whole setup is just wrong. Potah is on the council, so he will help decide who I'm Anointed with. It's like he's taking stock of my options. But I don't want to be Anointed with Saeri.

I stir my coconut milk-braised sand lizard. Our maid, Chassi, does a good job, but sometimes I miss Ki'Rhen Dalayn's cooking, simple though it was.

The dining room is opulent, spacious, and shining, light reflecting off a crystal chandelier hanging overhead. Potted cacti and decorative plants line the walls, and the setting sun can be seen through an enormous glass window that takes up almost the entire western wall, an extraordinary decadence. I'm not used to any of this.

"Surely better than fine!" Hael says in a brusque voice that matches his physique. "We on the council have heard almost nothing else than what an intelligent boy you are." Hael grins, showing lizard meat in his teeth.

Saeri looks up at me with pale blue eyes that contrast against her black hair. She smiles and winks before looking down at her meal again. Heat creeps into my cheeks.

"Could you pass me the salt, Saeri?" Aiyan asks. Her nose is sharp and stern like a desert hawk's beak. The way she looks at me is similar. Our salt bowl is within arm's reach from where she sits.

Saeri stretches out her arm. The floor is so clean that it's eerie—thanks, Chassi—but there is a crystal vase in the corner that Potah keeps full of sand. Two prongs of it swirl from the vase, and Saeri brings them over to the table. Each tendril wraps around the bowl and moves it across the table, not spilling a drop, to place it in front of Aiyan.

I raise my eyebrows. Strength in Shaking is genetic, but control like that only comes with practice.

"Thank you." Aiyan takes the spoon and sprinkles salt over her meat.

"Saeri is also doing well in school, I hear," Motah says. She lifts her cup for more of the tea she's always drinking.

Chassi steps forward to refill Motah's cup and then resumes her place in the corner. I blink. I'm still not used to her lurking there all the time.

"Yes, yes," Hael barks. "Her studies are coming along nicely. A little too nicely if you ask me. Saeri should spend less time on books and more time practicing Shaking."

"What need has she?" Aiyan says. "She is already quite skilled."

Saeri blushes and glances at me, and I try to smile back. Thoughts of Norah keep popping up in my head. I take a bite of meat, tender and flavored of coconut. I look back at Chassi and give her a covert thumbs-up. She grins, round cheeks shining.

"She is very skilled." Potah cuts into his boiled plantain. "I could use more Shakers like her in my quartz and glass business. Even though times are difficult, sand still needs to be shaped for the Forgers."

"Yes." Hael nods and reaches for the salt bowl over his wife, who gives him a sideways glare. "Harvest is approaching, and yet there's nothing to harvest. Nothing is growing, even though the rains keep the canals full."

Potah frowns, thin brows making a crease. His hair is sandy blond, like mine. But where mine curls into a hopeless mess, his is stiff and straight, hanging to his shoulders. "The plateau walls are eroding at unprecedented rates, and sandstorms are coming at odd times, something that can't be accounted for by a simple famine. A hard year is ahead for all of us."

I clear my throat. Potah will be pleased if I am part of the conversation. "What will it mean if the walls keep eroding so quickly? Will the village have to find a different plateau?"

Potah chews for a moment. "That's a difficult decision the council will have to make if it comes to it."

"Traveling the sands is dangerous, and relocating expensive," Hael adds. "That will only happen as a last resort."

"But it has happened before," Aiyan says. "Not for generations, but it can be done."

"Are there any habitable plateaus left that we know of?" I ask.

"A difficult question," Potah says, "since so much of the ocean of sand is unexplored. But, if it comes down to it, there are other oceans of sand. It would be quite a journey, but if To'Rahn erodes away, we may have no choice."

Saeri glances around the table. "Isn't it strange? The famine has gone on for over three years. The plateau is eroding faster than ever. Plants fail, even though the rains still come. Why is this happening?"

"An excellent question, daughter," Hael says. "One we would all like answered."

Potah sips water out of a crystal glass. "Quite right. I have been looking into it myself."

"Have you discovered anything?" Aiyan asks.

Potah pauses a moment. "No. I haven't."

Hael guffaws. "Now if only Atoille's missing eye could be found, wouldn't that solve things?" He takes an enormous bite of food.

Potah waves a hand. "Really, Hael? That's a legend. To'Rahn is in possession of the only moonstone."

"Yes, yes. You're right." Hael's eyes twinkle. "But have you ever been to the ocean of water? That's where the stories say the moonstone must be. So mysterious!"

Potah's smile is strained. "No. I've never been."

Motah takes tiny bites of plantain, leaving the meat untouched. She stays silent, and Potah doesn't try to draw her into the conversation. I tune it out, focusing on my plate and ignoring Saeri's bright eyes staring at me.

When Chassi clears away the dessert dishes—dessert!—I take a deep breath and look up at Saeri. "Would you like me to show you our rooftop garden?"

Saeri beams and stands. "Yes!" Aiyan eyes her sideways, and she adds, "Thank you."

I glance at Potah, and he smiles. I flush with pride. But, speck, now I have to take Saeri up and spend time with her. Alone.

Saeri walks around the table and holds out her hand like she expects me to take it. I freeze. Potah nods, and so I take Saeri's hand and guide her toward the stairs that lead up to our roof. My stomach squirms.

Norah.

I lead Saeri up the stairs and drop her hand as soon as we reach the top.

"Well, here it is." The garden covers our entire roof, with a stone path winding its way through the bone-dry plants. Most of the plants are functional—this is where Chassi picks our herbs and bristlebrush fruits—but many are planted just for their beauty.

Of course, it's not very pretty right now. "Sorry," I say. "Potah says the plants usually look better than this. But with the famine, they all wilted." In the two months I've lived here, everything's been scraggly and brown.

We walk down the path past sad-looking bushes and shriveled, flat cacti.

"The sky is gorgeous," Saeri says, looking at the dusky orange sunset. Atoille's outline, rising on the eastern horizon, becomes sharper and clearer when the sun goes down. "And it's nice to get out of the house."

I smile and nod.

"You were amazing today," Saeri says. "I can't believe the Ki'Rhen made you fight a Shaker and Forger both."

"Uh. Thanks."

We round a bend in the path and come to a fountain that's as tall as our knees. Water gushes out of crystal forged into a twisting pattern.

Saeri's eyes widen. "Wow."

I nod. It's a ridiculous extravagance. "You did, uh, really well today, too."

"Thank you!" Saeri loops her arm through my elbow before I can do anything. I swallow, and we continue to walk down the path. We reach the edge of the roof and look out over the city, the flat rooftops extending out to the edge of the plateau, the orange sand turning gray in the dimming light.

Saeri's breath catches, and she leans on the railing. "It's beautiful."

I nod. Besides the several-story buildings where the Ki'Rhen-raised children are housed, our home is the tallest in the city.

Saeri turns toward me. "Can I ask you a question?"

"Errr..."

"Do you ever think there's something wrong with our system?" She throws up her hands. "I mean, come on, shouldn't we be able to choose who we marry? I don't want to be partnered with someone I don't like. For life. That is just speck. Who thought of these rules?" Saeri puts her hands over her face. Her voice comes out muffled. "The Anointing Ceremony is in half a moon cycle. Just half! What if I'm partnered with Erno Rofort? What would I do then?"

I blink. "Yeah..."

"What are we supposed to do?" She peeks through her fingers.

"Umm..."

Saeri huffs and turns to walk back down the path. "I'm cold. Let's go back inside."

I follow her, hurrying to catch up.

That was weird.

"You're right," I say. "It is specking scary. Not to know who you're going to spend the rest of your life with."

She glances at me, and, for some reason, she blushes. "Exactly my point."

"But, I mean, they can't let us choose, right?" I shrug. "If you feel...love, there goes your sand gift, and then who would defend the village? And there's always genetics to think about. It's important to keep the sand gifts strong." *Atoille, I sound like Ki'Rhen Hainan.* I refrain from smacking myself in the face.

Saeri stares at me for a moment before shaking her head. "Of course. You're right."

I pull open the hatch that leads back into the house. "After you."

She gives me a smile before heading back inside. I follow her down the steps and let out a quiet breath. I'm glad that that's over. Potah will be pleased.

5

NORAH

"Norah! What did you and Zadock do today?" Shrey bounds into our home, throwing aside the woven cacti fiber door that keeps the blowing sand at bay. Her blonde curls seem to float around her head, especially during these two weeks that Atoille is in the sky. She's eight years old but short for her age. I think she'll always be a baby to me.

I can't help but smile from where I stand at the counter, peeling and slicing plantains. Motah shells spiny bristlebrush fruits at our quartz kitchen table. She gives me a look, one eyebrow raised. I drop the smile. Motah knows how much I care about Shrey, and she disapproves. Shrey has a sand gift. She still has a chance to be strong.

"Shreyen, come and help me with this," Motah says.

Shrey groans but drops her school bag and comes to help. She collapses into a chair beside Motah and grabs one of the fruits.

I chop off the stem of a plantain a little harder than necessary. "School was pretty boring. Then Zadock helped bring water up from the well, and I gathered herbs from the grow walls. Nothing too exciting."

"Ouch!" Shrey stares at her finger where one of the fruit spines has stabbed into her skin and broken off. I hurry to her side, ready to help her, but Motah holds up a hand. "Let her do it."

Shrey reaches underneath the table and scoops up a handful of sand from the floor. She cups it over the thumb that's bleeding, closes her eyes, and takes a breath. The sand glows and dissipates. Shrey opens her eyes and shrieks with delight, showing Motah her hand. "I did it!" The cut has healed, and she holds the spine in her palm.

"Well done." Motah gives Shrey a nod of approval.

Shrey beams. She slides the fruit spine into her pocket, then meets my eyes and places one finger over her lips. I smile and keep my mouth shut. We both know what Motah will do if she finds Shrey's collection of things that have stabbed her. Even showing too much love for objects is not allowed. Though why Shrey couldn't think of other things to collect is beyond me.

Out of the corner of my eye, I see Motah studying me, a frown on her face. Her dark eyes are full of concern.

"You're worried," I say. "Did the council discover something? There have been so many meetings lately."

Motah pauses. Her long dark hair is loosely braided, a few wisps escaping. Motah's face is lean and hard, at odds with large brown eyes and lashes that graze her cheeks. She is stunning. She could ask the council and the Ki'Rhen to assign her a new Anointed partner, but she hasn't. "The whole council is worried, trying to find a solution to the famine. The weather."

I know before I speak what a useless question it is, but I say it anyway. "Is there anything I can do?"

Motah stares at me for a moment before answering. "No. But thank you." She continues to peel. Shrey helps, watching for spines more carefully this time.

"I'm glad you made yourself useful at the grow walls today, Norah," Motah says.

I continue to chop, keeping my expression steady. Was that supposed to be a compliment?

"Did school go well?" Motah meets my eyes. "Did anything happen?"

I bite back a sigh. I get this question about once every moon cycle. For whatever reason, Motah still has hope that my gift will show.

"Nothing happened. Motah, I've been thinking..." I focus on my knife, made of quartz, like almost everything else in our village. Only the wealthy can afford real metal and real wood when they're so scarce, and it's simple for Forgers to turn sand into quartz.

Atoille, this is painful to say. "At school, it's...difficult...watching the other kids train with their sand gifts." Just saying that, how hard this is day after day, feels like I'm peeling back the layers of my heart and exposing them to her. But if I can get her to change her mind, it will be worth it.

Motah's hands slow, but I keep my eyes on the woven cactus fiber cutting mat. "Sitting there and watching my classmates practice while I can't—" I swallow. "I do want to be useful." I meet Motah's gaze. "Please, Motah. Let me train with the spear. I can still fight and defend To'Rahn. I want to—"

"Norah." Motah's voice is hard. She sets down the fruit she's peeling. Shrey glances between Motah and me. "You will continue to go to school. You will continue to watch the other students practice. Unless you're an Extractor, you won't need a spear. Someday your gift will show."

I set down the cutting knife. "No, it won't." I've never challenged her on this before. I've always accepted her word. It was a comfort to me when I was five, six, seven years old. I knew she was right, that even though I was late, someday my gift would show.

I do my best to keep my voice calm. "Motah, *no one* has ever shown a sand gift at this age. I'm different. There's something wrong with me." Stupid specking tears start pooling in my eyes. If only I could make her understand, if only I could reach her. I could be truly useful if she'd let me. "I'm different, and no lack of love is going to change that."

Shrey has stopped peeling, and her teeth are nibbling on her bottom lip. Motah opens her mouth, but I push on. "If not the spear, I could work on trading ships and sail the sands like Potah—"

"No. I will not allow you to sail the sands."

"I will never have a sand gift!" Saying the words out loud is like a stab in the gut. "But I can do other things if you just give me a chance—"

Motah's eyes darken, and I close my mouth. Shrey scoots back her chair. The sand that floats about a foot off the ground rises even higher around Motah, shifting and swirling in patterns. "You will not fight. You will not sail."

I unclench my teeth and press on. "Potah knew. Potah knew that I would never have a sand gift. That's why he taught me to sail, so I could have some useful skill, but you won't ever let me use it!" The anger is rising within me that I tried so hard to quell. "Potah—he loved me." I leave the unspoken words hanging in the air. *You don't.*

Motah's face reddens. Suddenly, a whip of sand lashes out and wraps around my ankle. I fall backward with a cry and land hard on the ground. Sand seeps up around me from the floor, crawling over my legs and arms, holding me in place. I scream and fight against it. I can't move.

Shrey shrinks back against the wall. I hate that she's seeing me like this, lying on the floor, helpless. I'm her big sister. I'm supposed to take care of her. I glare at Motah, fury writhing within me.

Motah stands over me. The anger on her face is gone, replaced by a cold calm. "Would holding a spear be able to save you from that?" She raises her hand, and the sand lifts me up. "What about this?" She turns me upside down, and the world spins. "Or this?" She forms a knife out of sand and sends it flying toward my face. I shut my eyes.

"There's only one way for you to protect yourself and others, Norah." Motah's voice is low and soft. Disappointed. "Develop a sand gift."

When I open my eyes, I see the sand knife turning in front of my face, an inch away from my nose. Motah flips me back upright.

"I hate you," I whisper.

Motah's eyes tighten, and for a moment, I wonder if my words have hurt her. But then her gaze hardens again. "Good."

The sand holding me unravels, and I drop to the floor with a jolt. I stumble to my feet and run from the house before Motah can see the tears in my eyes.

☾

WITH A CRY, I swing my spear around in an arc and miss Zadock's ear by a hair. It's a practice spear, only made of hardened cacti fibers and not sharp quartz, like the spears Extractors take to battle.

We trade blows in rapid motions. Zadock's face is set with determination, sweat dripping down his temples. "You're pushing really hard today."

I grit my teeth and step forward, getting in another swing that he blocks. Atoille pulls on my feet, lifting me higher, making my lunges take me farther. "Yeah. I guess I am." I glance at the guard at the top of the tower on the outskirts of To'Rahn. They're probably watching us, in between keeping an eye out over the ocean of sand, watching for To'Morat ships. But if we're lucky, the guard won't be able to recognize our features in the dusky light.

Because neither of us is supposed to be out here doing this.

At the edge of the plateau, we can find relative peace and solitude. The open sandy space between the rows of houses and the drop off into the ocean of sand is our playground. The sun is setting, the sky a hazy orange, and the intense heat of the day is being exchanged for the cold of the night, but I barely notice through the sweat dripping off my brow. It feels good to work out some of the frustration of the day.

We take turns striking, neither scoring a hit. Atoille's ashes, Zadock is *strong*. My muscles are screaming, barely blocking each blow before he gets in another one. I step backward, the sandy ground slick under my feet as Zadock edges me closer and closer to the plateau's edge.

I duck and then swing my spear and hit Zadock's shins with a *thwack.*

"Ouch!" Zadock bends at the waist.

I sweep my spear toward his neck and tap it against his skin. "You're dead," I say, even though we both know that if he used Shaking, I wouldn't stand a chance. It still gives me grim satisfaction when he leans on the practice spear, breathing hard.

We come out here at least once a week to practice. Zadock knows I love it. I revel in the feeling of learning a new skill, a skill that may save Shrey's life one day. The feeling of doing *something.* So even though I'll never get Motah's permission to fight for To'Rahn or sail the sands, at least I can do this.

I pass Zadock our shared waterskin, and he takes a long gulp. He smiles at me, and my heart flutters. "You're getting really good, Nors."

I blush, and I'm glad that the sun has fully set by now and that we're talking by the light of Atoille. About half of the moon is showing on the eastern sands, rising a little more each night. The desert chill sinks its fingers into my skin. I shiver. "Thanks," I say. "You, too."

Zadock shrugs and passes back the waterskin. "Seriously, Nors. You beat me nine times out of ten. Maybe you should show your motah. She might change her mind."

I look away, bending to run my hand through the sand that floats about a foot off the ground. It swirls through my fingertips, and I can pretend I'm Shaking it.

"She'll never change her mind, Zadock. Practicing in secret is the only way for me to learn something." *And at least if I ever need to protect you or Shrey, I won't be totally powerless.*

"Well. All right. I don't mind practicing with you."

Zadock will never be asked to use a spear. The sand is a much more powerful weapon for him.

"Again," I say.

Zadock grasps his spear in both hands and charges forward,

leaping across the sand. I smile. Zadock always likes to be the one to make the first move.

I duck under his wild swing, my balance solid even in the shifting sand. I spring forward, using Atoille's pull, and slash with my practice spear. Zadock jumps back.

"Ha!" He shouts with a triumphant grin. He wastes no time and brings his spear forward in a jab, and I sidestep and duck. His spear plunges, tip down, right toward me, but I manage to get my spear up in both hands to knock his away.

His spear goes up, and there's an opening, but I've pushed too hard. I'm losing my balance. My momentum carries me into Zadock, and we both tumble into the sand.

"Oof!" Zadock shouts as he falls and rolls. We skid to a stop, laughing. Zadock is right on top of me, his hands on either side of my head and his face inches from mine.

He looks into my eyes for just a moment, my heart thundering. Then he laughs, pressing himself to his feet. "You got me."

I stand, dusting sand off my clothes, and retrieve my spear. My eyebrows raise in a question. "Again?"

☾

ZADOCK and I sit side by side, dangling our feet over the edge of the plateau, overlooking the sea of sand. It's beautiful this time of evening. The white light of Atoille shines on the orange sands, washing them to gray. The ocean of sand stretches on until it meets the horizon. It's comforting to watch the waves swell and retreat, to listen to the *shhhhh* sound of sand sliding against sand. We're both sweating and breathing hard even in the cool desert air.

"Not bad, speck." Zadock grins at me sideways.

I jab him with my elbow. "Stop it."

Waves of sand crash and spray against the plateau far below us. Kind of like the ocean of water, I've been told, though I have never been there myself. Way too dangerous, with waves big enough to encompass our entire plateau.

The sand waves will get rockier now that Atoille is rising in our sky. For two weeks, the ocean of sand will be rougher to travel, and then for two weeks, it stills.

Zadock looks at me with that half smile I have known my whole life. "You should tell someone. Ki'Rhen Dalayn or—"

"Zadock. No."

"But you can fight, Nors! If the To'Morat come—"

"They will come, and I will be ready to protect Shrey. That's all I can do. If Motah found out what we do out here—"

"What?" Zadock plays with the hovering layer of sand. "What is so bad about learning to fight?"

I roll my eyes. "It's a waste of time. I should be working on feeling less love or whatever I need to do to make my sand gift manifest so that she doesn't have to be disappointed by a useless daughter."

Zadock's face softens. I shrink in on myself, wishing I could take the words back. My heart is exposed and open, bared for him to see the holes.

He hesitates a second before putting his arm around me. We used to greet each other like this all the time when we were little, so why does my heart leap?

"I'm sure she doesn't think that, Norah."

I shake my head. We sit in silence for a moment, and Zadock removes his arm. The chill of the desert hits, and I wish he hadn't. We watch the waves of sand. Even from this high up, the sound of the spray is hypnotic. Then there's a *thud* as a solid chunk of rock falls to the sand, only to be sucked away.

"What was that?" I ask. "That was not normal. A piece of the plateau just fell off."

Zadock frowns. "Potah is worried. The council says that the speed of erosion is increasing. They don't know why." He looks at me. "No one knows what to do."

I lean back on my elbows, and sand twirls around my shoulders.

"We might have to relocate." We settled on this plateau over a hundred years ago, well before even Motah was born, so the thought both terrifies and excites me.

Zadock lies back on the sand and looks at the sky. "Potah says that there aren't many plateaus left. They're all being eroded away. To'Rahn may be one of the last."

"What?" I whisper. What would the village do if we couldn't find another plateau?

"The council will figure something out."

I lie next to Zadock and point out a planet glowing amid the stars. "Look! That's Vernha, the closest planet to our sun. This is the only time of year when she's in her orbit far enough away from the sun that we can see her."

Zadock grins at me.

I elbow him again. "You have to know the stars to travel the sands." Not even Shrey knows how much I love the stars and planets. Only Zadock.

He settles his hands behind his head. "Well, go on then."

I point to another planet. "There's Gobehl, Vernha's brother planet in the old stories. Did you know he has forty-eight known moons?"

"What?" Zadock sits up on one elbow and looks at me. "Forty-eight? No way."

"Not as close as Atoille is to our world."

"That's amazing." Zadock sighs, leans back, and closes his eyes. "How do people even know that?"

I smile. "Forgers. They used to point their sand-glass lenses at the sky, too, not just across the sands. Old Forgers recorded a lot of knowledge that way before relocating plateaus became such an issue and they started looking across the desert instead of at the stars."

"And then the fighting started," Zadock says.

"Yeah." Resources became scarce. Villages turned against each other, and trade stopped.

The cold is starting to bite, and I think about scooting closer and sharing body warmth as we did so many times as children, looking up at the same desert sky. But I don't.

"Ooooh!" I point. "There's Tareh, the archer constellation. My potah talked about him all the time when he worked the trading ships. Tareh hardly moves at all, just rotates around our planet's pole."

"I don't see an archer anywhere."

"Right there." I point.

"Oh, I see it! There, right?" Zadock points in the opposite direction. I punch his arm.

I don't want to move, but I get to my feet and stretch tired muscles. "We better get going, or Motah's going to feed me to the deathstalkers."

Zadock shivers. "Those things scare the speck out of me. They're not real...right? Not the giant ones that people say exist out in the sands? You and your potah never saw one?"

"Of course they're not real. And no, Potah and I never saw one."

I look out across the sand one more time. Zadock stands beside me.

"For something so dangerous, it sure is beautiful." Zadock echoes my thoughts.

I grin at him sideways. And then I jump.

The edge of the plateau soars away from me. Wind rushes through my arms and fingertips, and I'm flying. The night air fills my lungs. For a moment, I'm free.

The waves of sand get closer and closer, and my heart leaps into my throat. I scream, a cry of terror and joy escaping my lips as I fall faster and faster, and then—

I lurch to a stop atop a platform of sand.

My breathing slows, and I look up and see Zadock standing at the edge, his arms outstretched, particles of sand drifting from atop the plateau and the platform he has created for me. I wave, and he lifts me up, leaving a trail of dust behind.

Zadock brings the platform to the top of the plateau, and I leap off onto solid ground. The sand disperses around us.

"Norah." Zadock sighs. "You just about make my heart explode, wild girl. Quit doing that."

For some reason, his words warm me from the tips of my toes to my head, and my cheeks heat. Atoille, what is wrong with me?

We grab our practice spears and start the walk back to the village huts, fires alight in the distance. "Thank you." I smile sideways at him, a real smile, unguarded. "For catching me."

Zadock smiles back. "Always."

6

ZADOCK

I stop at Norah's house after school the next day, but she's not home. Shrey points me to the boathouse at the edge of the plateau.

"Shhh." Shrey puts a finger to her lips. "Motah doesn't know she's there."

I nod solemnly. "I'll keep it secret."

I jog through the streets of To'Rahn, wind tossing my hair and desert sun beating down. I haven't got much time before Potah notices I'm gone, so I've got to hurry. He thinks I'm at his glass and quartz business, shaping sand for the Forgers. I don't like deceiving him, but it's such dull work. I just had to get away for a moment.

I break free of the rows of homes. The edge of the plateau comes into view, the ocean of sand beyond. Atoille shines on the outskirts of deserts even in daylight, a white orb in an otherwise blue sky. About three-quarters of the moon is visible above the horizon now. Her craters, darker pockets of gray, mar the white surface.

I pass the guard tower and glance upward. An Extractor stares out over the sands like always, on alert for a To'Morat attack. The guard is always an Extractor because energy from the sand can keep them awake.

I frown. Why can't things be different? Why can't we all solve the problem of the famine together?

When I reach the boathouse, I see Norah immediately. She's the only one here, and most of the stalls for housing the ships are full. No one's sailing. No one's trading.

Norah's hunched over the wood of her family's boat, wearing a sleeveless shirt, tanned arms scraping away hardened sand. I smile. She's so proud of that boat, real wood, even though most ships on To'Rahn are made of quartz-reinforced cactus fiber.

She stops scraping. Her fingers trace the letters engraved on the side, where her potah carved them when he named the boat. *Norah.*

She doesn't notice me watching. Even though I don't have a lot of time, I take a moment to just look at her. Her features are delicate—small nose, narrow face framed by straight brown hair. I know from experience that a guy could lose himself looking into those deep brown eyes.

"Hey!" I say. "You busy?"

Norah jumps and looks up. "Don't do that!" She throws a polishing rag at me, and I catch it with a smile.

"C'mon," I say, extending a hand to help her up. "I had an idea. I want to run it by you."

She blows out through her lips before grabbing my hand. "All right."

I hoist her up, and she's light as a puff of desert sand. Beautiful, even with a trickle of sweat running down her temple.

Norah blushes and releases my hand. "So, what's this idea?"

"You'll see."

We walk back through To'Rahn, and the streets are busy, people wearing sand cloaks bustling every which way. Some pull a camehl with a load of goods behind them. The camehls have wide, flat feet, perfect for navigating the shifting sands.

"Does Shrey still want one of those?" I ask.

Norah rolls her eyes. "Of course. But only a baby one."

We turn out of the community houses and enter the market district. It's less crowded than normal, with only a few stalls of merchants selling wares where there used to be dozens.

Norah shakes her head. "It's sad seeing the market like this."

We pass a stall of produce—pre-peeled bristlebrush fruit and yuca tubers. They're a little withered, but this stall actually has several people bartering around it. The stalls selling quartz jewelry and camehl-hair clothing are empty. Forlorn shopkeepers stare at their wares.

Norah stops to listen to the people argue. "What are we going to do, Zadock? What are we going to do when the food runs out?"

I take a deep breath in and out, feeling this urge to protect her, to wrap my arms around her and let her know it's going to be ok. "It won't. The council will figure it out. The famine will end. Something." I pause and put one hand on her shoulder. "Nors. Does your family have enough to eat?"

Norah just stares at me for a moment. "We're ok."

"You'd tell me if you didn't?" I put my other hand on her other shoulder, forcing her to look into my eyes. I don't care that people are staring.

"I would, Zadock."

Her words make me feel a little better. I'm lucky that Potah and Motah took me back when they did. My family is one of the wealthier ones in To'Rahn. We are still eating regularly. But if the food runs out, there won't be much I can do to help anyone.

I hate to think of how the Ki'Rhen-raised kids are doing. Who's looking out for them?

I give Norah's shoulders a squeeze before I release her, a blush creeping into my cheeks that I pray to Atoille she doesn't notice. I can't do that anymore, just touch her like that. We're older now. It means too much.

We continue to walk through the market, the sounds of angry bartering filling my ears.

"Let's try to hurry," I say, a sheepish grin on my face. "Potah doesn't know I'm gone."

Norah grins sideways at me but picks up the pace. "What? Could Faharic Penvaren's loyal son really be sneaking around behind his back? Whatever for?"

I poke her with an elbow. *Gahhhh. I have to stop!* "Anything to see you, wild girl."

Instantly I know the words are the exact wrong and exact right thing to say. Norah hides her smile behind her fingers, and her cheeks flush.

I turn away. I can't unscramble my thoughts when I'm looking at her.

A man hunched over with age peruses the stalls. I stop and bow, and Norah follows suit. "Good afternoon, Threh'hai Saiyen." I add the respect honorific for a male.

Threh'hai inclines his head toward us. He is the head of the council and one of the oldest members of To'Rahn. Sallow hands clutch his cane, and the wrinkles on his face increase as he smiles. "Good afternoon, Zadock Penvaren and Norah Saranyi. Wonderful to see you."

"You as well, Threh'hai Saiyen," Norah says.

"I am taking my walk through the village. I like to get a feel for the market." He pauses, looking down. "I'm worried. Times are hard, and the end is not in sight."

I'm itching to keep moving, trying to think of a polite way out of this conversation.

"Has the council proposed any solutions?" Norah asks. "Is there anything we can do to help?"

Threh'hai's eyes crinkle when he gives a weak smile. "The council is still discussing. Zadock Penvaren, you're a promising Shaker, and your potah is a member of the council. Some of us argue that we should send a party to the ocean of water. What are your thoughts?"

"The ocean of water?" Norah frowns. "What in Atoille's name for?"

I shrug. "Some people think that the legend of the other moonstone, Atoille's other eye, might be true and that the second moonstone could be found at the ocean of water."

Threh'hai nods. "In the story, Atoille gave one eye to land and one eye to sea. If the two stones are ever united, it is said that the sand gift powers will be boosted to incredible heights."

"The ocean of water... Has anyone even been there?" I ask.

Threh'hai smiles. "Oh, not in your lifetime. But it has been done, yes."

"Threh'hai Saiyen," Norah says, "even if the legend were true, the stone found, and all the sand gifts strengthened, would it be enough to save To'Rahn?"

The old man closes his eyes. "Not from starvation, no. The sand gifts can't do anything about that. But an attack from To'Morat, yes."

I swallow. He talks about it like it's inevitable.

Threh'hai opens his eyes and glances at each of us in turn. "It may only be a legend after all. But some members of the council argue that the stone might do more than just heighten sand gifts. They say that the second moonstone being lost for so long is the reason the natural laws of the world are being strained." Threh'hai pauses. "It may be that if the moonstones were reunited, the sandstorms would be predictable, the plateau erosion slow, and the rains would make the plants grow again."

Threh'hai eyes Norah for a long moment and opens his mouth. But then he closes it again and shakes his head.

Huh.

Norah puts a hand over his atop the cane. "We'll figure something out, Threh'hai Saiyen. It will be ok."

"Thank you, Norah." Threh'hai nods to her and then to me. "Zadock."

We continue through the market, and Norah glances my way. "Another stone? Really? Could the story be true?"

I shake my head. "If the council is discussing it, things must be desperate."

We come into a district where new homes are being built. Two Shakers hold up a wall of sand while a Forger presses her hands against it to change it into quartz. The transformation is slow, but she's almost done, and the part that she's finished is stunning and blinding in the sun. Other workers pad the quartz with cactus fibers and sticky clay mud so it's not so bright and harsh.

A group of children is watching the process, supervised by two of the Ki'Rhen. They clap and jump with delight when the wall is complete.

A wealthier family comes down the street, riding a platform of sand. I don't know them, but their clothes are colorful reds and blues, so, at the very least, they can afford precious dye.

"Look at them!" Norah gawks. Behind them walks a man who must be the Shaker, lifting his arms to keep the platform afloat.

I shrug. "Potah says it's the new trend. He wanted us to hire a Shaker platform. Thank Atoille Motah refused."

Norah shakes her head in disbelief. "Wow. That's ridiculous."

"Almost as ridiculous as jumping off the plateau and expecting someone to catch you."

Norah punches me hard in the shoulder, but she laughs.

Speck, I love that laugh.

"C'mon, c'mon, let's go!" I say.

We jog down another road that runs parallel to the canals. I hear the water rushing before I see it. All that glorious water, almost ankle-deep.

"Seriously, where are we going?" Norah asks.

"Almost there," I say.

We come to the wells, where a group of Shakers is lifting sand from holes dug deep into the ground, so deep that they tap into water reservoirs that lie underneath the plateau and the shifting sands. Shakers bring the water-soaked sand up and let the water drip off into the canals. The canals run to the grow walls, cellars dug into the sand to cultivate herbs and roots that otherwise wouldn't grow. But now, even with the water, the grow walls are empty.

We slow down along the canal, and I stop at one of the wells, a deep hole in the ground surrounded by a knee-high wall of quartz. No one is working at this one.

"We're here!" I say.

"Ok. It's a well."

I smile. "Look inside."

Norah starts to lean forward but then stops. "Are you going to push me in?"

I feign indignation. "I? Never. Really, just look."

She leans forward and looks down. The well is deep enough that the bottom is black. The walls are made of sand that has been turned into quartz. The well's got a diameter of about four feet, big enough for Shakers to reach down and bring up sand soaked in water. The rains pour rarely, but when they do, they pour hard. Besides that, this is our only way of collecting water.

Norah looks up at me. "It's dark. It's deep. So what?"

I grin. "Watch."

I grab a special quartz bucket that I asked Henli to Forge for me earlier. Attached to it are a series of ropes and a pulley with a long quartz handle.

Norah stares. "Did you make that?"

"Yes, I did. Well, I designed it, and Henli Forged it." Suddenly I feel a little shy. I would never show this to anyone but her anyway, but now I'm nervous. I bite my lip. "So. Shakers spend lots of energy bringing up the sand and holding it over the canal, letting the water drip off. It takes so much time, and it's a lot of work, right?"

Norah folds her arms. "Right."

I set the quartz rod over the top of the well and lower the bucket down, down until I feel the pressure of sand and water. "We rely on our sand gifts so much, but I think engineering might work better here." I turn a handle I've attached to the pulley, bringing the full bucket back up. It's heavy, and my arms are starting to ache, so instead, I Shake the sand, wrapping it around the pulley handle, and then I *push*.

The handle spins in a whirl and the bucket jolts to the top. I grab the handle. Now the bucket feels like it weighs more than a camehl, so I wrap sand around the handle and lift it over the running water in the canal.

I turn to Norah and smile. "Watch."

Using sand, I press a switch on the bottom of the bucket, and it falls away on a hinge, revealing a fine mesh underneath. Water drips through the sand and falls into the canal.

Norah's mouth drops. "Wow. That's ingenious."

I can't help but beam. "Thanks. If we had a series of these buckets attached to ropes dangling over the canal, we could be much faster than Shakers holding sand and working one at a time. Extractors could even Extract to power the buckets' motion. We could increase the amount of water flowing. It might even make a difference in the famine, who knows?"

Norah smiles. "You care about this so much. And you're really good at it."

"Thanks."

"You need to tell your potah."

"Norah—"

"He's on the council. He can do something about this, make it a system that everyone uses."

I shake my head. "No. I can't. You already know that I can't."

"Well," she glances around, "pass the design off as mine, then, if you don't want him to know you love engineering. But really. He wouldn't believe that I thought of this."

I frown. She's right.

The water's done draining from the bucket, and I overturn the damp sand onto the bank of the canal and then roll up the ropes and pulley. "Can I keep this at your house?"

Norah crosses her arms.

"Please?"

She sighs. "All right. But I really think you should show your potah. Once he saw how capable you are, what good ideas you have, he would see that you need to be an engineer."

I lower my eyes and sling the bucket over my shoulder. "Yeah. And then he would send me back to the Ki'Rhen. The only reason he wants me now is so he can start grooming me to take his place on the council. If I told him I don't want that..." I trail off, feeling a little sick.

We begin our walk back toward the village. Norah's hands go in her pockets. "Was it so bad there?"

"No," I say. "Not at all. Most of the Ki'Rhen are very kind, but there were things I didn't like, like never having your own possessions or your own space. Always being surrounded by other kids. Not having someone to look out for you because you were theirs." I run a hand through my hair. "Does that make sense?"

Norah looks at me with those wide, dark eyes. "Yeah. It does."

"Here." I put the bucket in her hands. "Thanks for taking care of this."

She looks from my contraption to me, her lips on the verge of trying to convince me more.

"I've got to hurry," I say. Her eyes meet mine for a moment. I feel something swirling in my gut. Not a bad feeling. What is this?

My body leans toward her almost of its own accord. I want to hold her. Atoille, I want to kiss her.

The moment snaps. "I have to go. I'll see you!" I turn and run toward Potah's business, the fire in my lungs and sweat dripping down my face driving everything away.

I can't feel this way about her. I could lose my sand gift. I could lose my potah.

My sandals *slap, slap, slap* against the hot sand. I don't look back.

7

—————

IMWRAETH

The plateau of To'Shahera burns before me.

I sit atop my retahn. Her wide hooves kick up sand, and her black mane weaves about her horns. She wishes to join the battle, to fight and kill as she has been trained.

Atoille shines almost directly overhead, an enormous white orb filling half the sky. The cold of the night is a stark contrast to the heat of the fires. The smell of smoke punches my nose.

The To'Morat are attacking. And nothing can stop us.

The dried cactus strands that fill in the cracks of the To'Shaheran quartz houses burn away, leaving behind shells of buildings. War cries blend with screams of the villagers. My people burn and raid, causing chaos in the streets. I watch an armored To'Morat warrior ram his spear through the gut of a villager with sand flowing through his fingers. I force myself not to turn away.

"An excellent plan, Favored One," Councilor Lienos says. His long gray beard brushes his saddle. "The To'Shaheran didn't stand a chance."

Truth.

Lienos rides his own retahn, and she is fidgety as well. Both animals are bred for violence. They hate standing here, watching the scene before them. Almost as much as I hate it.

"You have done well planning and coordinating, boy," Lienos says.

Lie.

I roll my eyes and don't acknowledge Lienos with a reply. I don't even need my uncanny ability to tell when someone is lying. We both know this plan was his.

Instead, I watch the homes burn. Listen to the villagers scream. My warriors that carry the torches are careful to stay away from To'Shaheran storehouses. Though we are a ferocious people, none of our wars are for sport. We always have a purpose. And right now, that is survival.

I'm supposed to get some kind of joy out of this, "feel the glory," and whatnot. I'm supposed to be watching for which warriors to give accolades to, which fighters to promote. But I don't.

I scrub a hand through my short red hair. My stomach clenches. I should be used to this by now. My heart pounds even though I'm sitting still, pumping blood and adrenaline.

Is this what it feels like to run?

I put one hand into the sand I always keep in a satchel at my side. I breathe in and Extract. The glow that emits from the sand is visible even through the canvas bag. Energy pours into my veins, and the beating of my malformed heart calms. Without sand to settle my pounding heart, it would beat harder and harder until it burst. If I wasn't an Extractor, if I couldn't borrow energy from the sand, I would've died a long time ago.

Lienos watches. He tries to hide it, but I notice the subtle twist of disgust on his face, the downward curve of his lips.

The To'Morat despise weakness. As part of their schooling, each To'Morat child goes through harsh courses of physical endurance, practices with weapons until they are proficient, and learns how to kill without mercy.

I fiddle with the retahn's reins, wishing we could take what we need and head back to To'Morat already.

A To'Shaheran Shaker runs toward us with a cry. It's obvious where he's from by the way he's dressed, brown pants and a loose shirt, very different from our black and red heavy armor plates. His hands are outstretched, gathering sand before him. I'll never know what he planned to do, for Lienos uses his own Shaking to wrap the man in sand and toss him screaming into the air. Lienos uses his other hand to lift a spear of sand and impale the villager with a sharp thrust.

Lienos is particularly good at that move. It's the reason he's stayed behind to guard me. Extracting gives me the energy to stay alive, or go without sleep, food, or water if I need to—handy, that, in a desert—but it cannot heal, not like Absorbing can.

The To'Morat have many strong Absorbers, one of the reasons we have been so successful at conquering other plateaus. Our village has spread onto three nearby plateaus in my reign, an achievement that I should be proud of.

But all I can think about is the people we have killed. The children's screams.

And still, not enough food. Never enough food.

Our warriors herd prisoners onto the bare stretch of sand before me, using their spear points, restraining others with loops of sand. The crying. The begging. I want to cover my ears.

Our Absorbers are busy at work behind me, healing warriors who have been wounded so they can head back to battle. Each To'Morat Absorber has taken a turn at working on my heart.

"Birth defect," they say.

"Congenital heart abnormality."

"We cannot reshape already malformed tissue."

"It's impossible to fix."

"Impossible."

I would have been hurled from the plateau, thrown to the sand at birth, like all children born with physical disabilities are. If not for one thing.

I was born on one very specific day. A day when Atoille was aligned with our sun. A day when the sky turned black at noon. The day that Atoille chose the next leader of To'Morat.

And that was me.

(

THE PRISONERS KNEEL in the sand, all those who are left of the To'Shaheran. The village burns behind them, but already our Shakers are dumping sand on the flames to put it out. Others head into the scene, raiding each home and storehouse, gathering supplies. The To'Morat have always fought, always wanted to conquer, but now our raids are even more crucial. We will starve without them.

The famine has stumped me and my councilors, Lienos and Therah. Even with regular rain, our gardens are dry as dust, the sandstorms coming without warning are tearing us apart, and the plateau is eroding away at unprecedented speed.

So what is the answer for the To'Morat? More raids. More stealing. Take care of ourselves, let others die.

It's the only logical thing to do.

The alternative...well, there is none. We've already tried planting more. It's just not working.

Rows upon rows of people cower before me. Their hands are clasped together and held above their heads, a sign that they will not use the sand against us anymore. There are women and children. Babies' cries echo in the night.

When I look overhead, through the smoke of the burning houses, I can see stars.

"Your coat, Favored One?" Therah halts her retahn next to mine and offers me my camehl leather coat. She has a motherly face beginning to show her age, with cheeks like wrinkled dates. I roll my eyes, but I put it on.

Warriors round up the last stragglers, throwing them out of their houses, using spear points and sand to bring them to their knees and join the rest of the To'Shaheran.

The To'Morat break into song, voices sounding in harsh and joyful tones. I watch my warriors carry boxes of supplies to our wagons—dried meat, fruits and vegetables, seeds and herbs. We round up the To'Shaheran camehls and a few more retahn, herding them into larger trailers. Even after all this killing, we haven't gained that much. To'Shahera is suffering just as much as we are.

The fires are burning low now, the village of To'Shahera a skeleton of smoke and ash.

A few of the To'Shaheran turn around and cry out at the wreckage and at our theft of their supplies. A mother rocks and comforts her wailing child. Most of them stare at the ground and weep.

They know what's coming next.

We could just leave them to die here. We've taken their food, their animals, their weapons and stores. They would die slowly in the hot sun, desperate to keep their children alive and failing.

What comes next is a mercy. It is.

Warrior Tysian mounts his retahn and rides forward to give his report. Pale blonde hair is tied back in a long tail down his back. It's always bothered me that his prominent eyebrows are black. Does he charcoal them?

On the right chest of his armor, Tysian bears the red-painted markings that show he is Blood Rank One. He has achieved the highest of accolades that our warriors can and is my military general. Which means that he orders our warriors around and pretends that those orders come from me.

Tysian doesn't give a full bow, as is proper, but instead inclines his head from where he sits in the saddle. "Favored One, all the remaining To'Shaheran are here. Our warriors have searched their homes for anything of value, and what we've found has been loaded into the wagons. We may head back to To'Morat as soon as the prisoners have been taken care of." Tysian jerks his head toward the side, where warriors are fighting to get two struggling girls into one of the wagons. "We found two Absorbers."

"Only two?" I watch the girls. One is young, about seven or eight, and the other older, probably about my age.

The younger one is solemn and silent, her eyes huge as she stares at the fires. Now that the chaos of battle has calmed, I can hear the older one screaming. "Stop this, PLEASE! NO—" And then the wagon is shut and locked.

Tysian shrugs. "These two were found Absorbing and healing their wounded. There may have been more, but you know how the chaos of battle makes these things so difficult."

I nod, keeping my face straight to hide my disappointment. Absorbing is rare, but not *that* rare. They could have found more, if they'd really tried. My people have given up on healing me.

Tysian grips the retahn's reins, his muscles flexed. They're nothing to brag about. My Blood Rank One is what some people, certainly not me, might call *scrawny*.

But he didn't get to the highest rank because of his muscular prowess.

"Thank you, General Tysian." I turn away from his gaze. "Well then. There's no reason to delay, is there?"

I want to reach into my bag of sand again and still my thundering heart. Why does the thought of ordering hundreds of deaths bother me so much? Me and no one else?

I press my lips together and swallow. Then I give Tysian a nod.

The general grins and dismounts his retahn. "Shakers Mylarah, Riah, and Behlron, to me!" The three Shakers, our strongest, take their places around the prisoners, one at each corner of the rows that we've formed. Their arms move and swirl, stirring up the sand, causing it to flow through the prisoners.

The To'Shaheran cry out. Some of them attempt to Shake the sand away, but my warriors are too strong, and the sand presses forward.

I sit. I watch. I force myself not to look away.

Lienos, to my left, sighs. "Such theatrics."

Councilor Therah snorts and holds out a water bag for me. "Are you keeping hydrated, Favored One? We so worry about your health."

Lie.

Even without this lie-detecting ability I've had since birth, it doesn't take a genius to know that if I was out of their way, Councilors Therah and Lienos would be in power.

"I'm fine, Councilor Therah."

Warrior Tysian stands at the front of the line of prisoners, who are now screaming and pleading. Some of their Shakers stand and push back, and my Extractors hurl quartz-tipped spears, bringing on more screams.

Tysian raises his hands. He's the only Shaker I've ever seen strong enough to do this.

In an instant, all of that floating sand becomes needle-sharp. It's like he changes the structure of the particles themselves. Tysian throws out his hands, and the sand particles burst inward in one intense wave.

I can't help it. I close my eyes. But I know what happens now. I've seen it before.

The prisoners are stabbed with a thousand miniscule needles. Pinpricks of sand leave innumerable tiny holes in their skin, burrowing to bone-level. The screams cease.

I open my eyes again. Every single To'Shaheran, save their two Absorbers, lies dead on the ground, bleeding into the sand. Every. One.

Tysian turns around and meets my gaze with a grin.

My stomach heaves. I turn my retahn away, her wide, flat hooves staying atop the shifting desert floor. My councilors follow close behind me.

"The supplies we gathered should sustain our village for a while longer, at least," Lienos says. "Long enough to plan our next raid."

I hear the warriors behind us mounting retahn, more padded hoof-falls following us across the sand in a column. Camehls will be pulling the wagons. We'll head back to the boats, make the three-day journey across the sands, and back to To'Morat.

"Yes." *Speck.* "Our next raid." I shut my eyes. We must raid again, of course. My people will die if we don't. I have another plan formulating, but the chances that it will work are slim, and we can't afford the consequences if it fails. My people are starving. "Where do you suggest next, councilors?"

Therah looks at me sideways. Her eyebrows are almost as intense as Tysian's. "To'Rahn. It's the obvious choice."

Lienos closes his mouth, then opens it again. "I have to say that I agree with Councilor Therah in this matter. To'Rahn, by all accounts, is faring better than other villages. They still have enough food to feed their people, though what they have is dwindling. We must strike soon."

We stop at the edge of the plateau and watch warriors finish loading our supply wagons onto the barges. Our ships are wide at the bottom, tall at the sides. There are stations at the back where Shakers will work to propel us across the sands. A door in the side of the ship is opened, and a ramp is extended downward so the supplies can be loaded.

"The To'Rahn will be more able to fight back if they are better fed." I protest even though my opinion doesn't really count for anything. What I wouldn't give to prove them wrong, to have some real power? To not have to stick my hand into this Atoille-cursed bag of sand to sustain my life.

"Our warriors are strong," Lienos says. "But if we wait too long, that strength will fail. The time to attack is now."

"Yes." Therah nods. "We must take these supplies to To'Morat, let our warriors recover, and then raid To'Rahn. It's our only chance to live through this cursed time."

I find myself nodding. I don't remember the last time I disagreed out loud with them. "To'Rahn next, then."

So that's three days back to To'Morat, a week to recover and organize the supplies we captured, and then we begin the seven-day journey to To'Rahn.

Less than a moon cycle until we attack.

8

—

ZADOCK

I almost drown while extricating myself from the downy multitude of blankets that cover my enormous bed. My toes dig into the camehl hair rug on the floor. I pass a wooden armoire (whatever that is) and wash my face in a quartz basin on the other side of the room. I study my reflection in the sand-glass mirror.

It's been two weeks since the sandstorm on the boat, but I keep dreaming about it. About her.

Norah was so close. I held her in my arms.

Shaking that sand, holding it up to protect her, was the hardest thing I've ever done.

The sand fought against me, against the emotions tumbling inside me. It felt heavier and pushed back against my control. My arms strained and burned while I was trying to hold up something that should have been simple.

Until she pushed me away. Until she asked me not to touch her.

Keep it together, Zadock. It's a big day today.

Today is the Anointing.

My stomach whirls. I lean forward against the water basin, trying to calm myself. It's not marriage, not yet. That doesn't have to happen for another year or two.

I'm going to be sick.

Trying not to think about it too hard, I hurry to get dressed in my traditional white Anointing robes.

Potah raps his knuckles on my door. I know it's him because Chassi doesn't knock. She just bustles in and starts cleaning. It's not Motah because she rarely leaves her room, just stays in there, drinking her tea.

"Come in." I straighten and fiddle with the sash that's supposed to go around my waist.

I turn, take in Potah's stern face. His smile doesn't reach his eyes. "You look ready," he says. "With a good wife at your side and a little more polish, you'll be ready to take my place on the council."

My stomach does another flip. I could tell him about my ideas, that I want to be an engineer, but not now. "Well, I have to be voted in first, right?"

Potah walks closer and ties the sash around my middle in an expert knot. I haven't tied the one around my upper left arm yet, the one that my Anointed will move to my right arm during the ceremony. Potah takes the fabric from off my bed and works on that band as well. "My influence is growing on the council. By the time that doddering Threh'hai is gone, it will be easy to sway the others into voting you in. Especially with a powerful family like the Rahlens backing me."

Doddering Threh'hai. I'm surprised that Potah would talk that way about the man who is essentially the leader of To'Rahn. "Do you know...am I to be Anointed with Saeri Rahlen?"

Potah's lips quirk up. "You like her, I know, but I can't say anything just yet. You'll find out soon enough."

The pit in my belly gnaws at me.

I don't want to be partnered with Saeri. But I don't want to disappoint my potah.

He finishes tying the band around my arm. "I will meet you

downstairs for breakfast, and then we can ride to the ceremony together."

The door clicks shut, and I glance at my reflection one more time.

What would potah do if I told him my thoughts?

If he knew how I felt about Norah, he would do everything in his power to keep me away from her.

I grip the sides of the wash basin and lower my eyes. And if I told my potah that I don't want to be on the council, that I want to apprentice to an engineer, what would he do then?

Would he send me back to live with the Ki'Rhen? I was happy there, but to have my real parents want me...

I take a deep breath and clench my jaw shut. I will not mess this up.

I follow Potah down the stairs to the table, where Chassi is laying out breakfast and pouring tea for Motah.

I will not mess this up.

☾

THE WORSHIP BUILDING IS HUGE, with a domed ceiling reaching far overhead and enough stadium seating for the entire village of To'Rahn. I sit next to my classmates in alphabetical order around a circular quartz platform Forged to look like Atoille. The work is detailed; the sand was shaped to create pockets and craters that match the ones on Atoille's face.

Norah loves this platform. To me, all those holes look like tripping hazards.

On the other side of the circle, prominent members of the Ki'Rhen sit in pristine white robes. Dalayn and Hainan are among them. Behind the Ki'Rhen, the wall is pure glass. Quartz is easy, I'm told, but only a skilled Forger can make glass. This building has an entire wall and ceiling made of it.

Through the glass, the bare plain of sand stretches to the edge of the plateau. And far beyond, I can just make out the sea of sands.

Atoille is directly overhead, halfway through her orbit on our side of the planet. Even though it's midday, the moon is visible in the sky.

Potah and Motah are seated in one of the rows close to the front of the room. Potah catches my eye and gives me a reassuring nod.

I turn back to face the front and wipe sweat off my forehead with my ceremonial sleeve. Great. Very dignified.

Because we're in alphabetical order, Norah Saranyi isn't too far from me, a Penvaren. There are about twenty of us graduating, all of us age seventeen. Past those who sit alphabetically are those who I grew up with in the Ki'Rhen. Those whose last names are known only on secret records.

I wonder if Potah watched me grow up, if he kept track enough to know that I was his. Or maybe he didn't, and he was disappointed when he was told that I was a Penvaren, and not another of the youth who sit around me.

I try to push those thoughts away. My classmates fidget and whisper while we wait for the Ki'Rhen to start the ceremony. I see Norah's motah and Shrey wiggling in her chair out of the corner of my eye, and I can't help but smile.

With the last name Rahlen, Saeri is sitting right next to me, her elbow resting on *my* chair's armrest. I try to lean away from her without seeming like I mean to. Erno Rofort sits next to her, chewing his nails and eating them.

What if I'm partnered with Saeri? Could I really live like that, watching Norah with some other guy? What if I'm not partnered with Saeri? Could I bear Potah's look of disapproval?

My stomach twists in knots.

Next to Erno sits Norah, and I lean forward to look at her and smile. She smiles back weakly, her face pale.

I look at the faces of my classmates sitting around the Atoille platform. Vaerhi Bael looks like she's going to throw up. Melric, last name unknown, fiddles with the sash tied around his arm, chewing his bottom lip.

It's strange that this marks the last day of our studies, the day we become adults and contributing members of the community. Most of us don't look like we're ready.

If Ki'Rhen Dalayn made the decision, I know she would pair me with Norah. She's one of the only adults in our community who advocates for more love in the partnerships. But then look where it's gotten her.

At last, Ki'Rhen Hainan stands, passes us students waiting anxiously, and takes his place in the center of the moon dais. A hush goes over the audience, but I still hear Shreyen's excited shriek.

I never liked Ki'Rhen Hainan. He always taught To'Rahn history in school, and his long gray face and dull, monotone voice just weren't that exciting.

He straightens his white robe with elegant fingers and clears his throat. The room is engineered so his voice can be heard throughout the building.

"Welcome to this year's Anointing and graduation ceremony." Hainan smiles out over the audience, then turns his gaze to us students. "Our youth have worked hard over the years, learning our history, learning to use their sand gifts, learning to defend our nation. And now they are ready to join the community as adults."

Hainan's wizened lips turn upward. "I will call each student up in order and then their decided partner. Both will join hands, transfer arm sashes, and receive the Anointing water that will bind them forever. This is done for the good of the community, to protect our sand gifts, and to keep our posterity strong."

Hainan gestures to the side. Ki'Rhen Dalayn steps forward and hands him a paper. I squint, but I can't see any of the names written there.

With a grand sweep of his hand, Hainan brings the parchment to his face. "We will begin." He looks up. "Eliyah Altanin."

Eliyah stands up and steps forward onto the dais. We used to play sand discs when we were younger. Eliyah's hands are shaking as he comes to stand by Ki'Rhen Hainan.

Hainan looks up. "Eliyah Altanin will be partnered with Shaeris Nuvoro."

Shaeris' eyes open wide. She runs a hand through her yellow hair and hurries to the platform.

The two join hands and awkwardly avoid each other's gaze. Hainan pours a drop of water from a quartz jug onto their clasped hands. "Eliyah Altanin and Shaeris Nuvoro, you are Anointed, to be partnered for life. The community of To'Rahn welcomes you into its arms."

The audience claps, and I join in as Eliyah unties Shaeris' sash and reties it on her other arm, then she does the same for him. Grinning like an idiot, Eliyah takes Shaeris by the hand and leads her off the dais and into the crowd to sit in the section reserved for "new adults of our community."

Ki'Rhen Hainan continues alphabetically. Each couple leaves the dais hand in hand to find a seat in the audience. More rarely, a name is paired with a younger member of our community, as there isn't an even match of boys and girls who are seventeen, and the ceremony is a little different. They clasp hands, and the water is poured, but the sash isn't untied and tied again. That will happen when the younger member of the pair comes of age.

My name hasn't been called yet, and as Hainan gets closer to the end of the alphabet, my nervousness ratchets upward. My fingers tap on the armrests of my chair. Not the one where Saeri rests her elbow and smiles sideways at me. I glance to the side at Norah, and she's still sitting, hands clasped in her lap, her back straight. Her name hasn't been called yet, either.

Trehi Olora, sitting next to me, is called up, and Shaysa is paired with him.

Oh no.

"Zadock Penvaren."

My legs wobble, but somehow, I manage to stand and climb the stairs. I walk across the face of Atoille, avoiding the craters. *Whew.*

I stand next to Ki'Rhen Hainan and look out over the audience.

Potah watches me with piercing eyes while Motah fiddles with something in her hands. Katiyah Saranyi meets my eyes and nods, and Shrey is, for once, holding still. She's clutching something in her hands...cactus needles?

It feels like an eternity before Hainan speaks. An eternity and no time at all.

"Zadock Penvaren will be partnered with Saeri Rahlen."

Saeri beams, her blue eyes bright. She leaves her chair to stand across from me, holding out her hands.

I stare at them.

No. No no no no no.

I can't help that I glance at Norah. Her expression is hard as quartz, but her dark eyes are wide and despairing.

Ki'Rhen Hainan clears his throat.

Oh. I am supposed to take Saeri's hands.

I could refuse. It's extremely rare and very frowned upon, but it's happened before. Society would look down on me, and I may be re-partnered, maybe not.

I'm not sure if I can face that, but how can I do this to Norah?

One whisper echoes through the room.

"Zadock."

Potah.

My arms lift almost of their own accord, and I take Saeri's hands.

An awkward laugh breaks through her lips, her smile frozen in place.

Ki'Rhen Hainan pours two drops of water over our hands. "Zadock Penvaren and Saeri Rahlen, you are Anointed, to be partnered for life. The community of To'Rahn welcomes you into its arms."

I freeze. I'm supposed to go first, but Saeri begins to untie my sash. "It's ok." She whispers, tying it on my other arm. "I'm nervous, too."

I'm ice.

I watch my fingers untie the sash on Saeri's left arm. I loop it around her right and tie it back on again.

It's done.

Saeri reaches out her hand, and I take it. We walk off the dais, and Saeri leads us to seats next to her family. Hael Rahlen pounds me on the back, offering congratulations. Aiyan Rahlen smiles at me and gives me a nod, then lowers her head with her daughter to confer in whispered giggles.

Norah...

What have I done?

9

NORAH

Zadock being Anointed with Saeri feels like a punch in the gut. I knew. I knew he would never be mine. Yet still, it hurts. It hurts so much. It doesn't matter now who I'm paired with.

Ki'Rhen Hainan opens his mouth, holding up the parchment to read the next name. I wipe my hands on my robe. Prepare to stand.

"Felhar Seryan."

My mouth drops open. Felhar stands up and walks to the front. He pauses halfway, glances back at me, and shrugs before continuing.

They skipped me.

Ice stabs into my spine. I keep my expression stony and clasp my shaking hands even as the pit in my stomach threatens to envelop me.

I glance at Ki'Rhen Dalayn. She stares at her lap, refusing to meet my eyes.

Anger begins to turn the cold into heat. How could they do this? *How could they do this?*

Felhar and his Anointed exit the platform. There are only two students left besides me. They are called forward, joined, and then walk away as adults. I just want to stand up and leave, but I'm afraid. Afraid to turn around and see the entire audience looking at me.

And there's that quiet voice, deep within, the one I always try to smother.

What is wrong with me?

"Norah Saranyi."

I jump.

I glance up at Ki'Rhen Hainan and hurry to blink the tears away. Hainan nods. My feet feel like they're made of quartz on my way to the front.

The entire community of To'Rahn stares at me.

Deep breath in. I am stone.

I see Shrey, her eyes red and puffy. I see Motah. Her face is hard, devoid of emotion. But in her eyes, there's...pity?

She is on the council. She had a say in this decision. Fury burns like coals in my chest.

I see Zadock sitting with Saeri's family. She whispers something in his ear.

My heart sinks down into my feet.

Strong.

Potah's voice.

You are strong, my Norah.

"Norah Saranyi," Ki'Rhen Hainan says again. "The community of To'Rahn welcomes you into its arms." Hainan gives me the tiniest reassuring smile, which looks strange on his gray lips. Gently, he takes the white band from my left arm. I watch him untie it, knot by careful knot.

He puts it in his robe pocket.

Hainan pats my back, and I walk on shaking legs down the dais steps, past the other young Anointed couples, past Zadock—oh, Atoille, if I look at him now, I'll cry—back to join my family. I take a seat next to Shrey. She puts her hand on my arm.

Motah doesn't even look at me.

Ki'Rhen Hainan gives closing remarks, but I hardly process what he's saying. Shrey's tiny hands pry open my clenched fists. In my open palm, Shrey places her precious cactus needles.

"For you," she whispers, sniffling.

Tears fill my eyes. I bend down close to her ear. Close enough that I know no one will hear. "I love you."

☾

I SLUMP as I walk through the doors of our home. Without a word, I go to the room I share with Shrey and let the cactus fiber curtain fall behind me. It's not much privacy, but it's better than nothing.

It's ok. You can cry now.

But nothing happens.

I take off my ceremonial robe and change back into my usual form-fitting brown pants and a loose cactus fiber shirt with laces up the front. I fold up the robe and shove it deep down into the bottom of my clothes chest. Stupid thing.

I sit on the bed. Stare at the floor straight ahead.

How could they?

How could *she?*

I'm suddenly thrown back to all the times in school when I felt alone. When all the other students would practice their sand gifts, and I would sit off to the side.

When all the other kids were assigned tasks to help around the village, according to where their gift would best serve. And I was assigned to pull weeds.

An especially painful memory floods my brain. I was young but old enough that it was odd I didn't have a sand gift yet. Felhar, who I've never liked, was embarrassed because I answered Ki'Rhen Dalayn's question correctly after he got it wrong. Later, in the schoolyard, he threw a wave of sand over me, smothering me and pinning me to the ground. Even gasping and struggling, I heard him say, "At least I can do that."

"Stop it, Felhar!" Then the sand was lifted off me, and there was Zadock. He punched Felhar with a fist of sand right in his face. They were both escorted from the schoolyard, but Zadock looked back at me and smiled.

Zadock.

The Anointing comes tumbling back, my heart clenching at the memory of today. I hug my knees to my chest and bury my face in my arms.

"Norah?" Shrey's voice comes from behind the curtain that separates our room from the hallway. "Are you ok?"

I take a deep breath. "I'm ok, Shrey. I just need a minute alone."

There's a pause. "Ok." Her footsteps are soft as she walks away.

Shrey's small act of love finally bursts the dam holding the tears back. I let them fall, my body shaking with silent sobs.

It's not fair, Atoille. Why did you do this to me?

The tears halt. The anger overtakes me like a sandstorm. I find myself getting to my feet, rage powering my movements.

I burst through the curtain and storm down the hallway. Motah sits at the table, a platter of bristlebrush fruits and a knife in front of her. She stares straight ahead at nothing, but when I walk into the room, she turns.

"You knew." Bitterness leaks from my voice.

Motah hesitates. Then she nods.

"You helped make this decision." I'm breathing hard now, my chest rising and falling. "How could you, Motah? How could you let them do this to me?"

Motah takes a long, steadying breath. "It's for the best, Norah."

The words hit me like a physical blow, and I fall to my knees. "But—"

"It's done," Motah snaps. "You have to think of the village now. If you were Anointed and wed, you would have children. What would those children be like? Would they be like you? Would they be in danger, too?"

Her words crush my heart. But then I frown. "Am I in danger, Motah?" I rise to my feet.

Her eyes widen, and she begins to stammer, but I go on. "If I am, it's because you won't let me train with the spear and do something that could be useful! That could actually protect Shrey—"

"Norah, stop!" Motah shrieks. She puts both hands on the table. Breathes. "You don't think it was hard for me to be part of that choice?" She blinks furiously, and a single tear falls down her cheek.

I turn away from her and cross my arms over my chest. I refuse to see it. She doesn't get to cry over this.

We both jump at a knock on the door.

"Is Norah here, Katiyah Saiyu?" Zadock's voice. He addresses my motah with the respect honorific for a female.

I hurry to wipe my cheeks.

Motah stands and walks past me to answer the door, her back rigid. "She's here, Zadock."

Motah steps aside, and Zadock walks through the entryway to our home, the desert sunlight making a silhouette behind him. Atoille, he's so beautiful. His sandy hair is messy as ever, his blue eyes full of concern. I want nothing more than to fall into his arms.

Atoille's ashes. I cannot think these thoughts.

"Norah." Zadock manages a weak smile and steps into the room. Motah closes the door behind him. "Are you ok?"

I think my heart is going to break.

The back door opens with a slam, and Shrey bursts around the corner, her thick blonde curls tied back in a kerchief that's coming loose. She rushes to Zadock and buries her face in his shirt. "My lucky cactus needles didn't even help." Her voice is muffled.

Motah folds her arms and frowns.

Zadock strokes Shrey's hair, but he looks at me. "This is a load of speck, Norah." Motah's frown deepens at the choice of words in front of Shrey.

She unburies her face long enough to mouth the word. *Speck.*

"They can't do that to you." Zadock looks at Motah. "Katiyah Saiyu, you're on the council. Can't something be done?"

Motah opens her mouth, but I step forward and hold up my

hand. "It doesn't matter, Zadock. Let it go." *I don't know if I want to be partnered. Not anymore.*

There's a hard knock at the door, and Motah sighs. "What now?" She turns and opens the door. Shrey lets go of Zadock and looks up at him with tear-filled eyes. *It helps, just a little, that Shrey feels so much of my pain.*

Zadock places one hand on my shoulder. "I'll talk to my potah. I'll do whatever it takes to get you Anointed." He gives me a small smile. "Don't worry, ok?"

I can't help the tears that fill my eyes. I can only shake my head. *I don't want to be Anointed. Not to anyone but you.*

"Did you say you need to speak with me, Zadock?" Faharic Penvaren strides into our entryway and shakes out his sand cloak. "Bit dusty out there." He grins and stamps his polished boots to rid them of sand. He's obviously pleased about the Anointing.

"Potah," Zadock says. His hand flies from my shoulder.

"Faharic." Motah nods.

"Whatever it is, it can wait." Faharic turns to Motah, his good mood falling. "Katiyah, we are needed urgently. An emergency council meeting has been called."

Motah's brows turn down in concern. She grabs her sand cloak from its peg. "An emergency meeting? What for?"

Faharic glances at the rest of us before speaking. Shrey takes my hand and looks up at him with wide eyes.

"Well, I suppose they'll know soon enough." He sighs. "We've just received word. The To'Morat have attacked To'Shahera. They left none alive."

Motah brings a hand to her mouth. Zadock gasps. I am frozen in place.

No.

To'Shahera is farther from us than To'Morat or any other of the major plateaus. I've never been there. I don't know anyone from there. But if the To'Morat are massacring entire plateaus...

Motah ties her sand cloak and adjusts her skirts. "I'll be back soon, girls. Peel that bristlebrush fruit for me, please?"

I nod. My whole body feels numb.

Motah hurries through the door, and Faharic follows. Before he shuts the door behind him, he turns to his son. "Zadock. You will go to Saeri Rahlen's home. She is your Anointed. Your friendship with Norah ends now."

Zadock stiffens. "But Potah. I can't—"

Faharic raises one eyebrow, and Zadock hesitates. "Please, Potah. Norah is—"

Anger darkens Faharic's face and Zadock swallows. "Yes, Potah." He looks at me then, a long, mournful glance.

I didn't think my heart could fall any farther, but it does. It sinks straight to the bottom of my feet.

Shrey opens her mouth, but I squeeze her shoulder, and she bites back whatever she was going to say.

Zadock waves and tries to smile. "Bye, Nors."

Atoille, no...please... Tears brim in my eyes. "Bye, Zadock."

10

IMWRAETH

I stir food around my plate at the Warrior's Feast, the customary post-battle dinner that I have to sit through with my Blood Rank One and Two warriors. If you're Blood Rank Three, you just don't get the pleasure of dining with your disabled leader, I guess.

After tonight, Lienos and Therah will help me oversee re-supplying the ships and making sure the retahn are well-rested. Seven days to prepare, and then my warriors will make the seven-day journey to To'Rahn.

Two weeks. Two weeks until another attack.

Laughter echoes through the dining hall, a large room lined with intricately Forged crystal pillars and burbling water fountains. Torches are lit strategically to reflect off the crystal and make light dance throughout the room. Servants make their rounds with trays of food and drink, bringing smells of spices and seared meat. The chamber is filled with the sounds of chatter and cutlery clinking against crystal plates.

Through long windows, Atoille sets on the western horizon, far across the ocean of sand. Tomorrow night begins the two weeks of darkness without Atoille in the sky. I sit heavier in my chair without the moon's gravity pulling me upward.

Warriors dine at four long banquet tables, and I am seated at the head of one. I'm far enough from my companions to maintain some respectful distance, allowing me to nod and smile and gracefully stay out of the raucous conversation.

General Tysian sits on my right, the most coveted spot at the table.

I take a bite of spicy camehl steak with butter and dates, but I don't have much appetite. Which is a shame because my plate is the fullest of everyone's at the table. This "feast" isn't much to speak of. If the kitchens have to resort to slaughtering retahns, we could be in real trouble.

"An excellent dinner, Favored One. I am honored to be seated next to you," Tysian says.

Lie.

I nod and take another bite of food to avoid starting a conversation with him. I try not to think about how tomorrow evening these same warriors will set sail for To'Rahn for another round of slaughter.

I want to lead these people to greatness. Not greatness through conquering and killing. I want them to flourish in trade, to work with other nations to solve the problems we're facing. I want to be a good leader. I want to keep my people alive long enough to survive this curse on the land so that we can thrive.

But I haven't a clue how.

Councilors Lienos and Therah are both seated at the long table opposite me, talking with esteemed warriors next to them. Therah catches my eye and gives me a nod. Time for another speech from our figurehead leader.

I stand, legs shaking. I hate giving these speeches. I am aware that I'm not very tall, that my red hair and pale skin don't make for an imposing figure, and that because of my heart, my physique is, well, unimpressive. I stand in front of a crowd of well-built fighters, their frowning faces turned toward me.

Councilor Therah gives me an encouraging smile. Lienos just scowls and drums his fingers on the table. Even from across the banquet, I can see his eye roll.

I clear my throat and try to sound strong, but my voice comes out in a squeak. "Warriors, in a week we embark for To'Rahn!"

A few cheers sound around the table.

My heart starts to beat faster, and I feel the irregularity in its pulses. Not again. I put my hand into my satchel to Extract.

Lienos leaps onto his feet and motions for me to sit down. I sigh and do as he suggests. Everyone knows there's something wrong with me, but Lienos does his utmost to make sure people are not reminded.

I don't care that he takes over. Not really. Extracting gives my heart a breath of relief.

"We will fight an honorable battle against a worthy foe," Lienos says. "Our people are counting on you, warriors. So we will fight, for the glory of Atoille, for the glory of the To'Morat!"

Lienos raises his glass for a toast, and warriors around the table shout and lift cups of cactus blossom wine. I lift my quartz goblet to my lips. It's the first time I've touched it this whole meal, per Lienos' request. He knows I can't hold my liquor worth speck.

The liquid sloshes into my mouth, and immediately, I know something is wrong. The cheers around me echo in my ears like they're coming from underwater. The drink tastes foul. My tongue burns.

I hurry to set the quartz goblet down and take deep gulps from my water glass, but the burning on my tongue remains, and now it's spread to my throat.

Don't panic. Don't panic.

I jam my hand into the pack of sand at my side. Extracting is different than Absorbing. Though both involve taking sand into one's body, Absorbing uses the sand and turns it into energy to heal.

When I Extract, I use the sand to give strength to my body. I can use it to go without food, water, or sleep. I can use it to power my muscles for a short time. I can use it to sustain my heart with a wound that will never heal.

Right now, I use it to force the poison out of my skin.

I grab a fistful of sand and squeeze, Extracting the energy from it. A soft glow emits from the bag, and the sand in my hand disintegrates. Pure energy pours into my skin, a burning heat inside of me, seeking the poison.

Beads of sweat break out on my forehead, and I hurry to wipe them away with a napkin. Good. The poison is coming out. I dab at my throat and face, one hand still in my satchel. It's getting low on sand. I'll have to refill it after this. The sand I use is nothing special, just regular desert stuff. I have to carry some with me always, and that is what sets me apart.

Tysian is looking at me sideways. His eyes go from my sweating face to the hand in the bag at my side.

I could be imagining it, but he doesn't look surprised. In fact, his frown of disgust almost appears forced. His lips keep quirking upward, almost into a smile.

My heartbeat slows, the sweating stops, the pain in my throat and tongue lessens. Sound returns to my ears, bit by bit.

Well. That was terrifying.

I take a deep breath and look Tysian right in the eyes. I deliberately lean back in my seat, lounging. I take a sip of water. "Terribly hot this time of year, eh, Blood Rank One Tysian?"

"Yes, Favored One." He takes a bite of food and chews, a confused frown on his face. Someone at the other table starts up a drinking song.

Someone poisoned my drink. But who? And why? Only an idiot would try to truly assassinate me by poison. Everyone knows that I am an Extractor and plenty strong to get rid of all but instantaneous poisoning.

So the poisoner was not trying to kill me but to send me a message. But what?

If I can get Tysian talking, I may be able to catch him in a lie. He is the highest on my suspect list of people who want me dead. He is Blood Rank One. My death could vacate a place for him to take until a new Favored One is chosen and comes of age, anyway. Therah and Lienos would also be candidates to take that space, but they're on the opposite end of the table.

"Good winds for our ships, though," I say. Not that I know anything about that.

Tysian swallows and wipes his mouth with a napkin. Again, I'm struck by how small he is, how much like me. He's never had a need to exercise his muscles much, and I've never been able to. Yet somehow, we are both in positions of power. I frown at his dark eyebrows, a stark contrast to his light hair.

"Yes, Favored One. The journey to To'Rahn should go smoothly," Tysian says.

"Yes. It should." Speck. I am terrible at this. How does one go about asking in a discreet way about one's would-be assassins?

I push my cup a little farther from my plate. "Awful stuff, this. The palace cellars have been emptier as of late."

Tysian skewers a piece of roasted cactus flesh. "Yes, Favored One. But everything's emptier as of late." He turns to his neighbor as if to end the conversation with me.

"Blood Rank Tysian, try mine, won't you?" I have to shout to get his attention. "I swear to Atoille it's worse than normal. Let me know your opinion."

Tysian freezes. He turns back to me. I scan his face, looking for signs of discomfort. Of course, they are there. But what does that mean?

"No, thank you, Favored One. I would not want to sully your drink with my lips." Tysian turns his back to me.

Hmm. I still don't know much.

I eye Lienos from across the room. He smiles at me and lifts his glass. He's probably thrilled that I'm finally engaging my Blood Ranked warriors in conversation.

But could it be more?

Lienos has never liked me. He could also stand to gain from my death.

Lienos lifts his glass in a toast and takes a deep drink, smiling at me from across the room.

Did Lienos put poison in my glass? Why? Was he truly trying to kill me or trying to send a message?

I take the glass and raise it toward Lienos. I lift it to my lips, hoping that he doesn't notice my hands shaking, and I tilt my head back.

I don't drink. But I want him to see.

I scan his face for a reaction. He smiles, eyes glittering, then turns to Therah and chats with her.

I set down my cup, and it rattles against the table.

I'm not sure what's going on, but I know that my next steps have to be very careful.

11

NORAH

Seven days.

That's how much time has passed without Zadock in my life.

An eternity.

Atoille will set tonight, dipping beneath the western horizon to cross the other half of our world. For two weeks, the night sky will be darker, the stars brighter. Everything is heavier.

My footsteps drag across the sandy kitchen floor. I pick up a knife and begin chopping withered yuca tubers that Motah left out for me.

The sting has faded to a dull numbness. Nothing brings me joy anymore. Zadock and I have, for once, honored our parents' wishes and stayed away from each other. I haven't even met him on the edge of the plateau for practice sparring.

I think we both know that it wasn't truly our parents that brought about this moment. We were separated the moment he and Saeri were Anointed.

I've lost him. My best friend is gone.

I make deliberate cuts in the yuca roots, pressing my knife onto the mat in even, rhythmic strokes. I helped Motah pick these yesterday, and they're already wrinkled like they've sat on the counter for weeks.

Zadock.

He is studying under his potah to take his place on the council, and I spend my time helping tend the Ki'Rhen babies and the grow walls. It's killing me. I can't live like this. I can't.

I chop another tuber. Harder.

Shrey practices Absorbing on the ground at my feet, the glow of the sand shining through her fingers. "Do you have any ouchies I can take care of?"

"No, Shrey. Thanks."

Her lower lip sticks out. "C'mon. I need to practice. Did you fall and scrape your knee on the way home from school?"

"No school, remember? I have a job in the community now." *Yay.*

Shrey drops the sand, and the glow vanishes. "Well, did you poke your finger on a needle? Perhaps impale yourself with a shovel?"

"No!" I throw aside a yuca that's gone moldy. "Atoille above, where do you get this stuff?"

Shrey stands and plants her hands on her hips. "You're not hurt at all? How am I ever going to get better at this?" Her eyes land on the knife, and she smiles. "Maybe—"

The door opens, and Motah enters in a rush. She whirls off her sand cloak and hangs it on a peg. Underneath, she wears her white council robes. Another meeting.

Zadock steps through the door behind her. The knife clatters to the cutting mat, and my heart leaps into my throat.

"Hey, Nors." He smiles, running a hand through messy hair. "You doing ok?"

I try to smile and nod. Atoille, why does he have to be so perfect?

"Your motah asked me to come." Zadock shrugs and puts his hands in his pockets, looking a little awkward and unsure of himself.

Motah smooths her skirts. "Thank you, Zadock. I have some... some news. Would you like to sit down?" Motah gestures to the table.

Zadock moves into the room, and I brush my hands on my

clothes. He's here, but I feel the gulf between us even more keenly. Why did Motah ask him to come?

"Did the council say something?" I take a seat at the table across from Zadock. He meets my eyes and gives me a tight smile.

Motah nods. "I am the bearer of an official assignment from the council. To both of you." She takes a breath. "Norah, you and Zadock have to leave. Immediately."

"What? Why?" An assignment from the council? For me?

Zadock's eyebrows lift.

"Shreyen, go to bed, please. It's getting late."

"What? But—"

Motah raises one eyebrow, and Shrey grumbles but goes to our room.

Motah turns back to us, fingers drumming on the table. She seems to notice and places her hands in her lap. "The council has discovered the location of the second moonstone of Atoille."

What?

Zadock looks at me, eyes wide. "But that's just a legend."

Motah shakes her head. "It's—it's real. And the council believes that if it could be found and put in its rightful place, our world could be fixed. Things would be made right again."

I stay quiet. I'm stunned.

"Food would grow?" Zadock asks.

Motah nods. "The unpredictable sandstorms would stop. The plateau erosion would slow. Plants would thrive. If we can find and reunite the second moonstone with its pair."

"How?" I ask. "How does the council know this?"

Motah shrugs. "It's a theory. But ancient records that speak of a second moonstone indicate that its loss may be what's causing this."

Zadock's eyes widen, and he blows out through his lips.

"Why now?" I ask. Something feels off here. "We've never had a second moonstone before. So why is it that in the past three years, all of a sudden, things have gone wrong?"

Motah swallows. "The council doesn't know. It could be that the moonstones can be separated for a time with no ill effect, and we've reached the end of that time." She shakes her head. "I'm not sure. But. If you two can go to the ocean of water and retrieve it, it could mean the salvation of our entire plateau. Of all the desert nations."

Zadock and I lock eyes, and I smile. A thrill of electricity runs through me. We could make a difference. We could save everyone.

And the council is asking me. Motah is asking me.

Zadock frowns. "The ocean of water?"

"Yes," Motah says. "The council has discovered records that point us to the conclusion that the second moonstone is on a pedestal, protected within layers of sand, somewhere on the east coastline. It may take a while to find it, but if you can..."

"We could change everything," I say.

Motah nods, a small, weary smile on her face. "Yes, Norah." She pauses. "To'Shahera is gone. And it's likely that the To'Morat will strike here next. By all accounts, To'Rahn is faring better in the famine than other plateaus. It's only a matter of time before the To'Morat attack."

Motah meets my eyes and then Zadock's. "You two may be able to change that. If food can be made to grow, if the weather can be righted, the To'Morat will cease their attacks. Many lives are depending on you. The ocean is a great distance from here, but not as far as people think. It will take you about seven days to get there, and you must leave tonight. We are running out of time."

Zadock bites his lip. "My potah didn't say anything about this."

Motah nods. "The council's discussions have been kept quiet. We agreed to send a small team like this, in secret, so that the To'Morat do not catch word and try to intercept you. If they hear what you are doing, they may try to take the moonstone for themselves instead of reuniting it with its pair."

This all feels surreal. It's happening so fast. "Why us?"

Motah's lips soften into something like a smile. She looks at me almost tenderly. It feels strange, and I bristle under her gaze. "You two were chosen because of your unique gifts."

Gifts? I almost jolt out of my chair.

"Zadock is the strongest Shaker our village has seen in generations," Motah says. "You'll need that strength to cross the ocean of sand, and quickly."

Zadock's face is bewildered. But then he steels himself and nods. "I'll do my best, Katiyah Saiyu."

Motah turns to me, that small smile still on her lips. "Norah. You were chosen because you know the stars. You learned from your potah, and he was one of the best navigators To'Rahn has ever seen. You can get Zadock there."

Something inside me warms and softens. Motah noticed.

Motah stands and gestures for us to follow her into the kitchen. She kneels and rummages through our pantry for supplies.

For a moment, I'm frozen at the table. Is this real? The council chose me, of all people, to go with Zadock. They saw my talent for star navigation and decided it was worth something.

Zadock follows Motah and grabs a sack of dried lizard meat. "We will do this, Katiyah Saiyu. We will figure it out."

A seven-day journey. It will be farther into the ocean of sand than I've ever gone, even with Potah, and much more dangerous than the little excursions Zadock and I have sailed before. The deep ocean of sand holds more hazards than its shores.

My hands tremble at my sides. Can I do this? A girl with nothing —no gift. I'm nothing special. And on the ocean of sand, if anything happens to Zadock, I'll be stranded. Alone. Powerless.

Zadock looks back at me with a smile. He packs another packet of food into a box. He believes that we can make a difference. He believes in me.

I kneel beside Motah and help her fill waterskins.

"Norah," she whispers. "Please be careful."

She lifts her hand, almost lets it touch my hair, then she snatches it away. "For the sake of the village. You must get Zadock to the ocean of water."

We carry boxes of supplies to the *Norah*, making the trek through the village streets and back. It feels strange to be packing the boat up again and getting ready for a journey after so long.

Bright stars are shining overhead, and a sliver of Atoille peeks on the western horizon by the time Zadock sets his last armload into the boat. "I should let my potah know we're on our way."

Motah shakes her head. "There's no time. Everyone on the council agreed that you need to go now."

Zadock hesitates but then nods.

Shrey bounds around the corner of the boathouse with a cry and wraps her arms around my legs. "I don't want you to go."

Motah frowns. "Shrey. Did you follow us?"

Shrey looks back at Motah with a sheepish smile. I wrap my arms around Shrey and hold her. "It's ok. We'll be back. Just seven days there and seven days back." I bend down to her level. Wipe the tears out of her eyes. "We'll be back. I promise you." I grip her tighter. If the To'Morat attack while we're gone...

"Shrey—one second."

Motah frowns. "Norah, hurry."

I race back through the village streets to our house, burst through the door, and dig through my chest of things until I find it. A doll I had played with as a child. I smooth the soft hair out of her face. Potah made her. When I didn't have any friends, I had this doll.

Motah and I used to play together with her, take care of her and feed her and pretend she was our baby until Shrey came along. Those early memories of Motah and me—those are some of the only happy times I have with her. She probably doesn't even know how much that meant to me.

I hug the doll to my chest one more time, a squeeze for comfort and luck. And then I run back to the boathouse.

Motah is frowning and tapping her foot.

"Here." I put my back to Motah so she can't see what I'm doing. Love for objects is discouraged, and if she knew I had kept this for so long, she would not be happy. I thrust the doll into Shrey's hands. "This is for you."

Shrey takes the doll and stares into her face with wide eyes. "Norah..." Shrey looks up at me, her eyes shining. She throws her arms around me. "Thank you."

I hold her tight, as tight as I can. "I love you," I say it so quietly into her hair it may have been carried away in the wind.

"I love you, too," she whispers.

I feel a stab of guilt.

Shrey presses something into my hand, and I feel a sharp prick. Cactus needles. I can't help it. My eyes fill with tears. "More lucky needles. Thank you, Shrey."

"They'll keep you safe." She gives me one more squeeze, then tucks the doll into her dress. I reach out and tug on one of her curls, making it bounce on her back.

"Hey!" She rubs her head, and I grin. I stand, blinking rapidly, and nod to Zadock. "Ready?"

Motah grasps my arm. "Norah. Find the second moonstone and get back as quickly as you can. To'Rahn is counting on you. I don't know how long we have until the To'Morat attack, but..."

I hear the words she doesn't want to say in front of Shrey. The attack is coming, and it's coming soon.

I look at Zadock and give him a determined nod. The village—the world—needs us.

I will get us to the ocean of water.

12

ZADOCK

Holy speck. My parents... I didn't get to say goodbye. But Potah is on the council. He knows what he's doing.

Katiyah puts her hand on Norah's shoulder. "May Atoille be with you, my daughter."

Norah stares at her motah. Then she gives her a sharp nod and turns away. She doesn't see that Katiyah's face falls. "Let's go."

I nod and we both climb in the boat. The *Norah* is small compared to the huge trading vessels I've seen that Potah uses, but it's still got enough room to walk a dozen paces across on all sides. Our gear and supplies are stored under our feet.

There's a single mast, I think it's called, and two sails, a smaller and a larger, that Norah flaps open. She's tried to teach me how to do this part a million times, but Norah's always been the sailor.

Norah lets out a whoop of joy as the boat lurches. "Push us off!"

Benches rim the inside edge of the boat, and I take a seat at the back. I Shake the sand underneath us, lifting us up and forward, giving one final wave to Katiyah and Shrey. We plummet off the plateau. Norah shrieks, her face lighting up with delight.

We fall, and I move my arms, lifting the sand beneath to catch us. Above us are countless glittering stars.

We hit the ocean of sand, and I propel us forward. When I glance behind, Katiyah and Shrey watch us from the edge of the plateau. It gets farther and farther away until they are just tiny dots.

I let out a breath. Atoille's ashes. We're really doing this. I wonder what Saeri will think when she finds out that I left without saying goodbye.

I've been avoiding her this past week. I didn't want to see her, even though now we're expected to spend more time together and get to know each other better. Not to grow in affection, but to come to an agreement of when we'll get married—ack—and what our future will be like.

Potah has been all smiles all week long, congratulating me over and over and taking me with him to the less important council meetings. I put on a smile and pretended to be happy, because I didn't know what else to do.

Being out here with Norah... It's like that moment when the sun is setting and the desert is the perfect temperature after a day of stifling heat. I can finally breathe.

She looks beautiful. Perfect. She sits at the front of the boat, her head tilted to gaze at the stars. She'll let me know which way to go, and I trust her completely. It's late, but I'm full of energy and ready for a long night of travel.

I move my arms back and forth, working the sand like it's an extension of my body. I can feel the sand beneath the boat, and it's easy as thought to move it, driving the boat forward.

Norah glances back at me, and her face lights up in a grin. "Zadock, it's—it's so good to be with you." Her eyes soften. "You doing ok?" she asks. "That was so sudden."

"Yeah. I'm ok. You?"

"I'm glad we're doing this. I'm scared." She bites her lower lip. "But I'm ready, you know? Ready to do something to help."

I smile. "I know."

"I missed you, Zadock." Norah glances down. "This past week was so hard without you."

I swallow. "I missed you, too, Nors."

"I don't want things to be like that when we go back," she says. "I know you're Anointed. I know. And we can't change that, but…" She looks up at me with hopeful eyes. "I still want to see you. I'm still your friend."

Her words warm me from head to toe. The sand is getting harder to work. "Me, too, Nors. I don't care what anybody says. Saeri—" Her name tastes bitter in my mouth. "—won't mind. She's your friend, too."

Norah nods. Uncertainty clouds her face, but then she smiles.

I focus on the sand, the sliding of each grain past another. The weight of the boat. Because if I focus on Norah, I'll lose control.

13

NORAH

It feels so normal to be out here with Zadock, like we're just going for a sail instead of setting out on an epic quest to save the desert nations. Like things are back to the way they were, the misery of the past week erased.

Motah was right. If anyone can save us, it's Zadock. I look back at the plateau, a dark, hulking shape against an otherwise empty horizon. I swear I see two tiny points at the top, still watching.

We keep going for hours, Zadock steadying and guiding the sand, and I help as much as I can. I keep my eyes on the stars to guide us. If Motah is right, all we have to do is keep heading east. At this time of year, that will mean following the Weeping Woman constellation. I keep our bowsprit pointed straight toward her tears.

By the time the sun blinks over the desert, we're both exhausted. Zadock's posture is slumped where he sits at the stern. "I can't do this much longer, Nors."

"Just a little farther," I say. "We'll sleep during the day and travel at night when I can use the stars to guide us."

When the sun climbs over the horizon, the sand calms and stills. It still shivers and shifts, but the waves are gone. Somehow the sun balances the gravity of the moon, changing the pull on the sand. The boat still rolls on gentle waves, but Zadock doesn't need to guide us quite as much. He drops his arms to his sides and shakes them out.

Zadock climbs down the steps to join me at the bow. "Speck, that was one long night." He gives me a small smile. "We're really doing this."

I smile back. It feels good to be doing something, anything. I plant the tiller in the last place I saw the Weeping Woman constellation and tie it down. Now any wind that guides us forward will be putting us in the right direction.

"Norah." Zadock puts a hand on my arm, and I feel the heat of it go through my whole body. I look up at him, into his deep blue eyes. "Your motah cares for you."

I start. It's not what I expected him to say. "Why do you say that?"

"You might not have noticed, but it was hard for her to say goodbye."

I look away.

"I know she's hurt you."

Zadock's gentle voice. The *shhhh* of the lapping sand.

"But you might try, you know, forgiving her?"

I close my eyes. Feel the heat of the desert sun on my shoulders. Zadock doesn't understand. He hasn't been there for the worst moments between Motah and me.

I open the hatch that leads to the hold. "Let's rest while we can." I glance back at Zadock. My heart pounds harder. This isn't a large boat, and for all the times we've been out on it, we've never stayed overnight. The hold is tiny, and it's crammed with all our supplies. The ceiling is low, with barely enough room to crawl around the boxes. There is one small sleeping pallet off to the side. When I was younger, Potah and I would share it. But we rarely ventured far enough to need to sleep. He didn't take me on his longer voyages.

"Ummm."

"What is it?" Zadock's eyelids are drooping.

I step aside. "You take the bed. You need the rest more than I do."

Zadock closes his eyes, shakes his head. "I'll sleep up here. You take it."

"No way. You just worked all night. We need you to be fresh tomorrow night so we can do that again. It's the only way we'll make it there and back in time." I squint at the rising sun. "It's way too bright out here to sleep well."

Seven days. Seven days there, and seven days back. Sooner if we push hard. And that's assuming that finding and retrieving the moonstone doesn't take more time.

Zadock takes my hand. A jolt sends shivers up and down my spine. He smiles weakly. "We both need to be fresh. Our people need us. C'mon."

Zadock leads me down the stairs into the hold. It's darker in here, the only light coming from the opening hatch that leads to the deck. Zadock cracks open one of our crates of supplies, and we both eat a small meal of dried bristlebrush fruits and sand lizard jerky. We pass a waterskin back and forth, and when my hand brushes his, that tingle hits me again.

We leave the hatch open to let in some fresh air. Zadock climbs onto the narrow bed and sheds his coat that I had handed him sometime in the night when it got cold. Underneath it, he wears a sleeveless shirt that shows his defined shoulders. I blush and hurry to glance away. Zadock lies down and outstretches his arm. "C'mon, Norah. Nobody is sleeping on that hard deck."

My breath catches in my throat. Is this doing to him what it's doing to me?

"But Saeri. She's—"

"Not here. And she'll die, along with our entire village, if we don't succeed." In the dim light, his dark blue eyes meet mine. "Rest."

Slowly, awkwardly, I lie down next to him. His body presses against mine so I am perfectly fitted to him. I lay my head on his arm. Close my eyes.

I have never felt this. This closeness.

Zadock hesitates, but then he places his other arm around my waist. "Is this ok?" His voice, a breath in my ear.

I tremble. "Yes."

"Good night, Norah," Zadock whispers.

"Good night."

In moments, his breathing deepens. I lie awake, my heart pounding so hard I hope it doesn't wake Zadock. I want to stay here forever.

I breathe in his smell. Earthy and warm and so...Zadock.

My heart is aching. I wish he was mine.

I close my eyes.

14

NORAH

"You're getting better at keeping the boat smooth," I say to Zadock on the third night. "I barely feel like I'm going to throw up anymore."

"Ha, ha. You're hilarious."

I grin.

We're making good time. The winds are favoring us, urging us onward. I can't help but think that Atoille herself is helping us, though she's gone from the night sky. The sands are calm, even out here in the deep ocean of sand. It's a good season for traveling.

I love this. Every moment with the sand spraying over my calves, the hot wind whipping my hair, my fingers gripping the tiller. This is what I was born to do.

On every horizon is sand, just sand. Miles and miles of it. The waves are soft, gentle. We are completely alone.

It's a strange feeling. We are so far from home, so far from anywhere, that there are no plateaus in sight. Just fine, orange sand as far as I can see. The line of the desert meets the stars somewhere far away.

Something to our left leaps from the sand.

"Norah—did you see that?" Zadock yells.

"Yeah. Keep watching."

After a moment, the thing emerges from the sand again, shell first. It's a creature about as long as my arm, with a hard gray-and-black-speckled oval shell. The head peeks up through the sand, and two black eyes stare at me. Long feathery antennae reach out to brush against the boat.

"Ugh." Zadock's mouth is turned down in disgust, and I can't help but laugh.

"What the speck is that? It looks like a giant bug."

"It's not a giant bug," I say. "It's a sand mole. It's exploring our boat, seeing if we're a source of food. So cute, right?"

"Ummm. That's not exactly how I would describe it."

I smile. "Watch." I reach out my hand and tap it on the shell. In the space of a breath, the creature dives face-first back into the sand, burrowing down deep. It's gone before I can blink.

"Whoa!" Zadock meets my eyes and smiles.

"Yeah, they're pretty neat," I say. "Potah loved them. You only see them out here in the deep desert."

Zadock's hands move back and forth, his shoulders working as he pushes the sand and moves us forward. "How do they move on the sand? How do they not get sucked under like we do?"

I shrug. "I don't know. Must be something about the way their bodies work, I guess." Why can't people learn to maneuver through the sand like that?

"Just hope we don't come across a blood worm," I say. "They are ruthless and will feed on just about anything."

Zadock pales.

I laugh and put a hand on his arm. "It's ok. Potah taught me how to shove them back under the sand with an oar. They're rare, anyway."

Zadock relaxes a little and continues working the sand. The heat of the day is fading, and I go into the hold and emerge with our coats. I help Zadock get his on so he can continue Shaking. One hand and then the other. I adjust it around his shoulders and then move around to his front. His face is so close to mine it makes my breath catch. I do up the buttons and then hurry to step back.

"Thank you," Zadock says. "You've seen some amazing things out here."

I take a seat again, glancing at the stars and adjusting our course. "The deep ocean of sand does get pretty weird. Potah always claimed it was magic out here." *Until that magic stole his life.*

Another sand mole—or maybe it's the same one—pops out of the sand closest to Zadock, on the other side of the boat now. Zadock stares into its bright eyes for a moment before poking it on the shell. It burrows away.

"You did it!" I give Zadock a thumbs up.

He grins.

"They're mostly harmless. Just don't let the antennae touch you."

Zadock's face falls.

"I'm kidding! I'm kidding." I can't help but laugh.

"Agh! You are so dead." Zadock grins back, but then he takes a deep breath, and his face turns serious. "We have to go faster, Nors. If the To'Morat attack while we're gone..." He pauses. "I want to see my family again."

"We will. This is the best thing we can do for the village right now. Go as fast as you can, but don't burn yourself out. We still have about four days to go, if Motah is right."

☾

ABOUT HALFWAY THROUGH THE NIGHT, clouds start to billow over the dark sky, obscuring the stars.

I frown. "We may have to stop."

"What do you mean?"

"I can't see the stars." During the day, I can set the tiller and let the wind take us in generally the right direction. But now, with Zadock actively propelling us, even the slightest misdirection in course could lead to major mistakes. "We can keep heading forward, but if we get off course, it could be disastrous."

I look back at Zadock, and he's chewing his lip. "If we don't get there in time, it could be even worse."

I stop and think, glancing up at the sky again. "Let's take a little break and see if the clouds pass."

Zadock nods. The boat stops moving forward, but Zadock still Shakes the sand to hold us as much in place as he can, flowing with the rolling waves. If it wasn't for Zadock, we would be overturned in a matter of moments.

I go into the hold and come back up with a waterskin and packages of seed crackers and dried plantains. Zadock needs his hands to work the sand, so I carefully hold the waterskin to his lips. For a second, I think about dumping it all over him, but we need to conserve, so I hold back. A wasted opportunity.

I feed him and myself, alternating putting a cracker or a plantain in his mouth and then in mine. It's strange, the exhilaration I feel at this small act, the times when his lips barely brush my fingers. I hope he doesn't notice the way I tremble at his touch.

Either his feelings have changed, or he's burying them down deep because I don't notice any weakness in his sand Shaking that would indicate he's feeling anything back.

After our lunch, I check the sky again. "The clouds are even worse." Droplets of rain splatter against my upturned face.

Desert storms can hit fast and pour hard on the plateau, and I've been out with Potah when they've hit on the sands. We need to hurry.

"It's starting to storm. Keep us steady," I say. The wind is picking up. I need to get our tarp up.

I hurry to fold in the sails and tuck them underneath my arms. I go below into the hold, store the sails, and then shove aside boxes, my hands finally touching the canvas that may save us. I drag it back up. The rain is pouring now, soaking through my shirt and hair.

"Norah?!" Zadock calls. "I can't see, and the sand is getting harder to control."

I hurry to both corners on the stern and tie the canvas to hooks there. Then I climb up the mast of the ship, using handholds, dragging the canvas behind me.

"Hang in there!" I call. "Just keep us afloat."

Zadock gives me a firm nod.

I try to smile back at him as I climb, wet hair getting into my eyes. "It's going to be ok. Just keep us above the biggest waves. They're going to get heavier now." I fasten the canvas to the mast. Just two more.

The rain is pouring hard, and I slip across the deck on my way to the bow. The canvas feels like it weighs more than a camehl, but I manage to drag it forward, and finally, I connect the last two hocks. I breathe a sigh of relief.

I brush sopping hair out of my eyes and wring out my shirt in our small shelter. Rain patters on top of the canvas. It's slicked with wax, so it won't get soaked, and it's designed so that the rain will collect at each corner.

I look at Zadock. "You holding up ok?"

His arms are shaking, and his teeth are gritted from the effort. "Fine."

I peek underneath the canvas. The waves are heavy, pushing against our boat. We rock and tilt, and I hurry to sit down. Nerves churn in my stomach. Potah was always able to keep us steady when a storm came, but Zadock hasn't had the practice. If our boat dips in the sand, if we're overturned by a large wave... "You're doing fine. We're going to be ok."

The boat gives another heave as a wet wave of sand tries to toss us to the side. I fall into Zadock, crashing into his arms. The boat lurches downward, and I let go so Zadock can regain control.

"Sorry!"

"It's ok," Zadock says, his face and arms taut with concentration.

I grab hold of the tiller and do my best to keep it steady. Anything to help Zadock through this.

Atoille curse this storm and the time we're wasting!

I hear a clicking noise, and my senses go on high alert. Then I turn around and realize it's Zadock's teeth chattering. With the adrenaline fading, I notice that I'm shivering as well. My coat and pants are soaked.

"We should change," I say, even though a blush brings some heat to my cheeks. "We could freeze out here in these wet clothes."

Zadock's face is focused, his arms moving to work the sand. "All right." He shivers. "But I don't think I should drop control of the boat."

I bite my lip and nod. I open the hatch and duck into the hold. It's a storage compartment, crowded with boxes, and only a spare corner open for the sleeping pallet. Not enough room to change.

Ok. Get it together, Norah. You have to change into dry clothes, or you'll freeze. It's purely an act of survival. I dig through our things for clothes for Zadock and me.

I emerge from the hold and stand there staring while Zadock works. The boat dips down a wave, and I stumble backward into my seat.

"You change first," Zadock says. "I'll close my eyes. I can feel the sand better that way, anyway."

"Umm. Ok." The thought of undressing in front of Zadock, even with his eyes closed, makes my neck burn. But eventually, the aching chill wins, and I take off my wet coat. Camehl wool is warm, but it isn't waterproof, and even my shirt underneath is drenched. I peel it off my skin and over my head. My bare torso is exposed to the cold, and I shake uncontrollably as I rush to get on a dry shirt.

Zadock stands at the rear of the boat, eyes closed, working the sand.

Next, my pants. I yank them down and pull on a dry pair while seated on the bench. I stand and jam them up to my hips. I breathe out. Dressed and dry, I feel much better. I only have one coat, so I lay it out and hope it dries fast.

Zadock is still shivering, eyes closed, directing the sand with his hands. The boat rocks with the waves, and the rain splatters on the canvas.

"You can open your eyes."

Zadock blinks. "Nors, I don't want to ask you to do this..."

"But if I don't, you'll freeze." I stand, determined to not make this awkward. He's my friend. He needs my help. "If you drop control of the sand, a wave could toss us under."

Zadock swallows. His jaw is clenched, trying to stop the chattering.

Ok, Norah. Don't make it weird.

I grab a clean shirt and pants for Zadock and carefully make my way across the tilting boat. I have to crouch to get around under the canvas. I unbutton Zadock's coat and strip it off his arms, one at a time. The boat dips with a wave. Zadock's shivering worsens.

I hurry to take off his wet shirt, trying to ignore his muscled chest and his bare skin so close to mine. My cheeks are on fire. I pull a dry shirt on over his head. My fingers brush the smooth skin of his chest, and the touch goes through me like a jolt.

The sway of the boat is getting rockier, and I wonder what's going through Zadock's head. What he's feeling.

His eyes meet mine, and there's tenderness there. I quickly look away.

I breathe out. Here comes the really tough part.

"I'm going to look away, all right?" Atoille, this is hard. But I don't have a choice.

I loosen Zadock's belt and undo his pants button, my stomach churning with nerves. I look to the side and yank them off. *Holy speck.*

I quickly grab Zadock's dry pair of pants and stare at his feet as he lifts one foot into the legs and then the other. Glancing away, I tug them up his legs. My fingers brush the sides of his thighs, and I swallow. The boat plummets down a crest of sand, and my stomach drops. Zadock falls to the bench.

I leave his pants button undone. He's covered enough.

"Thanks, Nors," Zadock says. His teeth have stopped chattering.

I clear my throat. "You're welcome."

We sit on the bench and listen to the desert rain. Like a sandstorm, it could be over in moments, or we could be here for hours.

"It's beautiful," Zadock says. "I don't think I've ever been out here during a rain."

I smile. "It is, isn't it?"

We're lucky, and it's only a short wait before the pattering quiets, and the rocking of the boat evens out.

"I think it's letting up." I peel back the canvas and blink in the starlight. The night is clear and black. What little body heat we had under the canvas dissipates, and the icy cold bores into my skin. My breath fogs in front of my face.

We both take long drinks of the fresh rainwater collected at the corners of the canvas, and I use what's left to replenish our waterskins before rolling up the canvas and putting it away.

I locate the Weeping Woman constellation among the stars. "Let's keep going." I point out the right direction. "That way."

Zadock nods, and his hands swirl with the sand as he controls the boat and moves us forward.

Our coats are still wet, and my teeth are chattering again. I look everywhere but Zadock, trying to think about anything except what just happened.

"Norah, c'mere."

I glance Zadock's way. He's moving the ship with one hand, and the other he's got stretched toward me. "It's easier to control now that the sands have calmed, and we're both freezing."

I scoot a little closer.

His eyebrows lift. "C'mon, Nors. We've got to survive to get there, no matter what. I realize that you just helped me dress, and you're probably feeling a little awkward, but seriously, it's ok. Let it go."

I swallow and meet his eyes, deep and kind. I slide down the bench into his arms and sink into his body heat. I sigh. He's warm and soft and...perfect.

His arm wraps around me and holds me close. We're both in sleeveless shirts since that's all we have other than the coats, and the bare skin of his arm covers mine. The shivering slows. I lay my head on his shoulder, suddenly exhausted.

The forward movement of the boat slows down as well, and I wonder if Zadock is having trouble working the sand.

At the moment, I don't care.

15

IMWRAETH

My skin tingles as the Absorber runs her hands over my bare chest. She grabs another handful of sand from the vase beside the medical bed and dusts it over my skin. I lie on my back, staring up at the light coming through the glass windows overhead. I don't want to look at her face. I don't want to know the person who is trying desperately to heal me.

Because I know what will happen if she fails, just as she does.

She is from To'Shahera. She is the elder of the two Absorbers that were taken while the rest of their people were slaughtered.

Shriveled potted plants line the walls, and two guards are stationed at the door, watching the Absorber work. The air smells sterile and distinctly sour, like medicine. It's a smell I've become accustomed to over the years. Every Absorber on To'Morat has tried their hand at healing me, of course, but when that failed, my doctors turned to other treatments. Nothing has worked.

The bed sheets beneath me are cool and soft, made of the finest camehl wool. Comfortable, but it still doesn't change the fact that I have itchy sand covering my chest.

The door opens and shuts, and Councilor Therah strides in with a disapproving frown. "Favored One! Lying on that hard bed without a stitch on above the waist and such a draft in here."

My face flushes bright red. Therah snaps her fingers and orders a servant folding sheets to get me another blanket. Therah turns her sternness to the girl working on me. "Hurry it up already. The Favored One is tired of this."

I bite my lip and refrain from saying anything. Therah is as close to a motah as I'll ever know.

Servants drape another blanket over my legs. The Absorber girl meets my eyes for the briefest instant, and I can't help it. I look back. Her eyes are the color of honey. They meet mine with pleading in her expression and a silent fear. Her hair is a deep mahogany that curls softly about her shoulders. I can't help but notice that she is quite lovely.

She is crying silently, one tear after another rolling down her cheeks.

Something deep inside me wrenches at my gut. I did this to her. I caused this pain. But it was necessary. I didn't have a choice.

"If this one fails, we'll bring in the other," Therah says, smoothing the blankets that cover my legs.

The Absorber jolts, dashing sand over my torso.

"Careful, girl," Therah snaps. She turns her attention to a sheet of dried cactus paper in her hands. "Favored One, let's go over the day's events."

I close my eyes, shutting out the bright light of the room, the servants seeing me in my weakness. It's bad enough that they're here and that there are also several guards posted around the room. I don't want Therah to see me like this as well. She's never shown open disdain, not like Lienos does, but of course she feels it.

"Not now, Therah. I'm sure the Absorber needs quiet to focus."

The Absorber runs her hands up and down my chest, the sand rubbing over my skin. Despite the grit, her hands feel nice. There's a faint glow.

"I will hear my schedule later, Councilor Therah." My fingernails bite into my palms. How will she react?

Therah's lips press into a thin line. "Yes, Favored One." She turns to leave. "Just remember that the warriors need your blessing before they depart for To'Rahn today. Servants are in your quarters packing your things as we speak. You are needed in your chambers after this to finalize preparations. And then—"

I tune her out as Therah proceeds to announce my schedule on her way out. Finally, she bows and closes the door.

The Absorber shuts her eyes now. Sweat drips down her brow. Her touch is gentle and probing, like a warm light in the cavity of my chest. I know what she'll find. I already know what she'll say.

"I think I can feel something."

It's the first time I've heard her voice.

"I feel your heart."

I sigh. Nothing.

"I feel the break. I feel the lump in the tissue that's causing a blockage."

I've been told this before. I begin to sit up. "Well, it's been a pleasure. I've got to—"

"I can do something about this!" she cries, her hands pressing me back down. "I can fix this!"

What?

I look at her. Take in her face. Watch every single detail. "Say that again."

She smiles. "I can heal you."

I jolt upright, and the sand slips from my skin.

Truth.

16

ZADOCK

Holy speck. This is hard.

My arms ache from working the sand. The wind pulls my hair back and forth across my face. It's up to me to keep us on course, above the sand, and going forward.

The boat lurches, and Norah shifts forward in her seat, one hand on the steering thing. She looks back at me with a smile that makes my heart leap.

She has no idea how hard that was for me yesterday to keep the boat going forward. To do what needed to be done to keep us alive.

I focus. Sand is constantly drifting into the boat, threatening to sink us and pull us under. I'm getting pretty good at getting the sand out of the boat and keeping us moving forward at the same time.

The night is deep and cold all around us, and the stars overhead are a jumble of lights. I wonder how Norah can make sense of it all.

Norah goes into the hold and emerges with food and water. She sits next to me and holds the waterskin to my lips. I drink, careful not to waste a drop. I can control the sand with one hand, but I'm faster if I use both.

Norah feeds me a dried plantain, sweet and chewy. The touch of her fingers against my lips still gives me a rush, and I have to focus on the sand.

"I checked our supplies," Norah says. "We're doing well. We should have enough water and food to get there and back, assuming the timeline Motah gave us is correct." She chews a cracker. "Assuming we don't need more time to find the moonstone."

"We have to have hope." I try to give her a reassuring smile. "Trust in your motah."

Norah glances away, to the desert behind us. Her eyes widen.

I turn. And then I see it. Something black in the distance, riding the waves. My heart skips a beat.

"Uhhh, Norah?" I point. "What's that?"

Behind us, far across the never-ending sand, there's a dark shape bobbing up and down on the waves. It looks almost like—

"It's a boat." Norah swallows. "There's another boat back there. Looks bigger than ours."

"Who is it? What do they want?" I ask, my hands and half my brain still focused on keeping us afloat.

"Well, it could be a trading boat."

"But trade is not happening right now."

"Yeah..." She trails off, still frowning.

I narrow my eyes, trying to focus on the dark blob. "It's not a giant deathstalker, right?"

"No!" Norah rolls her eyes. "The only thing it could be is another boat. The question is, where from? And what are they doing?" She shrugs. "They've probably got nothing to do with us."

"And if it's a To'Morat warship?" I ask.

"That doesn't make sense. From everything I've heard, they attack with a bunch of ships, right?"

"Right."

The wind picks up even more, and I throw my focus back into guiding the boat. The waves of sand are getting choppier, rougher. I grit my teeth. Wind sprays sand into my eyes. Why is this—

The boat is flung into the air, and for a second, we're floating.

A cry escapes my lips as we fly, and I furiously work the sand, trying to bring us down softly. We land with a thud and a spray of sand.

Norah's lips move, her face distorted with worry, but I can't hear what she's saying because the wind is roaring in my ears.

"SANDSTORM!" Norah screams.

Oh.

Speck.

We didn't even see this one coming, and it's upon us. How?

Norah scrambles to untie the sails. The sand slices through my coat and stings my arms.

I move my hands, trying to counteract the sand that's shifting erratically.

Sand washes overboard in a wave and spills at my feet. Our small boat starts to sink beneath the waves.

"Gahhhh!" I hurry to Shake the sand back over, but as soon as I do, more spills onto the deck. The waves are too choppy.

Norah has finally pulled the sails down, and she grabs my arm. "Cover us and keep us up!" She jerks me down with her. The boat dips and sinks. This is rockier than before when we were in sight of the plateau.

I put up a dome of sand around us, close and as tight as I can make it. When my eyes adjust, I can barely see Norah's outline in front of me. Her knees touch mine.

"We're sinking!" Norah cries.

I can feel the sand all around us even though I can't see it. Norah's right, the sand has filled the top of the boat, and it's starting to pull us into its depths.

Panic rises into my throat. I try to unbury us, try to move the sand and Shake us free.

"Use the sand underneath the boat," Norah says. "Push us up."

Deep breath. My heart is thundering. I focus on the vast sand underneath us. Heaving with all my strength, I begin to lift the boat on a platform of sand.

Slowly, I feel the entire boat rise. So heavy... My muscles are straining, aching.

I feel it when we break free. The sand slides off, and we become lighter.

"Keep going," Norah says. "We have to get above the waves, or they'll knock us back down."

I keep lifting us, higher and higher. The winds are rockier now that we're above the sand. I use the platform I'm Shaking to hold us as steady as I can, but we're still being rocked and roiled. I think I'm going to be sick.

The boat turns, and Norah cries out and falls forward into me.

My heart swells, and the boat drops down.

Norah pushes away and rights herself.

I clear my throat and hurry to rework the sand so that we're steady again. The darkness is so close around us, suffocating and hot, and it's even harder because I can't see what I'm doing. There's just her face in the dark, her eyes wide and bright, and she's counting on me to keep us alive. I work on holding us steady, not moving forward or backward, just holding us up.

"Thank you, Zadock," Norah whispers. "No one would be strong enough to do this but you." Even in the dark, I can tell her cheeks turn bright red. She averts her eyes.

Something warm glows in my heart, and as the glow brightens, my control over the sand leeches away.

Atoille, there's nothing in the world I want more right now than to kiss her. Holding her each day while we sleep is the worst kind of beautiful torture, a torment that I relish. I can't help it. I look down at her lips, and my body leans forward almost on its own.

The boat plummets.

Norah screams, and I wave my arms frantically, trying to gather the sand underneath us. It's not working.

The boat falls. If we splash back down in that sand, I don't know if I'll have the strength to pull us up again.

Adrenaline pounds through my system. I try to think about

anything else. Potah wanting me to be a politician like he is. Motah sipping her tea instead of ever speaking a word to me. Saeri and her bright blue eyes, her hands in mine as Ki'Rhen Hainan Anointed us for life.

I lift the sand to catch us.

Norah cries out as we jolt to a halt. The platform of sand is secure beneath us now.

I look down at my hands, pretending to be focusing on lifting us back up again, but really, I just can't look at Norah. I can't think about her.

I can't. Get. Distracted.

17

IMWRAETH

T ruth.

The girl had told the truth.

Sand blows through my hair in gusts as I stand on the outer rim of the plateau at the shipping docks, great quartz structures for housing the ships when they aren't in use. Thousands of people, nearly the whole village, have come to see the warriors off, as is traditional. I am supposed to be going with them to battle, also traditional, but with the Absorber's news...Therah had recognized that this needed to take precedence. Lienos had frowned and fixed me with those disapproving eyes, but he, too, had nodded.

So it is with relief that I stand here, anxious to get this over with. The sun is hot on my skin, but it will soon be sinking, replaced by starlight to guide the ships. I stand on a raised platform, overseeing the last-minute loading of cargo. Therah hustles up to me with my black coat in hand, and I shake my head. She frowns but stands off to the side.

I scan the crowd of my people who have come to watch, the families of those who leave to fight. Some of them clasp hands to shoulders. One couple even kisses. I turn away, averting my eyes from the unseemly display. Everywhere I look, I see lean faces, but proud and solemn. The goods we took from To'Shahera have helped, but feeding a nation is no easy task.

My eyes wander to the quartz pillar of To'Morat, standing thick and tall off to my right. It's covered in intricate, blocky markings, the ancient script of my people. It's said that it was erected when the To'Morat, a wandering people, found their home here, and the name of every great leader of To'Morat is inscribed there.

I feel a surge of pride in my people, and I wish that I was more.

Lienos strides up the platform steps and stands next to me. "A glorious sight, Favored One."

"Yes."

We continue to stare over the workers loading the ships. They're finishing up now, herding in the retahn and the empty supply wagons that will be used to haul away To'Rahn's goods.

"I will give your speech, Favored One."

I start, turning to stare at Lienos. "But—ah—"

Lienos's mouth quirks into a smile. "No need to strain yourself. My words will be enough. Oh, and Councilor Therah and I will be staying here with you, by the way."

"Hmm." I nod. I should say something, tell Lienos that I want to give my own speech, that I *can* lead this nation. But I don't.

Lienos steps forward and lifts his arms as he shouts. "Warriors of To'Morat, tonight we depart for To'Rahn!"

The people turn and raise fists in the air, cheering.

"Atoille is with us, for we fight for her and for glory! We are strong, undaunted—"

Lienos drones on, animating his words with grand gestures, pausing for cheers from the people. He does a better job of it than I would, anyway.

I tune back in to Lienos when it sounds like he's finishing up, but then out of the corner of my eye, I see it.

The quartz pillar of To'Morat is falling.

"Watch out!" My heart leaps out of control. People scream and scramble to get out of the way.

I stumble backward, acting on pure instinct, as the huge pillar crashes down. Running for the stairs is not an option. That's right where the pillar is falling.

Lienos cuts off at the screams and turns. He Shakes the sand, bringing it up to catch the pillar's descent, and it slows.

"Hurry. Move!" Lienos grunts.

I try to crawl away, but my heart is hammering out of control, and I can barely breathe. I grasp the wood of the platform, vision blurring, crawling forward inch by inch. No one has stopped to help me. They have all fled.

I hear Lienos cry out, and then the pillar slams into the platform behind me. I slide backward as it cracks and breaks. I have no air to scream, so I choke on sand instead. I slip down, grasping for splintering wood. Then I fall, fall, tumbling through broken wood and shattered quartz. My right leg snaps as I crash. I open my mouth in a soundless scream. Rubble falls and collapses over my head, but I am unable to speak. Unable to move.

Panicking, I grasp sand in my fists and Extract. The glow fills me, and my heart stills and calms. I gasp for air, my lungs heaving, rest my forehead on the sand. My leg is on fire with an icy hot agony.

I scream. "Help!" I'm buried in a pile of rubble, and it's dark save for a few shafts of dusty light slipping through. Wood is heaped on my back and legs, and I can't move. Pain shrieks through my right leg. It's stuck tight.

There are voices muted through the rubble, and one by one, the wood shafts come off. I claw through the wreckage and sand. My heart is pounding again, so I Extract some more and slow my breathing. The pain. The pain is everything. I can't think, can only respond to my body's need to get help.

At last, I gulp in clean air.

"The Favored One, he's here!" Warriors begin to pull me out, but I scream in pain, and they stop.

"Absorber," I cry. Vaguely, I hear someone running, feet pounding across the sands.

"Is he alright?" Lienos's voice, smooth and unconcerned.

"He's breathing."

My eyes jolt open. That was General Tysian's voice. Why is he still here? Haven't the warriors left yet? Does everyone have to see my weakness again and again?

Someone's hands are on me, and an Absorber's light blessedly fills my body. The fire in my leg retreats to a throbbing ache as the bones knit back together. Even scrapes and cuts on my face and arms seal shut.

I don't trust myself to stand yet, so I just sit and breathe. I nod to the Absorber, a young man about my age. "Thank you."

He nods and bows before rushing away.

Lienos strides forward. "Favored One, are you alright? How could this happen?"

"Yes." I cough on sand grit. "How?"

I turn in time to see the ships heading out, Shakers working together to lower them into the ocean of sand.

Therah rushes to kneel at my side. "Don't worry, Favored One, we will get the pillar erected again as soon as possible. Such an odd thing for it to fall."

I shut my eyes. Deep breaths. My legs are still shaking.

This was directed at me. The pillar didn't even have to crush me. Whoever is doing this is going straight for my greatest weakness—my heart.

Another attack. But from who?

18

____

NORAH

"We're almost there, Zadock!" I call, looking out over the bowsprit. The endless landscape of sand is changing, and something different looms on the horizon. Something glittering and long and black. It stretches out, dividing the endless sands from the sky. I can't quite make out what it is, especially with only starlight to go by, but it's not the ocean of sand.

A thrill swells within me. I've always wanted to see the ocean of water, and it's almost in sight. If all goes well, we'll find the pedestal with the moonstone and stop the fighting and the famine. Maybe Motah will even look at me differently after this.

We seem to have lost the other ship during the sandstorm, or they might've had nothing to do with us after all.

I smile at Zadock. Atoille, how my heart lurches when I look at him. He's exhausted, his arms dragging downward and his shoulders slumping, but he looks back at me with a smile.

"Can you see it?" he asks.

"I'm not sure. I see...something." I squint. Zadock's strong Shaking has gotten us here right on time, even with the delays.

It's been seven days. Every day we get closer to an inevitable To'Morat attack.

"Uhh, Norah. They're back."

I look behind us. It's hard to make out in the darkness, but there it is again, the same boat, a black splotch behind us, bobbing up and down in the sand.

"You're right. It must be following us. There's no way this is a coincidence, not after losing it in that sandstorm."

Zadock's arms continue to move, propelling us a little faster. "What if they're here to stop us?"

"Even the To'Morat want this famine to end. Maybe we can reason with them, whoever they are."

Zadock bites his lower lip.

"Don't worry." I smile. "We've got you, and we've got our spears. We're going to be fine." I have so much hope that I truly believe it. Things are going to change from here on out.

The sky turns pink and orange as we move closer to the dark blur in the distance. The sun rises in full, and the ocean of sand calms. We get our first full view of the ocean of water.

My hand falls from the tiller and drops to my side. My eyes widen. My breathing stops.

"Atoille's ashes," I whisper.

Zadock's mouth falls open. "Holy. Speck."

The water stretches on and on. It never ends. It just keeps going until it touches the sun. Fear squeezes my heart. At least the sand is predictable, and Shakers can control it.

And the waves.

"This is why no one sails on water," Zadock whispers.

I can only nod. A wave rolls forward, boiling in on itself and foaming like a beast. It's taller than the entire plateau of To'Rahn. The wall of water churns over itself and sprays foam, and I have to crane my head to see the top. Then it crashes down to collide with the sand.

As one wave sucks the sand under, another wave begins. The

ocean of water draws back in on itself, pulling sand with it like it's taking a breath. Then the water, blue crystal like the Atoille statue herself, rears up and up, reaching for the sky like it can touch the moon.

It's breathtaking and terrifying.

"Don't get too close!" I shriek, but Zadock's holding us steady a good hundred paces out from where the sand first starts to be slurped away. It doesn't feel far enough.

"Do you think we're in the right spot?" I can barely hear myself speak over the roar of the spray. I scan left and right. Sand and water for miles.

Zadock looks over his shoulder. "I don't know. I don't see a pedestal."

The blue water sparkles in the rising sunlight. The sand settles into a gentle shifting motion, and Zadock lowers his arms.

But the waves. The waves of water never stop, even with the daylight. They just keep rising, one after another, towering above us like blackish-blue monsters, then crashing and pulling away at the sand.

"It's incredible," Zadock whispers. "I have never seen anything like this."

The waves of sand drift us closer and closer to where water meets desert, and Zadock Shakes us back.

I take a deep breath. "Ok. What do we do now?"

Zadock looks behind us. "That ship is getting close."

I glance back. They're close enough that I can make out the red and black sails.

"To'Morat." Zadock's face has gone white. "What do you think they'll do if they catch up?"

"If we can fix whatever this is, maybe they'll just leave us alone." I put a hand on his arm. His skin is warm and smooth.

Zadock meets my eyes and nods. "All right. Do you think we're in the wrong place? Do we keep traveling up the coast?"

My eyes leave the ship that is getting closer and closer and scan the horizon. "I don't know. We followed the directions Motah gave us exactly, so we're in the right place. Unless the council was wrong." Nerves squirm in my gut. "We're probably going to have to look around."

Zadock nods.

"Could you Shake the sand out there and see if you can feel anything?" I *need* this to work.

Zadock nods and lifts his arms. "I'll try."

The sand before the water shifts, then starts rising in great waves, fighting back against the water. My mouth drops open as a surge of sand almost as large as the ocean waves meets the water.

"Zadock..." I whisper.

The ocean of water swallows the wall, and the sand is smothered. Even as far back as we are, sand sprays across my face, and I cry out, shielding my head with my arms. The wet sand stings where it touches me. The air smells like salt, sharp and tangy.

Zadock falls to his knees on the boat, lets his arms hang at his sides. "I don't...I don't feel anything out there. There's only sand." He gasps for air. "If there's something in the water, I can't feel it."

I look back at the waves, dread churning in my stomach. "Maybe —" A thick tendril of sand snakes around my middle and yanks me backward.

"Zadock!" I scream. His horrified expression gets smaller and smaller as I'm wrenched away from the boat. *No, no, no!*

I struggle and kick, screaming, sand getting into my mouth and lungs. Zadock stands, and he cries my name from far away. He lifts his hands, and his own sand tendrils lunge after me.

Sand wraps around my foot and pulls, halting my backward movement. I gasp. My leg feels like it's going to be wrenched off. Zadock's arms move, working to bring me back, but I continue to inch toward the To'Morat ship.

Zadock's sand slips away, and I'm jerked backward again. My stomach lurches. I hear Zadock's cry of panic even over the wind, and he raises his arms again. I slow. He's trying to take control of the sand that holds me. The sand around my middle squeezes tighter, and I struggle for air.

I'm wrenched backward again, even faster this time, and I scream. Then, with a thud and pain in my back, I land on solid wood.

The desert sun is blinding, so I only see the dark outlines of two figures standing above me and peering down.

I cry out and stagger back, as far as I can to the opposite side of their ship. It's wide and flat and bigger than the *Norah*, with two masts and two sails attached to each. I look over the side at the sand, know that jumping off will mean my instantaneous death.

"Is it her?" A feminine voice says.

I face my captors, my breath coming in rapid pants. What do they want from me? Why? They're both dressed in black armor with the strange symbols of the To'Morat painted in red on their shoulders. The woman has long red hair pulled back in a tail and one hand outstretched, Shaking the sand to hold me. The other is a tall man with a short, clipped beard almost as black as his armor, and he stares at me and frowns.

"It must be."

I wish I wasn't so completely and utterly helpless. I don't even have my spear. I glance over the man's shoulder and see the *Norah* getting closer. Hope leaps in my heart.

The man glances behind him. "Take care of the boy. Then let's go."

No...

The woman glares like she doesn't like being ordered around. "Fine." She turns and lifts her hands to Shake. The sand holding me slips away.

"NO!" I shriek, leaping to my feet and bounding across the ship. The man's iron arms wrap around my middle and hold me back. I kick, screaming and fighting, pounding with my fists. I plant one foot on the boat and kick backward with the other, aiming for where I hope it will hurt most.

A cry escapes his throat, and he drops me to the deck. I leap across the boat, but the redhead just absently stretches one hand behind her and wraps my legs in sand. I fall. I struggle and flail, trying to free myself from the sand holding me down.

With one hand, the woman hurls a massive wave of sand at Zadock.

"NO!" I scream. "STOP! Please leave him alone. PLEASE!"

The wave smashes into the *Norah*. Zadock's incredible, but he's exhausted. He lifts his arms to fight against it, but the wave barely slows. The sand smashes into the *Norah*, sinking the front of the boat deep into the ocean of sand.

I'm frozen in horror. My throat feels clogged.

Zadock moves to the back. He tries to Shake the sand out of the boat, but the *Norah* is already sinking.

"Best to be certain," the woman says. She lifts her hand again, and a giant wave comes from behind the *Norah* this time. Zadock turns in time to see the sand hurtling toward him. He lifts his arms, and then he's buried. He doesn't come back up.

"NOOOOOO!" Tears stream down my face. This can't be real. This isn't real.

Why? Why?

The woman turns back around and releases the sand that's holding me. I fall to my knees, tears dripping onto the sand in the boat.

Zadock... My best friend. The boy who I grew up with, who became the man I fell in love with.

He's gone.

I know that as sure as I know I am stuck on this boat, at the mercy of the To'Morat. The *Norah* has sunk beneath the waves.

And no one can survive the sand.

A surge of anger and despair roars to life within me, drives me across the deck toward Zadock's killer. It's so unexpected that I leap upon her and rake my fingernails across her face. She screams and shoves me backward with a ball of sand, throwing me to the deck.

Ropes of sand hold me down, my arms at my sides. I wail, crying and thrashing.

The man's boot comes toward my head, and pain erupts in my temple, bringing unconsciousness almost instantly.

Zadock...

19

IMWRAETH

The girl runs her hands over my bare skin, the sand between us soft and fine. I try to ignore the pleasure of her touch. She's only doing her job.

I cannot deny that she is beautiful. She's braided her curls out of her face today. She has smooth skin and large honey eyes, eyes that seem to pass judgment on me whenever they meet mine.

There's the fact that my army just murdered her people, and she hates me hotter than Atoille's fire.

But right now, her face is impassive. A faint glow emits from her fingers as she Absorbs. She says it will probably take a while before I feel results. That she will need a week at least to work on me before I start to notice a difference.

Which feels suspicious since an Absorbing healing is usually very quick, but I know what I saw. There was truth in her face.

If I am patient, I will finally be able to run. Finally be able to walk free without carrying this bag of sand.

I smile.

I'm lying on the table in the medic room. Two guards are at the door, and several servants move about, stocking towels, sheets, and plenty of jars of sand. Sunlight streams through the windows.

The army left for To'Rahn two days ago. We've had communication via sand gull, and so far, their journey is going well. My people have already eaten through almost all the supplies we took from To'Shahera. It takes so much to feed everyone.

That is what I have to tell myself. That is how I have to deal with more killing. With the slaughter I know is to come.

But my warriors have sent word that they have captured the girl from To'Rahn. If the rumors about her are true, my worries could be over. If.

I look at my healer. "What is your name?"

"Does it matter?"

"Well, yes. To me, it does."

She raises one eyebrow and sprinkles another handful of sand onto my skin. "And no one else, of course."

I shake my head. "Does it matter if it matters to anyone else?"

She looks at me. I was hoping for a smile or something other than the blank stare she gives me.

I clear my throat and look away.

The girl pauses, one hand resting on my chest. "I will tell you my name. On one condition."

Now it's my turn to look at her with a raised eyebrow. I don't think anyone has ever said those words to me in my life. "And that is?"

"My sister and I will get our own room out of the dungeons." She looks at me with that hard stare, daring me to defy her request.

So the other Absorber is her little sister.

I shake my head. "Too risky. You'll run away."

"Then put up some guards."

"Sorry, the answer is no." I wish I could tell her yes. But I can't take that risk, not when she can save me. Plus, there is no way in the fires of Atoille's Hell that Lienos would ever agree to that.

She continues working. I think our conversation is over, and I feel...disappointed?

Then she speaks. "Can we at least have a walk outside once a day? With guards, of course." She waits until I meet her gaze. "We won't run away. I promise."

I scan her face. I'm surprised when I see truth.

"I believe you." I pause. "All right. A daily walk outside. Guards will accompany us."

"Us?" She frowns.

"Us."

She purses her lips before letting out a sigh. "Deal."

I reach out my hand to her, and she presses her fingers against mine before interlocking them, Atoille's ancient symbol of a promise. For some reason, my hands tremble against hers.

She quickly lets go.

"And? Your name?"

The girl looks at me and swallows. "It's Lylahn Velare."

"Lylahn." I smile. For some reason, learning her name feels like a victory. "I'm Imwraeth Jeriyah." I leave off my long string of "Favored One" titles on purpose. "It's a pleasure to meet you, Lylahn."

Again, no smile, nothing. She just keeps working, keeps that soft glow running up and down my skin over my chest. I analyze how I'm feeling inside. Nothing different. Nothing unusual. Nothing at all.

The door slams open, and Lienos storms in.

Oh no. Here we go.

"Favored One!" Lienos inclines his head. "Urgent news."

"Can't it wait?" I gripe. "As you can see, I'm half naked."

Lienos frowns in disapproval, twisting his already withered face. "It cannot wait, Favored One. We've received urgent communication I must discuss with you. The girl will have to go for now." Lienos nods to the guards, and they take her away without even looking at me for permission.

Lienos eyes Lylahn. "Has the other Absorber worked on you yet, Favored One?"

"No, not yet. If this one can fix me..." I shrug, trying not to let the hope bubble up in my voice.

Lienos presses his lips together. "Still. The other one should still take a look, I think. Otherwise, she's a useless waste of resources."

Lylahn stiffens and looks over her shoulder as the guards haul her away. She meets my eyes for an instant before turning back around.

I sit up, letting the sand fall. "Thank you," I say to her. "I will keep my promise." The door closes.

I take a white algohde cotton robe from a servant and face Lienos. "All right, tell me your news." I still haven't discovered who put that poison in my glass and who orchestrated the pillar's fall, and now might be a good time to cross-examine Lienos.

"The To'Rahn girl has arrived," Lienos says. "She is being held in the dungeons. She may be the answer to all of To'Morat's problems."

I nod. If this works, we will call off the attack. If not, To'Morat's armies are already in place.

"That is good news." I nod to the guards, and two of them escort me out of the room and through the white marble hallways toward my chambers. I find my mind drifting, thinking of Lylahn, looking forward to walking with her tonight.

"We must act quickly," Lienos says.

I let out a breath. "If this works, it could mean the beginning of an era of prosperity." I want so desperately for my rule to be one of peace, a new start for To'Morat. "We must hurry if we are to get her to To'Rahn before Atoille rises on the eastern horizon." I count in my head. "We have five days. Five days for a seven-day journey."

Lienos nods. "It can be done. Strong Shakers have been held in reserve for this purpose. A team of three on a swift vessel, switching out and never resting, could make it in time."

"Then make it happen."

Lienos turns and hurries down the hallway.

"Councilor," I say.

Lienos looks over his shoulder.

"I want to meet with her first." It will be hard, but I have to know. I can't condemn her to her death without at least speaking with her.

"Yes, Favored One." Lienos strides down the hallway.

I stand for a moment, hands clasped behind me. Am I really doing the right thing?

I stare at the dead plant in the vase before me and realize...it's not dead.

The cactus flesh is full and vibrant, green. The needles are sharp and straight. There's even a yellow flower blossoming at the top. *What?*

I smile and reach out to touch the soft petals. The girl's presence. It must be.

All the reports about To'Rahn hinted that they have fared better than other plateaus in this unending famine. It must have been because of her.

Maybe this really will work.

20

ZADOCK

I heave an enormous breath of air and gulp like I've never breathed before. I grasp at sand, trying to keep my head above the waves, but the desert sucks me in again. The force pulling me down is unnatural, magical even. Like the sand itself wants to devour me.

Blackness, drowning me. Sand and grit crushing every pore of my body. I can't breathe. I open my mouth, and it fills with sand. Unbearable heat scorches my skin. I'm pulled farther down, down.

My thoughts are fuzzy and heavy. I kick and flail, trying to swim upward, but I'm sinking. I Shake the sand below me, hardening it. I heave, trying to jet myself free.

The pressure is crushing. I spent everything I have getting to the ocean and then trying to get to Norah.

Norah.

I force the sand to lift me, and my muscles scream. The pressure tears me apart from the inside out. I'm moving up. I'm doing it.

Inch by slow inch, I fight against the force trying to pull me under. The sand is relentless, clutching and pulling.

Norah!

I dig up every ounce of strength I have and *push*.

I rocket upward, sand streaming around my body. Finally, my face breaks the surface. I guzzle air.

I eke out a bit more strength and create a platform of sand below me, lifting me above the sand. My entire body shakes. I can't stop it. Even my teeth are chattering despite the heat.

I survived. I was pulled under the desert, and I survived.

And then, bless Atoille, I see the boat, although it's overturned. I float over to it and set myself down on top. I'll have to right the boat before it sinks, but I just need a minute to rest. The shaking of my muscles dies down to a quiver.

I still hear the ocean roaring to my left, a monstrous thing with a life of its own. It's a lot closer than it was before. The cool spray hits my face.

I am entirely drenched in sand. It's everywhere, in every strand of hair, clinging to every spot of skin. Ugh.

I scan the horizon for a sign of the black ship, but nothing. The sun is blearing my vision. My head droops. They're gone.

A few more moments. Just a little while to recover. That's all I can afford.

I close my eyes and Shake outward. Sand flies off my body. I run my fingers through my hair, Shaking the sand free.

I slide back off the boat onto a platform of sand and use my other hand to Shake the boat. It's heavy, so incredibly heavy. But with another heave, I finally get it righted and collapse on the deck. Or whatever it's called.

For a moment, I just breathe and close my eyes, swaying with the waves of sand.

My throat feels like sandpaper, so I work up a little strength to open the hatch that leads below deck and crack open a box of waterskins. Praise Atoille that everything in the hatch is still there, even though the boxes and crates are jumbled.

I come back up to the deck and drink and drink. Then I lie down and close my eyes.

What am I going to do?

I know nothing of navigation. Nothing of boats. But the To'Morat took her and that no one knows it but me.

I have to save her.

If Norah was here, she'd probably tell me to keep looking for the moonstone. It's what will save everyone. We need it.

And I know that, but part of me is starting to doubt. Is it really out here? If it is, it could take a moon cycle or more to locate. And Norah needs me. Now. She doesn't have that kind of time, and I will not abandon her.

I sit up when some of my strength has returned. I rub a hand over my eyes and take a deep breath. The task ahead of me feels impossible. I don't know where to go without Norah.

Fighting against despair, I look up at the sky. The sun is blindingly bright. I haven't slept since the day before this one.

I squeeze one hand on the steering thing, the other hand reaching out to Shake and keep the boat steady on the waves.

What would Potah tell me to do?

I was so happy when he came to the Ki'Rhen and informed them he wanted me back. When I walked out of those doors with him, my heart swelled with pride.

I can see him in my mind. *"You have quite the gift, Zadock."*

And the unspoken question on my lips, something I have never had the courage to ask him. *"Why did you not want me?"* My heart wrenches in two. *"And then why did you change your mind?"*

The ocean crashes in the distance, tearing away at the sand. I hear a faint rumbling sound, too, almost too low to catch. I'm not sure what it is, but it must be part of the ocean somehow.

I snap my eyes open. The ocean!

If I put the ocean at my back, it will point me back to To'Rahn. I know that To'Morat is somewhere Northeast of To'Rahn, so if I head north... That should work. *Atoille, please let it work.*

The *Norah* drifts in the sand, floating toward what looks like a dip in the usually level desert plain. Huh.

Now to figure out if I can steer this ship by myself.

"Speck," I mutter. "Speck speck *speck*." No one's here, so I can shout it if I want.

There is only one bed in the lower deck of this boat. One. That means it is intended to be crewed by one person. Right? I put one hand on the steering thing and stretch out one in front of me, ready to try doing this by myself.

The *Norah* dips over that lip of sand. Now I see that it's the edge of a giant crater, large enough to swallow my home. The center is filled with chunks of quartz that sparkle in the sunlight, along with bones of dead creatures.

What?

"Oh. No!" I scream and try to lift the boat.

With a hissing roar, out of the center of the crater shoots the biggest deathstalker scorpion I have ever seen. It's bigger than me. Bigger than the boat.

"Holy. Speck."

The sickly yellow tail shoots out toward me, faster than my eyes can follow, and it's only because I was lifting the *Norah* already that the needle jabs a hole into the deck instead of my head.

Horror chokes me, and chips of wood spray everywhere. The deathstalker's front pincers click back and forth. Its outer chitin is opaque yellow, and its black heart pumps deep within its casing. Four black eyes —two in the center and one on each side of its carapace—narrow in on me.

I scream and push the *Norah* back. The deathstalker sweeps its pincers, and sand goes flying. Gusts of sand cover the *Norah*, and I slide back down into the crater. I can't see. There's too much sand. I Shake it to the sides and attempt to lift myself again.

The deathstalker stops for an instant, and then the back needle strikes.

I leap to the side, and the needle jabs into the boat again, spraying chunks of wood. Norah's going to kill me. The scorpion sweeps up sand in great gusts, trying to bring me down.

That's when I see it. Underneath the yellow carapace, tucked in next to the sand, is a shining red gem.

What?

The second moonstone.

It has to be. It's red as a bristlebrush shell, but it's the right size and shape.

Oh no.

I heave, Shaking a wave of sand back toward the deathstalker. Sand blasts over its ugly body, and it hisses and retreats backward. The moonstone rolls away, and I lose track of where it is under the deathstalker's body. I try to lift myself out of the pit, but I've sunk down farther now, and the needle strikes again.

Barely thinking, I bring up two waves of sand, one with each arm, and catch the tail in the middle. I will the sand into hardness, sweat dripping down my temples. I grit my teeth and *squeeze.*

The deathstalker makes a deep-throated grating sound, its eight legs scrambling across the sand, trying to get away.

I am using every ounce of strength I have to hold that tail. A drop of venom slides off the top and hisses when it makes contact with the hot sand.

The scorpion stops scrambling, and four eyes swivel toward me. My stomach drops. I lose control of the tail, and the scorpion leaps forward. I bring up a wall of sand in front of me. Claws grate and scrabble against it.

I hold the wall with one hand and throw up a screen of sand with the other, hoping to catch some in its eyes. The scorpion hisses and retreats, so I lower the wall and throw darts of sand, one after the other, almost as sharp as if they had been Forged. But the deathstalker's pale chitin is too hard, and my knives just bounce off and dissolve back into sand.

The deathstalker starts sweeping sand atop me again, and the *Norah* sinks in farther. I try fighting it, try lifting the sand underneath the boat, but it's too heavy. I reach out and try to take hold of the sand underneath the beast, trying to grab the gem. The scorpion pauses. I've almost got it.

The tail darts forward in a blur, and I jet backward off the *Norah* in a stream of sand. I watch from above as a powerful blow cracks the *Norah* in two.

My stomach drops. All my hopes are going down with that boat. The two pieces are sucked away, buried in the sand.

I keep myself afloat on my platform of sand and move in a little closer. I must be the only sane person to *willingly* move toward a deathstalker, let alone a giant one.

Wait until I tell Norah. They *are* real.

Norah. She needs me. And our village needs this stone.

The deathstalker scuttles back and forth, its claws making soft clicks. It sweeps more sand upward, hoping to catch me, and I dodge. With one hand, I reach out for the sand underneath the beast.

I feel it—there! I give the sand surrounding it a yank, but it's underneath the scorpion. I need it to move.

I sigh. Of course it couldn't be easy.

I move a little closer.

The deathstalker hisses and lunges forward, pincers slicing. I make a grab for the gem and then fly to the side. The scorpion misses me by a hair's breadth.

I float backward and bring the sand I've scooped up to my platform. I hold my breath and let the sand fall away.

A shining, faceted red gem falls into my palm. It's beautiful.

I heave a sigh of relief. Below me, the deathstalker shrieks. I push myself back farther. I'm not sure how far it can throw sand.

The creature gives one last grating roar and then backs into the center of the crater, burrowing down deep. Smooth, white shards of something—from the ocean of water?—fall back in to cover the hole.

I drift backward, farther away from the crater, my arms working to keep the sand platform afloat. I tuck the gem into my pocket. Then I close my eyes and take a deep breath.

Atoille's ashes. I'm in the middle of the specking sand ocean with *no boat.* My heart plummets. What am I—

I'm slammed from behind.

Water. All Around me. I'm spinning out of control.

My platform of sand dissolves, and panic grips my chest. Water forces me downward. I kick and struggle, but I spin helplessly. I can't fight it. My movements mean nothing. My body is at the mercy of the giant waves.

I try to scream, but salty water engulfs my throat. I gag and try to breathe by reflex, and more water fills my lungs. Panicking, I try to reach out for sand to Shake, and feel nothing.

I can't breathe. I can't breathe. Terror is the only thing I feel, air my only thought. I try to Shake again, and there it is, sand far below me. I try to lift it up—

Slam.

I hit sand, and the force of it stuns my entire body, freezes my bones with pain. It's only because I was already Shaking the sand, softening the blow by instinct, that I wasn't crushed.

I bury my fists in the sand and Shake with everything I have, freezing my body in place. The wave pulls away, and the force of it yanks at me, trying to drag me to Atoille's Hell.

Then the water's gone, and I gasp, heaving for air. The fuzz in my vision begins to clear.

I've got to *move.* But my body responds an inch at a time, still stunned from the lack of air and the shock of being pummeled by a wave. The ocean roars behind me, and wet sand cements in my grip, and I know another wave is coming.

I Shake the sand under my body and heave. The sand lifts me up.

I'm struck by another wave, barely buffered by the stranglehold I've got on the sand underneath me. Thoughts flee as I'm thrown about by the darkness, lost in the endless sea. I try to Shake myself upward, but the pressure is just. So. Strong.

I'm thrown down by the wave, hitting the sand again. I gasp, every nerve in my body stabbed by needles. I blink my eyes open and gasp for air, fighting to stay in place against the grasping current.

And then there's a red glint out of the corner of my eye. The gem. *No!*

I shoot one hand out, immediately slipping backward and losing control, but I manage to wrap the gem in sand and yank. The gem flies to me, and I grasp it in my hand and the sand combined, slamming my hand back down into the sand and cementing my grip there. I stop moving backward.

The roaring again. Another wave is coming.

"NORAH!" I hurtle myself upward in a jet of sand. The ocean sprays me, and when I look over my shoulder, I see the great, hulking beast of a wave, taller than our entire plateau. Its shadow falls upon me, blocks out the daylight.

In one burst, I break free, feeling drops of water strike my back.

"AHHHHHHH!" The cry rips from my throat, a scream of exultation and adrenaline. I did it! I, Zadock Penvaren, faced the ocean. And won.

I can't help but grin as I slow my jet of sand, molding it into a platform and taking a seat. I glance behind me, marvel again at the monstrosity and the beauty of blue sea.

I release the vise-grip I have on the gem in my hand and look at it. About the size of my palm, perfectly cut, round except for the facets that make up the sides. It has an inner glow, shining red from within.

It's a perfect match to the blue moonstone.

I found it. I found it!

Deathstalkers collect shiny things to draw in their prey. At least, that's something Norah told me one time when she was trying to creep me out. It worked.

The legend was true. The moonstone has been here all along, part of a deathstalker's hoard.

I stare from my platform at the ocean of sand around me. Reality sinks in and chips away at my excitement. I have nothing. No supplies. No boat. I'm alone.

Despair makes my stomach sink. My breathing starts coming in quick gasps.

I put the gem into my pocket again. I am thirsty and wearier than I've ever been in my life, but I push my platform of sand forward. Based on my earlier reasoning, I keep the ocean at my back and slightly to my right.

I have to make it to To'Morat. I have to save her.

21

IMWRAETH

I walk along the garden path with Lylahn at my side. Her sister is young, about seven or eight years old, and she flits along the path in front of us and then behind, stopping to examine the plants along our route. We're trailed by two guards, of course, but the garden is otherwise deserted.

The garden is pretty pathetic, just some scrawny plants strewn along a winding path surrounded by a low wall. The sun is low in the sky, and Lylahn looks...beautiful in the dusky light. She even smiles slightly as she watches her sister play.

This girl is starting to unsettle me, so much so that my heart pumps harder, and I have to put my hand in my bag of sand and Extract. How weak she must think I am.

Once I am healed, everyone will expect me to give the order for Lylahn and her sister to be killed. That's what has to be done. There just aren't enough resources to keep every prisoner alive.

I shut my eyes. Stop walking.

When I open my eyes, Lylahn is looking at me.

She looks away quickly, and we continue. "Well, it's a pitiful excuse for a garden, but it's not a bad place for walking," I say.

She says nothing, of course.

"What's your sister's name?"

Lylahn looks at me sideways, frowning. "Why do you care? Why ask about us now, after you took everything—" Her voice breaks. "Everything from us."

I look away.

The girl stands and pushes long brown hair, much like Lylahn's, out of her eyes. "I'm Kaera."

The corners of my lips lift. "Kaera. It's nice to meet you. I'm Imwraeth." She smiles at me before bending down on the path to get a closer look at a sand lizard scuttling along.

Lylahn gives her sister a weak smile. "She doesn't understand." Kaera follows the lizard to the side, where it dashes up a tall cactus. Lylahn's voice drops to a bare whisper. "She thinks that you took everyone prisoner. She doesn't know that we're alone."

Something clutches at my heart, dragging it down into the pit of my stomach. I stop and take a few deep breaths to steady myself. I am the leader of To'Morat. I have to take care of my people, and right now, this is the only way. I want to be a good leader. I want to be everything they need me to be.

So why won't this sinking feeling of guilt and horror go away?

We turn a corner in the garden. We're close to the outer quartz wall.

"It was beautiful before...everything."

Lylahn continues to stare ahead.

"Are you enjoying your walk?"

She stops and stares at me with those huge eyes. Says nothing. Then she looks away and continues forward, watching Kaera play and run along the path.

Lylahn is clearly not going to respond, so I just start talking. Why not? The guards are far enough behind us that they won't hear. There's no one else around. It's almost like talking to a wall. A perfect, lovely wall.

"I don't really want to be the Favored One, you know. But I'm stuck. How do they choose leaders in To'Shahera?" I don't wait for an answer. "I think I learned that once, in school, growing up, but I've forgotten. Well, here, if you are born on a specific day, the day when Atoille eclipses the sun in the sky, you are chosen by Atoille to be the Favored One. You are raised to be a leader when you are of age or when the previous leader dies."

I kick aside a pebble in the path. "And so, they're stuck with me, heart defect and all. If it hadn't been for that, I would've been thrown into the ocean of sand at birth. But you can't just do that to the Favored One of Atoille, can you?" I glance sideways, and Lylahn is staring at me. Kaera is picking up rocks and putting them into a pocket of her dress.

"I don't want to be the Favored One," I whisper. "But I really do want to take care of my people."

"By killing everyone else?" Lylahn glances away like she doesn't expect an answer, and she stops to look closer at a long-needle cactus on the side of the path. I'm grateful because all this talking and walking is wearing me out. I take the opportunity to sit on a nearby quartz bench. She doesn't sit next to me.

"And what would you do if you were in my place?" I ask quietly.

"I would find another way." She brushes away a tear on her cheek.

"If there was another way," I say, "I would take it." Speaking that to anyone else would only invite disdain. For a To'Morat leader, in this culture of warriors, to feel this way—it's wrong.

I clear my throat. My heart is hammering in my chest, and I put my hand into the bag of sand at my side. "Lylahn, I—" I swallow. "I wish things were different."

"Murdering others so that your people can live is wrong." Lylahn's shoulders shake with her cries. "You killed our two older sisters—Hyria and Bellah. They raised Kaera and me when our parents died. Kaera was only a baby. They were the only parents she knew." Lylahn rounds on me, her eyes red with fury. "You took them from us."

I look away and let her cry in peace. Nothing I can say will bring her people back.

I don't know what to do, so I just keep talking in the evening light. "You miss your family. I wish I could understand that." Lylahn pauses in her tears, and I know she's listening. Kaera hums and skips along the path ahead of us.

"I never knew my family, never had any friends." I look down at my hands. "My governess hated me. She loathed that I was going to be the leader of To'Morat—me, a weakling boy with a heart defect. Sometimes when my evening meal was delivered to the nursery, she would make me sit and watch while she ate it. I was so hungry, but I was so afraid of her that I wouldn't say anything."

Atoille's ashes. These memories are still sore within me. I had been so achingly lonely. "I had this soft sand lizard toy that I would sleep with at night. It was my only friend as a child. One day, she made me watch while she took scissors and cut the head off. I don't think I've ever cried so hard in my life." I try to force a laugh, but it comes out as a strangled croak. I didn't know this pain was still so raw. "I never told anyone that." I trail off, realizing how stupid this must all sound.

Lylahn doesn't turn around.

"My governess was chosen specially by the Ki'Rhen. I couldn't be raised by my motah, of course, way too much risk of love. I was already so weak." I close my eyes, rest my head on the back of the bench.

Atoille above, what am I doing?

I hear a rustle, and when I open my eyes, Lylahn is sitting next to me, staring straight ahead. My heart leaps.

She shivers and wraps her arms around herself. The night is dark without Atoille, our footsteps heavier on the path. But the stars are brilliant overhead.

Kaera wanders back toward us, rubbing her eyes. "I'm tired, Lahnnie." She gives me a shy smile. "Thank you, Imwraeth."

"You're welcome, Kaera. We should get you both back. Our time is almost up."

"Yes," Lylahn says. "Back to our separate cells."

I stand. "If it's worth anything, I wish it could be different, but I—"

"You don't trust me."

"Er—well, no." I sigh. "Even if I did, my councilors would never allow me to give you a room out of the dungeons."

"And you always listen to what they say?" Lylahn stands, and we continue to walk down the path. Kaera takes Lylahn's hand and walks beside us, the guards following behind.

"Um. Well, yes. I do."

Lylahn stops and looks straight at me. "Kaera is only a child. Let her stay in my cell."

I meet Lylahn's eyes. Atoille, she is so beautiful. She wears a simple brown dress, one of the cheap things we keep for prisoners, but she wears it like a queen, tall and straight. Kaera glances between her sister and me.

"I will see what I can do."

Lylahn nods before heading toward the gate.

"Tomorrow, Kaera will be summoned to attempt to heal me. Make sure she's ready."

Lylahn freezes, then slowly turns back around. "Why? Why do you need her to try? I already said—"

The guards are approaching, so I step in close. Lylahn shrinks back but then stops herself. My heartrate speeds up from her nearness, and I can smell the sweet scent of her hair. I do my best to ignore it and lower my voice. "Convince me that both of you are needed. Otherwise..." I suck in a sharp breath.

"Imwraeth..." Lylahn trails off.

"It will be all right. Just say that both of you are necessary."

The guards grab Lylahn and Kaera by their arms and pull them toward the exit. I stand there a moment longer, breathing in the night air, watching them go.

Lylahn looks back at me, her eyes full of fear.

2 2

———

NORAH

I can't breathe.

The prison walls around me are made of quartz, but we're so far underground that the only source of light is a torch in the hallway.

There are no windows. There isn't a door, for Atoille's sake.

After two days of sweltering heat in the hold of the To'Morat ship, we landed, and I was blindfolded and hustled through the streets of the plateau in the depth of night like I was a secret to be hidden. Then my captors dumped me in here. A Forger turned the quartz back into sand, shoved me in, and then Forged again. I'm sealed tight.

The floor is smooth, swept free of sand. I plant my hands on the quartz and take deep breaths.

Why?

Why did the To'Morat capture me and leave Zadock to die?

I close my eyes and bury my face in my hands. It doesn't feel real. It seems like he'll come bursting around the corner at any minute to rescue me, a grin on his face. But the hallway is quiet. Empty.

And no one survives falling into the sands. I see a different hand, reaching out as he was sucked under the waves. Potah was a strong Shaker, too.

And then, just like now, I was helpless.

Tears slide down my cheeks as it sinks in. Twice now, when it came down to it, when I had to save someone I love, I had nothing. Nothing.

I bite my lip and try to hold back a sob. Then I don't care anymore. Who cares if they hear me cry? A wail escapes my mouth, and I cry and cry.

He's gone. Oh, Atoille. He's gone.

I jump when there's a grinding sound, and a small portion of quartz at the bottom of the wall, barely an inch high, trickles to sand. A plate of food, some kind of mushy grain with bristlebrush fruits, is slid through the gap, along with a skin of water. I take the water and drink it in slow sips. I know I should eat, but my heart is too heavy.

I don't know why my thoughts drift to Motah.

I'm running home from school on short legs, tears streaking my cheeks, clutching a doll in my hands. I brought her to school, hoping that other girls would play with me, but no one would touch my precious doll. All the girls had squealed and run away, saying that they didn't want to catch the "Norah disease."

It hurt. Oh, it hurt. And I'm falling into Motah's arms, sobbing big, fat tears. Wishing that I had someone, anyone to play with.

And then, Motah, taking the doll in her hand, walking it along the floor toward me, saying, "What shall we have for dinner tonight? Will you help me collect bristlebrush fruits?"

A hand presses against the quartz on my wall from the other side. I jump.

"Are you ok?" The voice is muffled but sounds female, and the fingers pressed against the glass are long and slender.

I edge closer to the wall. Slowly, I press my hand into the quartz.

"No," I whisper.

"What?" the voice says. Her face comes closer to the wall, and I can make out the blurry outline of a girl, probably about my age, with long brown hair.

"No," I say a little louder.

The girl pauses. "Did they murder your entire village, too?"

My mouth falls open. "Is that what happened to you?"

"Yes." She chokes back a sob. "My sister and I were spared because we're Absorbers."

"Why...?"

Her outline shifts. "You don't know? The leader of To'Morat always captures Absorbers. He's looking for healing. Is that why you're here?"

"No, I'm not. I'm from To'Rahn. When I left, we were preparing to defend against a To'Morat attack." I shiver. "I'm so sorry."

The girl looks away and lowers her hand. She doesn't speak. There's nothing to say. Nothing to be done for the unbearable tragedy she has suffered.

And then I start talking, and I don't even know if she can hear or understand me, but it just all falls out. "I left because I wanted to end this. I thought if I could get my—my best friend to the ocean of water —" I choke, and tears fall down my cheeks. "We could right whatever is wrong with the world. I thought we could stop all this. I thought we could make everything better." I pause to breathe. "And now—now the To'Morat are probably sailing for To'Rahn already. And my—" A sob wrenches from my throat. "—my best friend is..."

Suddenly there's a light and a grating, jarring sound coming from right outside my cell. I hurry to wipe my eyes.

The quartz where a door should be gives way to sand, crumbling into my cell and into the hallway. Two guards wearing red and black To'Morat armor step over the sand and enter. One is carrying a spear tipped with a quartz point.

"Time to go," one of them says, a tall woman with black hair sticking out from under her helmet. She motions with her spear.

The other is a man. He's not wearing a helmet, and his hair is pale blonde, almost white, and hangs to his shoulders. His thick eyebrows are dark, nearly black. He moves his hands, and tendrils of sand creep toward me and snake around my arms and legs. I stagger backward and fall, but the sand lifts me into the air.

I have always been strong for Shrey. Always hidden away that part of me that longed for a sand gift, that longed to be more. I will hide my feelings now. I will be strong now.

I grit my teeth and meet my captor's gaze, my feet floating off the floor, my arms and legs wrapped in cold, compacted sand.

"And here she is." He scowls and turns to his companion. "Was it for her that we were left behind? To'Morat's strongest Shakers, left out of what could be the greatest, most crucial, battle of our time?" He glares at me. "For what?"

I squirm and wish that I hadn't because I can't get free. Instead, I will my muscles to stillness. Will my thumping heart to steady.

The woman frowns. "Voicing these thoughts goes against the Favored One's wishes, Blood Rank One Tysian."

He walks around me, taking in every angle. I swallow.

"Yes. You're right, Riah. We must always honor the Favored One's wishes." There is venom in his voice. "Come."

They walk ahead of me, and, with a wave of Tysian's hand, I'm floating in sand after them. I glance at my neighboring cell and see an outline of the girl watching. Then we're down the hallway, and she's out of sight.

"You are angry," Riah says quietly.

Tysian glances sideways at her as we ascend a staircase. "Are you not? After all we have done for To'Morat, we deserve to be there. To witness and take part in the glory of our people."

"There's nothing to be done."

I sense there is more here that is going on than I know, but then that's not a surprise. Why did they spare my life?

What do the To'Morat want with me?

Tysian pushes open a door, and we enter another hallway, this one decorated with rugs and potted plants. I stare, my eyes widening. The plants are actually green and beginning to bud.

We continue down the hallway, servants stopping to gawk at me, floating along behind my captors.

My mouth is free, so I dare to speak. "Where are you taking me?"

Tysian stares straight ahead, but he says, "We are taking you to the Favored One of Atoille."

☾

WE ROUND A CORNER, and servants push open a carved wooden door. Tysian drags me behind him into a chamber lined with quartz pillars. I gasp at the size of it. At the end of a long black and red patterned rug, sitting on a crystal throne, is the Favored One of To'Morat.

He's younger than I thought he would be, with short red hair and a bored expression. He slouches in his seat, one elbow on the arm of his chair and his fist supporting his head. Only his eyes move when I enter. His eyes are dark, almost black, and they slide toward me, inspecting.

On either side of him sit two older people, a woman with knitting needles clicking away with lavender thread and an older man with a long, neatly trimmed gray beard and stern eyes. The woman glances up at me, and the knitting needles stop. The man frowns.

Two other To'Morat warriors, a man and a woman, enter the chamber from a side door and join Tysian and Riah. My eyes widen. It's them! The two who captured me and murdered Zadock. I fight against my bonds, hatred surging within me. I note with a small degree of satisfaction the four red scratch marks on the woman's face.

The sand tightens against me, and I stop squirming.

We stop in front of the Favored One's throne, and Tysian waves his hand so that I am moved forward. I hate this sand. I hate how helpless I am.

I float in front of the Favored One and meet his eyes.

"This is she, Favored One," Tysian says.

There is a moment of silence while he regards me. I take even breaths and do not look away, even though my heart is pounding. Even though every second without Zadock tears me apart a little more.

The Favored One opens his mouth and looks like he might say something, but the older man to his left plows ahead. "Thank you, General Tysian."

Suddenly, I can't take it anymore. "My name is Norah Saranyi. I am from To'Rahn. We have no quarrel with you and only want peace. Now tell me why you have murdered my friend and taken me captive." My voice shakes, but only a little.

The Favored One's eyes widen. The man to his right scowls and the woman to his left looks up from her knitting.

"We will be doing the questioning, girl," the man snarls.

The Favored One simply nods with his eyes still wide. "Councilor Lienos, please tell our four strongest Shakers why they have remained behind from the battle."

The older man, Lienos, I guess, nods. "Shakers Tysian, Riah, Mylarah, and Behlron, you four have been held in reserve for a special purpose, a purpose that could save To'Morat from destruction."

I can't see Riah and Behlron—they're behind me—but Tysian nods, and Mylarah folds her arms and raises an eyebrow.

Atoille, this sand is so itchy and hot. It wraps around my arms and squeezes my torso and legs. I can't move an inch.

Lienos continues. "This girl, Norah Saranyi of To'Rahn, was long thought to not possess a sand gift at all."

Tysian glances at me sideways. I feel my cheeks flush. But why did he say "long thought"?

"She is, in actuality, what is called a Sustainer," Lienos says.

I catch my breath. *What...?* Is this possible? Is this real? It seems more likely to be some To'Morat trick.

"A Sustainer?" Mylarah asks.

"I've never heard of a sand gift like that." Riah's voice, behind me.

The female councilor resumes her knitting and focuses on the yarn, but the Favored One studies me intently. I meet his stare and hold it.

Lienos nods. "Ancient sand gift records indicate that Sustaining used to be as common as Shaking or Forging. But it has been lost for quite some time. Until now."

Lienos' eyes meet mine in a discerning gaze, and I force myself not to look away. But my mind is reeling. Could this be true? Could I have a sand gift? And if I do, why have I never been able to use it?

"Councilor Lienos, what does Sustaining do, and why is it so important?" Tysian asks.

The Favored one glances from Tysian to Lienos, his mouth opening like he wants to respond, but he stays silent.

"It is a sand gift that encourages life and growth," Lienos says. "Sustainers of the past could absorb sand to make plants thrive in the desert, even in harsh conditions. They could balance the weather and prevent the sudden sandstorms or encourage rain. Now, without them for so long, the plateaus are eroding away. Plant life is failing. Sustaining may have been the most powerful and crucial of all sand gifts, and it was lost."

I want to ask a million questions. "How do you know this?"

Tysian moves to strike me, but Lienos holds up a hand. Tysian's arm lowers.

"Ancient To'Morat records indicate that it was so."

I frown. It seems odd that To'Rahn wouldn't have had this information. But what do I know? It could all be a lie.

But if it's true... A sand gift! Tears prick my eyes. I spent all those years praying to Atoille, feeling useless and alone and different from everyone else. I had a sand gift all along. Could it be true? And how do I use it?

If I can figure this out, it could change everything. I could Sustain food for my people.

"One more thing," Lienos says. "The Sustainers could give something miraculous to their communities. Every newly rising moon, the night where the sky goes from dark to showing just a sliver of Atoille's light on the eastern horizon, if a Sustainer threw themselves to the sand, an enormous burst of life and prosperity was granted to the world. Enough food grew to feed the villages for a hundred years just in that one night. Through the Sustainers' deaths, the world flourished and prospered."

The Favored One moves his gaze to my face, studying me. I try to keep my features still, but my insides are turning. Fear squeezes my heart. At last, I know why they have kept me alive. I try to think of how many days it's been since Atoille sunk beneath the western skyline.

"You're wrong about me," I cry. "I don't have a sand gift. I never have. I can't—I'm not—"

"Silence, girl!" Tysian sneers and waves his hand. A tendril of sand drifts upward until it covers my mouth.

Lienos continues. "In ancient times, when plague or starvation threatened their villages, the Sustainers gave themselves willingly. One life to save the world? It wasn't even a question. But then they started being murdered for wealth and power. Whatever the reason, Sustaining was lost." He looks straight at me, and I feel my skin crawl. "Until now."

Behlron frowns. "So if we kill her, food will grow?"

Lienos smiles. "Yes. Enough food to feed everyone, not just To'Morat, for at least a hundred years. And the plateau will stop eroding so fast. The sandstorms will stop coming without warning. The world will be made right again, for a time. Long enough for us to figure out what to do next."

"Is killing her really the best option?" The Favored One speaks up. His voice is quiet and small. "If she's alive and can use her gift, won't that be better?"

Lienos waves his hand. "Have you seen her using Sustaining, Imwraeth? She doesn't know how, and records give no indication as to how Sustaining works. It's obviously very different from the rest of the sand gifts. And To'Rahn is faring only slightly better than To'Morat, so we know her presence alone isn't enough."

Imwraeth shifts his gaze to me again. He looks sorrowful. Which is strange for the leader of the vicious and cruel To'Morat.

Lienos scowls. "She must die."

"So get it over with," Behlron, behind me, says.

"Not here. Not now." Lienos clasps his hands in his lap. "She must be thrown to the sands the first night that Atoille rises, or it will be for nothing." He glances at me and frowns. "And she must be killed on To'Rahn, the land of her birth. Otherwise, it won't work. This is why you four have been kept in reserve. You must get her there in time." Lienos' lips turn up in a smile. "If killing the Sustainer is everything we hope and the world is saved, To'Rahn will be spared. If not, our armies are in position to attack."

I see Tysian grin out of the corner of my eye. My stomach whirls. Sweat breaks out on my temples although I am frozen in place. It's too much. It's too much to take.

"Atoille will rise in five days." The woman looks up from her knitting. "You must go swiftly, rotating between you, never stopping. Get her to To'Rahn in time. Everything depends on this."

Five days. I swallow.

Tysian nods to Lienos and then to his comrades. "We will do as you say, Councilor Lienos." He turns to the Favored One and inclines his head. "We are loyal to you, Favored One."

For some reason, the Favored One jolts upright, his eyes enormous.

Tysian pulls me behind him out of the chamber, the three other Shakers following.

This information could change everything. But only if I can do something about it. I try to nurture the hope within me. Can I figure this out?

Five days. Five days to learn how to use Sustaining, or To'Rahn will be attacked, and I will be killed.

23

───────

ZADOCK

omehow, I keep going.

I float on my platform, leaving a stream of dust behind me, the waves of sand crashing below me. I've long since left the ocean of water behind.

Thirst grips me in a vise. My throat is so raw I can hardly swallow, the last of my saliva long gone. Hunger hollows my stomach.

And I'm so. Specking. Tired.

It's been over a day. Over a day of pushing on, never stopping, never sleeping. My head droops, sleep threatening to overcome me. But if I sleep, I die.

And still, nothing. No ships, no plateaus. Just endless sand.

My muscles keep going by memory, forced and locked into position. I'm pushing on only by will.

My brain is giving up on me. I hear voices. See images.

Motah, turning away, refusing to look at me, teacup in hand.

Potah, smiling, joining Saeri's hand with mine. His voice, saying what a wonderful couple we'll be.

"No." I croak. "I don't want that."

Norah. Screaming.

My eyelids jolt open, and I heave the sand platform upward again. This is the third time I've fallen asleep and awoken during the drop.

Something black in the distance.

Could it be?

"It's not real," I whisper. "It's not real."

It gets closer.

It's a deathstalker scorpion. Don't go to it.

Still, I find myself drifting that way. So tired. So weary. The thing dips in the sand, and when it rises again, I see the black and red sails.

"A ship..." I lift my head, trying to get a better look. I've never been so happy to see a To'Morat ship.

"Help." I force the muscles in my throat to swallow. "Help!" I drift closer, urge the sand to go faster, but still, I inch along.

Someone aboard points toward me and shouts something. It's real! *Please, Atoille, let it be real.*

Jets in the sand come up to strike me. I try to dodge to the side, but I lose what little control I have over my platform and fall—

Something catches me, and I cry out. I'm suspended by sand, not under my control. I force my eyelids to stay open. I'm carried back to the ship and lowered to the wood.

Wood. It feels like heaven. I almost cry I'm so relieved. I'm alive! I'm safe.

Sort of.

A warrior wearing To'Morat armor points a spear in my face. Sand wraps around my hands and feet.

"Who are you? What are you doing out here? How did you get here?" the spearman says.

"Looks like we found something interesting on this worthless scouting mission." A different voice.

"Water..." My voice rasps. "Water."

Someone holds a waterskin to my lips, and I drink and drink like I've never had water before. I drink until I feel sick. It's the best thing I've ever tasted.

I can't help it. My eyelids start to slide closed.

"The Favored One will want to know about this. Back to To'Morat."

Ahhh. Excellent.

Oblivion hits me.

24

IMWRAETH

I lie on the healer's table, cool white sheets beneath me, a quartz jug of sand to my left. I stare up at the ceiling, waiting. The guards were just sent to fetch Lylahn and her sister. By Lienos.

He sits off to the side, scratching away with a quill on some cactus parchment, Atoille knows what about. His long beard is more gray now than the black it used to be. He wears the mahogany robes of a Favored One's councilor. Lienos' eyes keep drifting upward, examining me and frowning.

I sigh. "I wish you wouldn't do that."

He cocks an eyebrow, and his pen stops scratching. "Do what, Favored One?"

At last, the door opens, and Lylahn enters. I can't deny the way my heart beats faster in my chest, almost to the point of pain. I can't help the smile that lights up my face when she enters the room.

But I see Lienos' calculating gaze, and I hurry to school my face to stillness.

I sit up on my elbows, aware of my pale chest and torso. My muscles are nothing to brag about. I've never worried about it until now.

Lylahn walks into the room, chewing on her bottom lip. Kaera walks in behind her sister and gives me a shy smile. She looks thinner than I remember, even from just a few days ago. I think to order more food brought to the prisoners, but there isn't any to spare.

Lylahn looks at me, and her face is, if not pleasant, slightly less hostile than it has been before. "Thank you for putting us in a cell together," she whispers.

I smile and nod.

"So these are the Absorbers," Lienos says. "They don't seem any different from the dozens of other Absorbers who have worked on you, Favored One." He sighs. "Perhaps it's time to—"

"I can heal him." Lylahn cuts in.

Lienos stands, fire in his eyes. I give my head a tiny shake, and luckily, he sits back down. "Yes. So I've heard."

"It's true, Lienos," I say.

"But I can't do it alone. I need my sister to help with the process," Lylahn says.

Truth.

Her face is smooth and straight. I scan her face, looking for a hint of a lie, but I can't find it. She's telling the truth.

I blink in surprise. I had told her to lie, but I do not find it in Lylahn's face. Maybe she really does need Kaera to assist with the healing.

Lienos returns to his chair, his gaze going back to his writing. "Get on with it, then."

Lylahn and Kaera walk to my side. Kaera looks up at her sister, her eyes wide and full of fear.

"It's ok," Lylahn whispers. "Just do your best, like we talked about."

I lie back down and try to relax as the two of them pour sand over my chest and torso. Lylahn's hands rest on my chest, and I suppress a shiver of pleasure.

"Just like we talked about." Lylahn's voice is barely audible.

Kaera looks from me to her sister. What is this about?

And then a soft glow emits from Kaera's hands, and the sand is Absorbed away. Lylahn begins working as well, moving her hands up and down.

I feel Lylahn's touch within my body. It's not unpleasant, just a tingling sensation that always accompanies a healing. I feel as she works on my heart, poking around the tender blockages.

But I don't feel Kaera.

I open my eyes and glance toward the little girl. She's moving her hands up and down, and the sand is glowing, but I don't feel anything.

I look up at Lylahn, and she's staring at me. Her wide, honey-colored eyes meet mine. Her hands are trembling on my chest. "Please." She breathes. "Please."

And then it hits me. Kaera isn't Absorbing.

She's Extracting.

It's so obvious now. The little girl shifts her feet, and her hands race up and down my torso like she's full of extra energy. And of course she is, with that much sand she's Extracting from.

I meet Lylahn's eyes and nod.

"I can feel it," I say. "Both of them working together is doing something even more."

"Good, good." Lienos doesn't even glance up from his writing.

Lylahn almost sags with relief. She takes more sand from the jar and sprinkles it across my chest. Then she meets my eyes. "Thank you," she mouths. She looks away and continues working.

Warmth floods my body.

Lienos sets his pen down and rubs his temples. "Favored One, I know you want to be healed, but—"

I sit up, and sand trickles down my abdomen. "She said they could do it. They're doing it. Give them time."

Kaera freezes, a glow of sand still emitting from her palms, but Lylahn keeps working.

Lienos meets my eyes. "People will lie to save themselves. She knows what will happen if she fails. If she could heal you, she would've done it by now." I open my mouth, but Lienos cuts me off with a wave of his hand. "It's time to end this."

Lylahn stiffens and meets Kaera's fearful eyes. She gives her a reassuring nod.

My fingers grip the blanket covering my legs. "Lylahn said she could heal me, Lienos. She wasn't lying. I know it."

Lienos gives me a long hard look. "Very well. The healing should go faster now that both of them are working on it, yes?"

Lylahn clears her throat, and I nod at her to continue. "This type of healing is unprecedented." She doesn't look at me and she doesn't look at Lienos, just continues to move her hands up and down my skin. "It's difficult to say how long it will take."

Lienos grinds his teeth. "One more day. You have one more day."

Lylahn meets my eyes, and hers are filled with terror. My mouth drops open. "One day? Councilor." I squeeze my eyes shut and take a moment before opening them again. "I could be healed. Please. Don't deny me this chance." I loathe with everything I am that I have to beg him, that I can't order it so. I could try, but he would just ignore me. Lienos could order a warrior to execute Kaera and Lylahn, and it would be done, with or without my knowledge.

"Give us two," Lylahn speaks up, and the fear is gone from her face. "Two days, but we will have to be with you at all times."

Lienos frowns. "What? Be with the Favored One at all times for two days? And out of your cells?" He turns to me. "Favored One, this is a ploy. Do not—"

"Say that again." I turn to Lylahn. "Say that again."

She meets my eyes. "If Kaera and I can work on you for two entire days without leaving your side, you will be healed."

Truth.

Truth!

"Lienos, she's telling the truth." I turn to him, hope lighting my heart. Two days. In two days, I could be running, I could feel my heart pounding in my chest without fear that it is going to burst. I could be free.

I would no longer be a liability to my people. I would be strong. Everything they need.

Lienos considers for a long moment. "If this is your decision, then we will give the Absorbers two days. If at the end of two days you are not healed, they will both be executed."

Lylahn's breath catches, and Kaera bites back a cry.

But she wasn't lying. She can do this. It's going to be all right. "And when they succeed?"

Lienos picks up his pen and waves his hand. "Then they will be given an appropriate reward for their station."

That could mean anything. But, if we get to that point, hopefully I can have some sway over what that reward would be.

I meet Lienos' gaze. And I nod.

Two days.

25

NORAH

The hold of this ship is huge compared to the *Norah*. It's got a passageway and multiple rooms, for Atoille's sake. It's also dank and dusty.

I sit on the floor, a little light coming through the slats of wood that make up the deck. Crates of supplies are stacked haphazardly around me. My hands are tied in front of me, the fiber cords biting into my wrists. My throat is so dry it's swollen.

But I don't dare move. Don't dare call out. I don't want to give them a reason to encapsulate me in sand again. At least this way, I am somewhat free. To do what, though?

I lower my eyes. Adjust the position of my feet. Above me, I hear them, the four Shakers who have been pushing the ship without rest for two days. One of the women, Riah, sleeps in a bunk to my right. The four Shakers have kept us going at an incredible speed, never resting, just rotating through.

I catch slips of conversation from above, the men arguing over who's reading the star charts correctly. Mylarah pokes her head into the room. "Riah, will you come tell them that I'm right? To get to

To'Rahn, we should be heading straight toward the Antarhes star, but Behlron doesn't agree with me."

Riah groans. "I'm trying to sleep, Mylarah. You know I'm terrible at navigation, anyway. You'll figure it out."

Mylarah huffs but closes the door.

For the past two days, my thoughts have been racing.

I know what I am.

But I don't know how to feel. I've just learned that I'm a Sustainer? So I do have a sand gift? This is...everything I ever wanted. Something that would make me not so different, not such an outcast. Something that I could use to protect those I love.

And I have it?

Sand covers the floor, scattered over the boards and crates and boxes. I watch Riah out of the corner of my eye, and I lean forward to grab a handful of sand.

I've tried this so many times before. Tried to Absorb, Extract, Shake, Forge, anything. But maybe now, maybe now that I know, it might be different.

I remind myself of everything Motah taught me during her grilling sessions that used to be so frequent when I was younger. Before she gave up hope.

Take the sand. Take it within. Use the power of life that is there.

And above all, do not feel love. Do not feel attraction. Do not feel empathy or kindness or well-being toward another soul. That will get in the way of everything and make your powers void.

I rub the sand between my fingers, close my eyes, and shut out all thought. I don't think of Shrey. I don't think of Zadock. I don't think of Potah. I shove them from my mind.

Instead, I think of Motah. I think of all the times she frowned down at me. The times she humiliated me. The times she sighed, shaking her head, turning away from me. How I am never, ever enough for her.

With a burst of anger and loathing, I squeeze the sand.

Nothing.

I let the sand slip through my fingers.

I lean my head back against a crate. Could Motah know? Could she know what I am?

Is that why she tried so hard to get my gift to show, to make me hate her so much in the hopes that it would?

More importantly, what's going to happen when we make it to To'Rahn? Will the village council try to rescue me? Should they?

My bound hands clench into fists. I'm so angry, so frustrated.

Wouldn't it be worth it to trade one life to save everyone?

I squeeze my eyes shut.

I'm not ready to die.

Questions still plague me. Supposedly the To'Morat learned about all of this from ancient records, but why didn't To'Rahn have this information? How come none of my leaders guessed at what I might be?

And how did the To'Morat know? How did they know that I was the one they were looking for?

I grab another handful of sand. I shove those questions aside and dig up the anger burning within me. It doesn't matter. Now I know what I am. I know that somewhere inside of me is the power to fix this.

If I can learn Sustaining, if I can right what is wrong in our world, it could change everything.

I squeeze another handful of sand. Take a deep breath.

2 6

IMWRAETH

My fingers drum on the polished wood of my desk. I sit in council with Lienos and Therah. My study is much cozier than the throne room. I'm on a real wood chair with cushions, and Lienos and Therah sit on quartz. We share a gorgeous carved wooden table where Lienos keeps shuffling and re-shuffling his papers.

Therah knits with algohde yarn, dyed a light blue this time. I honestly don't know where she gets the money for all these dyes. Or what she does with the stuff she knits. Her knobby fingers hardly look like they'd be fit to do all this needlework, but she's an Extractor like me, and she told me once that she uses the sand to give her the energy to keep going.

Two sparse bookshelves line the walls with squat potted cacti in between. A glass window overlooks the stable and palace grounds below.

I rotate the crystal goblet of water in front of me on the desk. I haven't touched it since Lienos came into the room. I can't be too careful.

My people are dying. I thought I had a plan to deal with it, but

Tysian lied to me. He lied! I've been mulling over what to do but haven't come up with anything yet.

It was when he said, "We are loyal to you, Favored One." So he isn't loyal. I felt the lie. I already knew that Tysian was not my friend, but would he betray me? Would he betray his people? What is he planning? Am I overthinking this?

The threat is likely gone now that Tysian is. His lie all makes sense if he is the one trying to kill me. So now that he's gone, I shouldn't have to worry. Unless he has others working with him. Atoille's ashes, it's too much.

Lylahn sits in the chair next to me, one hand on my bare neck. I try to ignore the pleasure I feel just from that simple, warm touch. She, too, carries a satchel of sand now, and she keeps Absorbing, taking from her bag to place sand on my neck and skin and continue to heal me. She's been at it all morning, and now that it's afternoon, she's slumping in her chair, her face haggard. I worry for her and want to say something, but now is not the time.

Kaera sits on the other side of me, one hand on my arm, Extracting. She sits up straight, taking in the room with bright eyes. She's full of nervous energy, bouncing in her chair. This must be so difficult for her. She's so young to have to bear this deception. Lylahn must think the same thing because she keeps looking worriedly at her sister.

Lienos stares at her in between paper shuffles, shifting between a disapproving scowl and muttering under his breath. At last, he sets his papers down and clasps his hands on the table. "Favored One, you called for this meeting?"

I clear my throat and shift in my seat so that not quite so much itchy sand is getting down my shirt. "Yes. Thank you. I need advice."

Therah's needles click together. Lienos raises one eyebrow.

"The Sustainer was sent away two days ago," I say.

Lienos waves a hand. "Yes, and messenger birds say that the Shakers you sent are making excellent progress. They have three more days before Atoille rises."

Therah nods and turns the blue yarn over in her lap before her needles begin to click again.

"Yes. I am glad they are making such good progress. But—" I pause. When I was young, I told Lienos and Therah about my gift, but neither believed me, dismissing any proof I gave as luck. I gave up trying to convince them. Lienos only believes my gift is real when it's convenient for him. "I have reason to believe that Tysian will not follow through with his orders."

Lienos inhales and closes his eyes. He rubs his fingers against his temples.

"A serious accusation." Therah clicks her tongue. "It is well you brought it before us and not a larger audience."

"And what basis do you have for it?" Lienos asks.

Lylahn dumps more sand down my back, and I jump. "He was lying when he told me that he was loyal to me. That is all the proof I have. But I know that it was a lie. He has some other plans, something else up his sleeve. I just don't know what." I look them both in the eyes before continuing. "This deal is crucial to the survival of our people. And Tysian is going to mess it up."

Therah's needles freeze. She stares straight ahead for a moment before glancing at Lienos.

Lienos just shakes his head. "It's not enough, Favored One. What do you expect us to do? We cannot call him back. There is not enough time. I know you do not like Tysian, but you must trust him. He has every reason to help this mission succeed. Trust him."

Therah looks back into her lap, and her needle-clicking resumes. I am seized by the urge to throw her yarn out the window, but I stop and take a breath.

Besides, Lienos is right. I've mulled over this problem and gotten nowhere. There is nothing to be done but hope that Tysian and the others can still make this work.

"Yes, Councilor Lienos. You're right." Atoille, how that galls me. I bow my head and close my eyes. Lylahn's fingers run over my neck.

A hard knock raps on the door, and a guard opens it.

A messenger enters the room and bows. "Favored One, we have captured a prisoner from To'Rahn. He was drifting by sand platform without a boat when our scouts intercepted him. We thought your councilors might wish to interrogate him."

I stand and nod. "Thank you, messenger. You did well to let me know. Lead on."

Lylahn stands and shifts her grip to my bare arm. Kaera follows suit.

Lienos sighs, but he and Therah both fall into step behind me. The messenger leads us down the hallway.

We make an odd procession, Therah and Lienos walking a pace or two behind me, along with Lylahn and the two guards that accompany us everywhere we go. Lylahn's hand glows on my forearm, and Kaera's glows on the other. We get quite a few stares. But Lylahn keeps Absorbing.

We enter the throne room, and I cross the red carpet and glistening white floor to take a seat on my throne. Lylahn and Kaera stand next to me, and the guards take their places on either side of them. Lienos and Therah sit in their chairs, and Therah sets her knitting in her lap.

Two guards enter through the far door. They aren't Shakers. Almost all of our warriors are gone now. They half drag, half carry the prisoner in with his hands tied behind his back and spears pointed at his neck. He walks forward, back straight, his eyes scanning us with intensity. His rumpled hair is dirty with sweat and sand.

The guards dump the prisoner on his feet in front of me, and he staggers. He stares at us, breathing quickly. The guards stand a pace or two behind, spears still pointed at him.

All right. Here I go. I can manage a simple prisoner interrogation. I—

"What is your name?" Lienos asks.

I grip the arms of my throne but say nothing. What's the use? Lienos wants to take over. I should just let him. Does it really matter?

The prisoner—about my age, I would say—opens and then closes his mouth.

"You were caught in To'Morat territory. Give us a reason to keep you alive." Lienos growls.

The boy glares at each of us, and when he speaks, his voice is full of desperation. "You have Norah Saranyi. Where is she? What have you done with her?"

I glance at Lienos, surprised. Didn't he say that whoever was traveling with the Sustainer was killed? Apparently not.

Lienos frowns. "What is your name, prisoner?"

He looks around uncertainly. "Erno Rofort."

Lienos glances toward me. Oh, so now he trusts my ability? I roll my eyes. "Lie."

The prisoner's mouth falls open. He hesitates just a moment too long. "No, it's true, I—"

"Tell us the truth," Therah says, quietly but firmly.

He glances between us, mouth working. "It's Zadock Penvaren."

I nod to Lienos. Truth.

"And where are you from?"

Zadock's eyes glance from Lienos to me. I give him a flat stare. Honestly, I don't know why it's so important to question him. We sent Norah Saranyi away. But if Lienos thinks we can discover something valuable here, I guess it's worth the time.

"I'm from To'Merah."

"Lie," I say. Too easy.

Zadock's eyes widen. "How are you…?"

Lienos frowns and nods to a guard, who pulls back and slaps the prisoner across the face before I can say anything. He cries out through clenched teeth.

"Look," Zadock says. "I will tell you anything you want. Anything! Just tell me where Norah Saranyi is." His expression turns pleading. "Please? Is she alive?"

"So," Lienos says, "you are from To'Rahn then."

Zadock's gaze turns to me. "Please? Is she here?"

I open my mouth, but Lienos reaches into a pocket of his crimson robes and pulls out something remarkable—a palm-sized faceted red stone.

My mouth snaps shut, and my eyes widen. In the desert, gems are *extremely* rare. Almost non-existent. The only one I know of is—

I inhale sharply. "Is that...?"

Lienos examines the stone and holds it up to the light. "And how is it that you came by To'Rahn's legendary moonstone?"

Zadock eyes the spear pointed at his neck. I nod to the guard, and he eases off. I glance at the stone in Lienos' hand, fascinated. And questions plague me. What is it? Why did this boy have it?

And most of all, why did my guards take it to Lienos instead of me?

"It's not To'Rahn's moonstone," Zadock Penvaren says.

I frown. "Truth."

Lienos' eyes widen.

"The moonstone is blue," Zadock says. "This is different. Just something I found on the sands."

Truth. I nod again, though something feels off. He's not lying, not exactly. But he's not telling the whole story.

"Well." Lienos pockets the stone. "We will keep it for further study. You mentioned Norah Saranyi. Who is she to you?"

Zadock hesitates. "Norah is my sister."

I sigh and shake my head.

Lienos gestures to a guard, who tightens his spear tip at Zadock's neck. "No lies," the guard says.

The sand starts to swirl at Zadock's feet and drift toward his hands. So he's a Shaker, then. But the guard presses the tip of the spear into his neck, and Zadock stiffens.

He swallows. "She's my—my friend."

Lylahn's hand freezes on my arm, sand falling between her fingers. "Your best friend?"

I look at her, startled. So does Zadock. "Yes," he whispers back. "She is."

Lienos lurches to his feet and slaps Lylahn across the cheek. "Silence, worm!"

Kaera screams, her hands flying to her mouth. Lylahn cries out and falls to the floor, sand scattering.

My mouth drops, and I come to my feet in a rage. My heartbeat explodes in a wild rhythm, so hard that it aches. "Councilor!" I put my hand in my bag and Extract. I reach out to help Lylahn to her feet. She jerks her hand away from mine and stands on her own.

There's a red mark on her cheek and pinpricks of tears in her eyes, but she places a hand on my arm and continues Absorbing.

I round on Lienos. "You—"

He stares at me, one eyebrow raised.

"Never. Again."

Lienos stands. He meets my eyes and raises one hand. My heart sinks down into my feet, and I reach out—

There's a sharp crack as he slaps Lylahn again.

This time she doesn't shriek or cry out, just turns away with an intake of breath.

I stare for a moment, stunned. My hands tremble in fists at my sides. "I—I—"

Lienos nods. "I think we're done here."

The guards turn and drag the prisoner away. They do nothing to stop Lienos' disrespect, his outright disobedience of my order. My jaw hangs open. I look to Therah, who keeps her eyes on her needles.

I turn back to Lienos, my mouth working. Yes, we've always known who the real power was, but this—this blatant disregard for my command—

"Please!" Zadock Penvaren calls as the guards drag him back toward the dungeons. "Where is she? Is she alive? PLEASE!"

He is pulled around the corner and taken out of sight.

ZADOCK

I pound against the quartz cell door over and over until my fists are bruised, but I barely feel the pain.

"NORAH!" I shout until my voice is hoarse. Is she here within these awful walls? Can she hear me?

I beat against every wall, feel in every crack, and there's nothing. No way out. I am trapped. There are slits at the top of the quartz walls on all sides to let in air, but I can only fit my fingers through. I want to scream in frustration.

I feel like I've been punched in the gut every time I think about this entire mission—and how I've failed.

They took the stone.

They took Norah.

I've handed the To'Morat everything.

My head sinks, and I drop to my knees in exhaustion and despair. To'Rahn was counting on us, and I lost it all.

The bottom of the wall begins to crumble away, and I hurry to stand. I Shake the sand, pushing it through the crack in a gust that I hope will sting whoever is standing behind, but all I accomplish is getting sand in the bowl of soup that is pushed through, along with a skin of water. Speck.

The sand hardens into quartz once more. I drink and eat despite the grit and then continue feeling the walls and corners of my cell, searching for any hint of weakness. Somehow, I need to figure out a way to save her. I'm the only one. It's all up to me.

What would Potah do? *What would he have me do?*

I drown in my own thoughts for what feels like hours. There's no way out of here. I'm trapped.

But. If they kept me alive, there's a reason. What do I know about the To'Morat? They are ruthless and brutal. And yet, I'm alive. Maybe Norah is alive here as well.

Is there something I have that they want? Something that I can bargain with? All I want is her freedom.

A blur of shapes moving beyond the quartz wall is my only warning, and then the quartz turns to sand again, and this time more of it pools onto the floor of my cell.

All right. This is it.

I grasp hold of the sand, ready to Shake—

The Favored One of To'Morat steps through the doorway. "Shake one speck of sand, and my guards will kill you." He gestures with one finger, and a guard steps in behind him, leveling a spear in my direction.

I freeze. Shaking is always what I gravitate toward. It's what I'm good at. But maybe there's another way out of this.

I hold out my hands, fingers spread wide. Sand falls to the floor. "All right. What do you want?"

The guard, a female, inches the spear closer. "You will address our Favored One properly."

"Fine. Favored One, what do you want?"

He frowns and crosses his arms over his chest. "I want to know more about that red stone. Where did you get it? It's important to you. You carried it across the sands even without a ship. Why?" He waits, staring at me with black eyes that contrast against his stiff red hair.

My mind races. I want him to know as little about that stone as possible. If there's anything I know about the To'Morat, it's that they will press any advantage they can. If they know how important it is... Well, I just can't trust them to hand it over to To'Rahn for the greater good.

But. Information remains my only bargaining chip.

I shrug and try to act casual. "Why should I tell you? As soon as you have what you want, you'll kill me. Favored One."

His mouth quirks. "Because I know where Norah Saranyi is."

I go still. All right, fine. He wants to trade information. I am willing to do that. I just have to be very, very careful.

The guard eases her spear away from me after a nod from the Favored One. I relax, but my thoughts sprint. "I'm willing to trade. You go first."

The guard hisses, probably at my lack of a title, but the Favored One waves a hand. Is there a way I can use this situation? Could I get around them and out the door? Maybe. But then where? I need to know where Norah is first.

"Is she alive?" I say, desperation making my heart pound.

"She is alive."

A sigh of relief escapes my lips. She's alive. I run a hand through my hair and blink rapidly. She's alive.

"She's very important to you," he says.

"Yes."

The Favored One's eyes soften. I'm surprised. This isn't a reaction I expected from the bloodthirsty To'Morat leader.

"Tell me what I want to know, and I'll tell you where she is."

I pause. "Can I trust you?"

He watches me for a moment, then he holds out his hand, palm erect. I lift my hand to meet his, and our fingers interlock. Atoille's sacred symbol of a promise.

It could mean nothing, coming from a To'Morat. But it's probably all I'm going to get.

I need to get Norah. I need to get that stone back. And we need to get out of here.

What do I do? Tell the truth and hope for the best? Make something up and pray that the Favored One can't tell? Potah would know.

I can't lie worth speck. And somehow, when the To'Morat were interrogating me, he knew every single time I was lying.

I take a deep breath. "It's a pair with To'Rahn's moonstone. By itself, I don't know if it does anything. But if the two are brought together, the world can be made right again. Everything that's happening is because nature is out of balance, and bringing the two moonstones back together can fix it."

The Favored One's eyes widen. He says nothing for several moments. The guard's eyes shift from me to him.

"That's all I know."

"I believe you." He frowns. "That is powerful knowledge indeed."

"What will you do with it?" I ask. "I have to get it back to To'Rahn. It could save everyone."

The Favored One eyes me. "I will think on what to do. Thank you."

I'm taken aback. The leader of the war faring To'Morat isn't at all what I expected.

"And Norah?" I ask. "You promised, you swore—"

"I know, I know." He holds up a hand. "She is on a ship. On her way back to To'Rahn."

My heart drops. "What? But, why—?"

"Thank you for your help." The Favored One gives me a nod and leaves. The door reforms into quartz before I can even think to Shake.

She's gone.

And back to To'Rahn?

Why?

28

IMWRAETH

Thoughts of Zadock Penvaren boil through my brain. I walk along the garden path next to Lylahn and Kaera, and it's silent save for the swishing of our feet on the dusty path. I have a lot to think on. Lylahn and Kaera each have one hand on my arm, constantly glowing. The sand against my skin is rough and annoying, but I don't say anything. If I can be healed, any price is worth it.

Kaera is quiet today, though she still walks with nervous energy like she longs to go faster. I can't imagine what this constant Extracting is doing to her.

But we're almost done. Less than a day now.

The sun is setting in a stunning orange-and-pink sky. The desert has hit that perfect time of day. It's warm, with the burning heat of midday retreating, but the freezing temperatures of night haven't set in. I inhale the earthy scent of the garden, cool and fresh. The wind changes, and I breathe in the scent of herbal soap. I glance at Lylahn. Her hair is clean, the soft curls flowing about her shoulders. Her skin is smooth and glows in the dusky light.

"Lylahn."

She glances in my direction. Her eyes are still hard and cold every time she looks at me. What more could I ever expect? How could I ever understand the hurt she is going through right now? And who caused it?

I did.

That crushing truth hurts my heart more than anything ever could.

"You look...clean." Ugh.

Her eyes widen, and her lips twitch in what could be the start of a smile. "Thank you."

"One of your servants let us take a bath!" Kaera exclaims.

"I'm glad."

We walk in silence for a few more moments. Two guards trail behind at a distance.

We round a bend in the path, and Kaera gasps at a cactus that has arms that reach taller than my head. It's still a withered, brown thing, but it's somewhat impressive. We stop for a moment. Kaera takes a step toward it.

"No, Kaera," Lylahn says. The girl snaps her hand back to my arm and continues Extracting.

We stare at the cactus, Kaera's eyes enormous.

"We're almost there," I whisper. "Then you won't have to do this anymore."

"And then what?" Lylahn snaps. She lowers her voice to a breath, her lips close to my ear. The hair on my neck tingles. "Your councilor's not going to let us live. And you don't have the backbone to do anything about it."

I suck in a breath. Ouch.

"I won't—I won't let that happen." I look at her. Try to force a smile. "I still have some power, you know."

Lylahn doesn't reply, just keeps her gaze straight ahead.

We turn and continue walking, passing wilted flowers and more dying shrubs.

"You could just—" Lylahn swallows. "Let us escape. With

Kaera's power, we could get over the wall. Probably faster than the guards could catch up. We could—"

"Lylahn, no."

She closes her mouth. Meets my eyes. Hurt and anger war in her expression.

"You wouldn't make it far. Think. My warriors patrol the streets of To'Morat. Even if you made it passed them, it's an enormous desert. You wouldn't survive." I pause and watch a row of fire ants scurrying across the trail. "And I need this, Lylahn. I need to be healed. If I let you go…"

Lylahn turns away and continues walking. Now I eye the trail, watching for when the path gets too close to the wall. The guards would catch up before they could escape, right?

"Why?" she says at last. "Why do you need to be healed so badly? You can function with your Extracting just fine."

I look at her, stunned. We step over the row of ants. No one's ever asked me that before. "In To'Morat culture, weakness is not tolerated. Our deformed are thrown to the sands at birth."

"Well then, maybe that needs to change, not you."

I look to the sky. It's deepening to purple, stars starting to wink overhead. "I need to be a good leader to my people. I need to be strong to do that."

Lylahn looks at me for a long moment. "Strength isn't just physical, Imwraeth."

I stare back. My mouth turns upward in the barest of smiles. "You said my name. I don't remember the last time someone called me that and not just Favored One."

For some reason, Lylahn blushes and looks away.

Even though that discussion was difficult at best, I can't help but smile as we round the last bend in the garden path.

☾

I JERK awake to starlight cascading across the coverlet on my bed. The aching cold of the night has penetrated my room, and I pull the comforter closer. I glance over at the floor and see Lylahn and Kaera, sleeping snuggled together on a pallet, shivering under a thin blanket.

I hesitate a moment before sitting up. I pull a blanket off my bed and tiptoe over to lay it on them. A guard at the door eyes me but says nothing.

I climb back into bed and watch Lylahn. The shivering stops. I sigh and sink deeper into my blankets.

It's risky, I know, having them sleep in my room. Lylahn has every reason to hate me and want me dead. But she insisted on continuing to work until late into the night, past when I was asleep.

Tomorrow morning marks the end of the two days.

Something swirls in my gut, dread mixing with hope. She probably just needs a little while longer tomorrow morning, and then I will be healed. She wasn't lying. It will be the first day that I drop my bag of sand and walk—no, run—free.

And then I know what Lienos will do.

I can't help but stare at Lylahn, at her long brown hair curling out around her face. She's like an angel. An angel I've broken. I close my eyes.

I lie there for a moment, trying to sleep and failing. What am I going to do? How am I going to fix this? Lienos has already shown me that he will not acknowledge my orders concerning her. Somehow, I will stand up to him.

When I open my eyes, the guard is gone.

I blink and sit up in bed. The guard—he was just by the door a moment ago. Now there's no one.

Is it a change of the watch?

I lie back down. If the watch is changing, I don't have the energy to address new guards. I just want to fall back asleep.

I hear the door creak open, but I keep my eyes closed. I lie still in the dark, counting breaths, in and out. I'll make Lylahn and Kaera citizens of To'Morat. I'll have to make Therah see that when they succeed at healing me, they should be granted the right to live. And if Therah agrees, then I'll have a better chance against Lienos.

Wind whistles through spindly trees. Inhale, exhale.

Footsteps, a whisper of a *pad, pad, pad* across the floor. Those are no guards' boots.

My eyes shoot open.

Therah brings a finger to her lips. She's dressed in a dark robe. For some reason, she's holding a knitting needle at her side. Is she knitting at this hour? "Shhh. It's me, Favored One."

I breathe a sigh of relief. These assassination attempts have made me paranoid. "Councilor Therah. Do you need something? It's the middle of the night."

Therah fiddles with the needle. "I have to ask you a question, Favored One. A very important one."

Truth.

In a flash, Therah punches her fist into my chest with brutal force. Sand dust filters through her closed fist. She's Extracting to make her hits stronger. Pain erupts in my chest, and I gasp.

"Don't you think it's time for a change, Imwraeth?"

Therah lifts the needle. A cry strangles my throat, and by jerk reflex, I roll to the side. The needle plunges into my left side, glancing off ribs and narrowly missing my heart.

I scream.

Wrenching pain tears through my side. I feel cold all over. Worse, my heart is thundering in my chest. I gulp down air, choking, never getting enough oxygen.

"I'm sorry, Imwraeth," Therah whispers. "You were never enough for this nation. You never will be." She raises the needle above her head.

Lylahn screams and tackles Therah from behind. Therah grunts and falls to the floor, Lylahn on top of her. Lylahn grabs for the needle, and her hand wraps around Therah's wrist instead. They struggle, kicking and screaming, rolling on the ground.

Where are the guards? Why is no one hearing this?

The pain in my chest is so intense I think my heart is going to burst. Where. Is. My. Sand? I reach for the side table where I keep my satchel. Empty.

Every movement is torture. I can't breathe, and my side is on fire with pain. I roll, inch by excruciating inch, and look over the side of the bed.

No sand.

Kaera stares at me with enormous eyes, clutching the blanket to her chin. The floor is spotless. There's no sand anywhere.

A shape emerges over the side of my bed. I wave a hand to try to block Therah, but I'm so weak. My vision fuzzes over.

A needle clatters to the floor. Through the blur, I make out Lylahn's face. She puts her hands on me and closes her eyes.

I feel sand through her fingers. Where did she get it?

She begins Absorbing, the sand glowing through her fingers. I let out a low moan. The skin on my side knits together, the blood replenishes. The searing pain fades.

My vision clears, but I still can't breathe. My heart is too weak. I've lost too much blood, even with the fluid the Absorbing restored. This is something Absorbing can't fix. I need to Extract.

"Sand," I croak.

Lylahn holds up the bag she was drawing from last night. But then she hesitates.

"Please." I reach for it, and she steps back.

"I—" A tear slips down her cheek. "I—I hate you. I wanted to kill you." She speaks through clenched teeth.

"Help him, Lahnnie!" Kaera cries.

I don't know if I can hold consciousness much longer. "Please," I whisper. I try to sit, inhaling and exhaling labored breaths that are accomplishing nothing. Panic lances through my body. My heart can't take this. It could give out at any moment. An iron fist closes around my chest.

Lylahn turns away, clutching the satchel of sand. She takes a step toward the door. "You gave the orders for my people to be killed.

Everyone I know, my friends, my sisters—" Her voice breaks. "The order for them to die came from you."

Beside us, Kaera lets out a soft gasp.

"Lylahn." My voice comes out strangled. "I'm sorry." Tears fall from my eyes. If there is one more thing I get to say, I want it to be this. "I'm so, so sorry."

My vision is going black. My chest is being crushed.

And then, suddenly, the bag is in my hand. Scrambling, I reach inside and take a fistful of sand and Extract.

My heartbeat slows. My lungs fill with air.

I just breathe, focusing on inhaling and exhaling. I Extract more energy. Then I open my eyes.

Lylahn sits on a chair beside the bed, her head in her hands. Therah's body is on the ground, the blanket I just laid on top of Lylahn wrapped around her neck. I don't know if she's unconscious or...not. All this commotion, and still no guards. Therah must've told them not to enter, no matter what they heard. A small part of me, underneath all the other hurt I feel, is stunned by her betrayal. The whole time, it was her.

Lylahn's shoulders shake with sobs. I sit and only hesitate a second before I wrap my arms around her and bury my face in her hair. Tears pour down my cheeks. "Forgive me," I cry. "I don't deserve it, but please. Forgive me."

Lylahn stiffens in my arms, but she doesn't pull away. "I can't," she whispers. "But I don't want anyone else to die."

I look into her eyes. "For my entire life, I have wished with everything I am to be normal. To be healed. To be able to run."

She glances to the side, averting her gaze from mine.

"But even more than that, I wish...I wish that I could take it back. I wish that I could bring your family back."

I pull away from her and bury my face in my hands. What have I done? What kind of ruler have I become? I can't blame Lienos. It was his plan, but it was my choice to allow it. Mine.

From the floor beside the bed, Kaera sobs.

29

NORAH

I cry out in frustration through gritted teeth and let the sand slip between my fingers. My wrists are raw, my fingers sore and tight from grasping so much sand. I've had to wriggle around the bottom of the ship, trying to find more.

And still. Nothing.

"Quiet." Mylarah rolls over on the bed, her long red hair dangling over the edge. "I'm trying to sleep."

I blink away tears. I've tried thinking of every painful memory I have of Motah, trying to bring up enough hate and anger to banish any trace of love within me.

There are only two people I love on the whole plateau—Shrey and Zadock. Are they the problem?

I squeeze my eyes shut. I cannot feel love. *I cannot feel love.*

And yet, isn't that why I'm doing this? Why is love so wrong, anyway? I want to help my people, save them, because of love.

And that is exactly the problem.

Almost four days of trying, and nothing. Four days of nonstop travel and some heated discussions that I couldn't quite make out above deck. Something is going on up there.

"Mylarah!" There's a muffled call from above deck. A moment later, the door opens, and Behlron sticks his large, hairy head down into the room. "Wake up." He grins. "We're here."

Mylarah leaps to her feet and hurries after him.

Four days? There's no way. He can't mean To'Rahn. Where are we?

"Get the girl." Tysian's voice.

Behlron comes below deck and doesn't even bother to Shake the sand. He hauls me up by the armpits.

He half-drags me through the hallway, up the steps, and into the light. I blink and allow my eyes to adjust. My mouth falls open.

A sparkling quartz structure, almost as tall as a plateau, juts from the desert sand. It rises above the sand like a flat-topped mushroom, with a thick trunk of quartz and a wide base. The engineering, the Shaking and Forging combined that would have had to happen to build this, is incredible.

To'Morat ships are moored to the trunk with thick rope, and there are crews of Shakers managing them in the relatively calm sand. More ships line the brim of the platform above. Through the blurry quartz, I can see shapes of people moving around. The platform is not wide enough to house a village forever, but it's enough to provide their army an excellent base for attack.

I glance around, squinting in the bright glare, but I don't see a plateau anywhere. But if the army has chosen to base its camp here, we must be somewhat close.

Tysian steps forward, his mouth set in a hard line. Riah stands beside him on deck, gripping her spear and staring at me.

"I don't like this, General Tysian," Riah says. "We should do what the Favored One instructed us to do."

"Tysian is right," Mylarah says, walking across the deck to stand next to them. "It's time for a change."

"What you say is blasphemy," Riah whispers.

Behlron releases my arm. Tysian waves his hand, and sand comes up the side of the ship to wrap around me. I stiffen. The sand is hot against my skin, and I bite my lip so I don't cry out in pain.

"The Favored One is too weak to lead this nation to greatness." Tysian nods to Behlron, who lifts his arms, and sand gathers underneath the ship. We rise toward the top of the quartz platform.

"Would you argue that, Riah?" Tysian hisses. "An attack on To'Rahn is not a solution. It's merely extending the inevitable. The world is *dying*."

Riah flinches. "The girl—"

"We have no way of knowing if any of that is true." Tysian's eyes bore into her. "It could just as easily be a ploy. We must be prepared for the future, and strong leadership is the first step. Don't you agree?"

Slowly, Riah nods.

We are lifted to the top of the quartz platform, rising through the hot desert air. We reach the top, and the full extent of the To'Morat army stretches before me. My mouth drops open, and my heart sinks. My people will never survive this. There are so many of them. No defenses we erect, no preparations we make, could stop this. They'll overwhelm us in a heartbeat.

The To'Morat are as endless as the sands. They walk through neat rows of pitched tents with the visors on their helmets pulled down to fight the glare of the quartz. Others march in formation, and even more groups spar with sand and spears. My breath catches in my throat.

I have to stop this.

My heart sinks, the enormity of the problem before me hitting me in full force. How can one person do anything against the vastness of this army?

We step off the boat, and I'm carried behind everyone else. I'm so tired of being dragged around in sand.

The four Shakers pull their visors over their eyes, and I have to practically shut mine because of the brightness. The army notices our arrival, and several warriors raise spears or fists in the air, cheering.

"Blood Rank One Tysian has arrived!"

"Our strongest Shakers are here!"

"Victory for To'Morat!"

Behlron pulls me behind them, and we make a procession across the platform. Warriors stop their activities to look up at us and carry on the hurrah, then their eyes drift to me, and the whispers begin. We pass warriors sharpening spears or Forging new ones, erecting tents in neat rows, or cooking over fires. Finally, we step into a shaded tent, and I blink.

Then I experience a shock so great it feels like a punch to the gut.

"Threh'hai Saiyen?" I cry.

The old man sits behind a quartz desk, his hands clasped over his knobby cane. He meets my eyes for a moment, sorrow weighing them down, and then he looks away.

I'm speechless. What is he doing here? Was he captured as well?

The four Shakers flank me, Tysian standing at my right.

"Here is the girl," Tysian says. "We have brought her to you, as was negotiated."

My thoughts grasp for a logical explanation. "Threh'hai Saiyen, what does he mean? Are we going home now?"

Threh'hai doesn't meet my eyes. His hands tremble, and he tries to cover it by gripping his cane. The pit in my stomach grows.

And then Faharic Penvaren enters the tent.

Zadock's potah. He is here. I blink in shock.

Faharic's hands are clasped together behind his back, and he walks calmly to stand beside Threh'hai. He wears a richly dyed green camehl wool sand cloak. His straight hair is pulled back into a tail. A sneer creeps onto his face when he sees me.

What is going on? Why is he here?

Zadock's potah looks me right in the eyes and smiles. "Norah. I trust that you are doing well."

"Zadock is dead." I choke back a sob. "Did you know that? How did—Why are—" I can't breathe.

Faharic nods gravely. "Yes. I was told about the accident with your boat, a necessity to obtain you. It's a shame. He was a good son. He would have followed in my footsteps well."

Threh'hai just sits at the desk, staring at his hands.

Tears stream down my face. Faharic's callousness makes me want to throw up.

Something he said makes me pause. *To obtain you.* "You're working with the To'Morat?"

Faharic only smiles.

"What about the moonstone?" I shriek. "You sent me and Zadock to get it. The whole council did—"

I cut off at Threh'hai's confused frown.

"There never was a mission," I breathe. "It was a lie." I struggle against the sand even though it's useless. "How could you?" I scream. "How could you?!"

Why did they lie? Why make up the story about the moonstone and the mission? To make it easier for the To'Morat to capture me?

Faharic leans forward and plants his knuckles on the table. "Sacrifices have to be made for the good of the whole. I gave up my son to the Ki'Rhen at his birth because I refused to let my sand gift suffer. The only reason I took him back was because he was close to you." He grins. "It's because of Zadock that I know you, Norah Saranyi. I know that you want nothing more than to be able to have the power to save those you love. I know that you would do anything to protect your people." He leans even closer. "Norah, you have that power. You can save us."

I writhe within the sand. "Threh'hai Saiyen...please."

The old man doesn't raise his eyes.

"She knows," Tysian says.

Faharic nods and leans forward. "Norah Saranyi. You know what you are."

I cringe and try to lean away. I hate him. My entire body aches with it, the complete loathing that I feel.

Faharic's lips quirk upward. "Your motah knows as well."

I jerk my head up.

"Oh, yes. It was she who told the council." Faharic grins.

Threh'hai holds up a hand. "Faharic, enough."

My stomach drops. *Motah knew. She knew about this. And she told the council.*

She betrayed me.

"Of course, we had to make a deal with the To'Morat." Faharic nods to Tysian. "We can't have it appear that we on the To'Rahn council would murder one of our own. But the benefits we'll reap will be for everyone."

Threh'hai looks up then. I try to glare at him, but tears are blurring my vision. It's too much. Losing Zadock. Motah's betrayal. Knowing that my own village has turned against me.

Threh'hai lets out a deep sigh. "Norah. Think. The village is dying. *All* villages are dying." His voice is thick and heavy. "I have our people to think of. And you can save them. You can save everyone. Or at least, buy us enough time to figure this out."

My breath comes in sharp gasps. "But—but can't we try to bring Sustaining back? Give me a chance. If I die, it's gone forever."

Threh'hai's eyes are old and so brown they're almost black. "You've been trying your entire life to manifest a sand gift, Norah. If you could've made it work, you would have by now. Something is fundamentally wrong with Sustaining. Something that cannot be fixed."

Faharic nods, a small, pleased smile on his face.

Threh'hai's expression softens into deep sorrow. "Even if your children have the ability to Sustain, they wouldn't know how to use their gift. Yes, your presence is helping To'Rahn somewhat. But it's not enough. You could not birth enough Sustainers to make a difference in this famine. We will all be dead by then."

I look away and squeeze my eyes shut, fighting back despair.

"This is the only way, Norah. We have no other choice. You can save everyone. You can give us enough time to figure out another way."

Motah knew.

"Enough," Tysian interjects. "She's not going anywhere. She doesn't need to be convinced. Now it's time to negotiate."

"I don't understand," Threh'hai says. "We already dealt with your Favored One. We already set the terms."

"Yes." Faharic frowns. "You will kill her and make it clear to the people that the To'Morat have done this, not us. In exchange, we are paying you quite a large sum. Not to mention that your people will be saved as well."

Tysian smiles. "Times are changing. Power is changing. Our Favored One is...no longer with us. Ailment of the heart, such a tragedy."

I look around at his comrades, though I can't see Behlron since he stands behind me. Mylarah crosses her arms and stares straight ahead. Riah clutches her spear with wide eyes. Neither of them challenges him.

"Either way, I have the girl. You will deal with me now." Tysian stands with his arms crossed behind him, a calm and confident smile on his face.

Faharic takes a seat and gestures for Tysian to do the same.

Threh'hai lets out a deep sigh. He looks at me for a moment.

"How could you?" I whisper.

"I'm sorry, Norah." He turns his gaze to Tysian. "Will you call off this army?"

Tysian's smile widens. "I shall. With only one provision. We sacrifice this girl as we already negotiated. You get to blame her death on us. However." He pauses. "To'Rahn will be under our rule as a province of To'Morat. You will acknowledge me as the Favored One of our kingdoms. You will pay tribute to us every season of twenty-five percent of your growth. I will allow you to govern your people underneath me."

Faharic's face darkens, and Threh'hai's frail hands clench into fists. "Absolutely not. We will not agree to these terms."

"I don't think that you have much choice, old man." Tysian smirks.

"We already made a deal with your people," Faharic says. "You must honor the previous terms. Where is Imwraeth Jeriyah?"

Tysian waves a hand. "I told you. He's dead. You deal with me now. We have the girl, and we have an army hanging over your heads. You don't have many bargaining tools."

Threh'hai opens his mouth. "But—"

Tysian holds up his hand. "Submit to our terms, or we will attack. And we leave none alive."

30

IMWRAETH

Councilor Therah is dead.

After checking that fact, I called a guard in to remove the body. The guard was stoic about it, keeping no expression on his face. What had Therah told the guards who were supposed to be watching over me at night? How had she had so much sway over them? And what did they think now?

I am losing control.

Truth.

I had the two guards who were stationed outside my door last night dismissed and removed from the palace. Lylahn, Kaera, and I relocated to another room to try to sleep, but of course, none of us could. I lay awake in bed the rest of the night, listening to Lylahn's whispering words of comfort and Kaera's quiet cries.

I despise myself and the ruler I have allowed myself to become.

Truth.

It's still a shock that the assassination attempts were Therah all along. The first two tries, the poison and the falling rock, seem so different than the third. More subtle. But I guess she was getting desperate?

Now I stand in the guest bedroom in front of a full-length mirror, donning formal Favored One regalia. The sleeveless crimson robe brings out the red of my short hair. I match it with a black belt and boots, warriors' accessories. I'm going to need every bit of help today to look commanding. I strap my satchel of sand across my shoulder.

Lylahn and Kaera continue to work on my exposed arms. Lylahn's hard breathing tells me she is almost frantic about it. Sweat drips down her forehead.

Today, the time is up.

Despite the insanity of the previous night and the fact that my hands are shaking still, I smile at my reflection in the mirror.

Today, I will be healed. I will become the ruler I was meant to be.

Atoille chose me as a leader. Me. The moon goddess must have known that I could be healed.

Lylahn removes her hand from my arm, and the glow of Absorbing stops. Kaera follows her sister's lead.

I meet Lylahn's eyes. "Is it done?" Giddiness bubbles inside me. "I don't really feel any different."

"Imwraeth," Lylahn begins, "I have to tell you something."

Time freezes.

The door bangs open, and Lienos strides in, trailed by two armored guards. "Ah, here you are. Why have you decided to relocate sleeping quarters?" He plows on before I can answer. "Well, it has been two days. How are you feeling, Favored One?" Lienos folds his arms across his chest and cocks one eyebrow. "Has this miraculous healing worked?"

I glance from my councilor to Lylahn, and then at Kaera. I clear my throat. "I—I think they need a little more time, Councilor. Maybe just—"

Lienos' face goes as red as an algohde blossom. "The arrangement was two days. It has been two days. Are there results?"

I glance to Kaera and then back to Lylahn. "Am I healed?"

Lylahn's eyes widen. "Yes." She clears her throat and stands straight. "Yes."

And then something very odd happens.

My internal lie detector, something that has never, *ever* failed me, gives me two different answers.

The first yes—*lie.*

The second yes—*truth.*

What?

I stagger backward, clutching at my chest as my heart begins to pound out of control. My thoughts are reeling. This isn't right—this isn't—

Gasping for breath, I reach into the bag of sand at my side and Extract. My heartbeat slows.

I close my eyes and sink to the floor. I put my head in my hands.

Lylahn lied.

When I look up, Lienos wears a smug smile. He nods to the guards. "Take them away."

Kaera screams as a guard grabs her under the arms. Lylahn kicks and fights, but the second guard holds her arms.

I stand on shaking legs. "Wait. Wait!"

Praise Atoille, the guards stop.

"They will not be executed." I try to put command and control into my voice, but it still quavers.

Lienos closes his eyes and rubs his temples. "Favored One. They have lied to you. They have not kept their promises. There must be a consequence."

Lylahn gasps, struggling, and Kaera's cries fill my ears. The guard points his spear at Lylahn's neck. "Be still."

She obeys.

I stand a little straighter. "Yes, Councilor. You are correct. They did lie." *Though how, I have no idea.*

Lylahn's breathing quickens, and she stares at me with those enormous eyes, pleading. Lienos smiles.

"But," I say. "But they also saved my life."

Lienos' smile vanishes. "What? What is this nonsense?"

I plow onward despite the surge of disappointment and hurt that threatens to overwhelm me. "Last night, I was attacked. By Councilor Therah."

And then something supremely satisfying occurs. Lienos' mouth drops open.

"It was she who was behind the assassination attempts all along."

Lienos blinks and closes his mouth.

"If it wasn't for Lylahn and Kaera, I would be dead right now." I smile at them. Tears stream down Lylahn's cheeks. "They saved my life, and I order that they are not to be harmed. In fact, they will be given special rooms in the palace and, how did you put it? Rewarded appropriately for their station."

Lienos's face reddens. Then he gives himself a shake and draws himself up. "No, boy. They will not." He turns to the guards and nods.

Without a glance at me, the guards drag Lylahn and Kaera away.

No... No, no, no!

I stare in stunned silence, Lylahn and Kaera's screams echoing in my ears, as the guards drag them, kicking and fighting, down the hallway.

"No!" I cry. "You will not! I order you to—"

Lienos smirks. "Everyone knows where the real power is in To'Morat, boy. It's time you learned it as well."

Lienos Shakes, stealing sand from my own bag, and wraps it around me almost quicker than I can blink. Before I know it, my arms are pressed against my sides, my legs cemented together.

"I will allow you to live. I am not like Therah. But I can't have you going after them and interfering." Lienos sneers as he watches me struggle.

I stop.

The sand encases me in one long, twisting tendril. Lienos thought he could trap me. Thought that I would be too weak to fight back. But he has forgotten one thing. This sand, the sand wrapping around me, has kept me alive my entire life. Has been a part of *me* much more than it has him.

I Extract from all of it at once.

A wild energy floods my veins. I fling the sand wide and break free of Lienos' snare. Sand hits him square in the face. He stumbles back, clutching at his eyes. I reach into his pocket and smile when I feel the smooth, faceted surface of the red gem. Lienos wouldn't keep it anywhere but on his person. I jam it into my pocket and hurry from the room.

"Imwraeth!" Lienos calls. "Get back here, boy!"

Energy bubbles inside of me, pushing me down the hallway. But even with Extracting, I can't do anything that would pump too much blood through my heart.

I've got to get to them. *Oh, please, Atoille, don't let me be too late.*

Lienos doesn't follow. Whether he doesn't want to cause a public scene or is still scrubbing sand from his eyes, I don't know.

I burst out of the palace doors and speed walk to the left, through the side courtyard that leads to the execution blocks.

Faster, faster.

I will my legs to move, will my heart to hold together as it thunders in my chest. I slam open the gate, and there they are.

The open courtyard is large, built to hold an audience. Quartz benches line the walls, and two slabs of quartz sit in the center. Lylahn and Kaera are tied to each one with ropes of sand, fighting to get free. Two Shakers stand above them with sand pressed to their necks. Two other guards, Forgers, stand ready to Forge the sand and crush their throats.

"STOP!" I scream.

The guards look at me. My body sags with relief. "You will not execute these prisoners." I gasp for air and can't seem to get enough of it, but I hold my ground. *Let them listen, please let them listen.*

The guards glance at each other for a moment. One of the Forgers removes his hand, then the other one. "Yes, Favored One."

"You will release the prisoners to me."

The guards nod in deference before striding from the courtyard.

Once they're gone, my knees give way, and I fall to the ground. Arms wrap around me, and I look up.

Kaera's hair is in my face, and she's squeezing the life out of me. But I put my arms around her in return.

"You saved us," she whispers. "I knew you would."

Lylahn sits up and climbs off the quartz, her legs shaking. "Thank you, Imwraeth."

Adrenaline drains from my system, giving way to pure, blessed relief.

Kaera pulls away and goes to her sister's side. I stand, my legs wobbling. That was way too close, and I'm afraid. Afraid of what is happening in To'Morat.

Worse still... I turn away from Lylahn so she won't see the bitter disappointment.

She lied.

I will not be healed.

I will not be the leader my people need.

"What are we going to do?" Lylahn says. "We are still not safe."

We are silent for a few moments.

I push aside the hurt. I can't process it right now. I turn. Lylahn and Kaera cling to each other, and they are counting on me. "Come with me. I know what to do."

31

ZADOCK

I pound the wall. Again. And again.

My hand falls, and I sink to my knees. Since that visit from the Favored One, the only interaction I've had has been when my food is pushed through the narrow opening in my cell.

I feel useless. Worse than useless. Norah is out there, in the hands of the To'Morat, Atoille knows where, and I'm stuck in here.

That specking gem, the key to everyone's survival, was in my hands. And I lost it.

My head sags into my hands. Crushing despair wraps around me like a sand cloak.

I blink my eyes open and see sand crumbling at my feet.

I scramble to stand. The quartz wall is coming down, more than needed just to slide food through. Something is happening. I won't waste this opportunity.

I raise my hands. Prepare to Shake.

Here we go.

The wall crumbles to sand. I take control of it, form it into a hundred knives. I've never seriously injured another human being with sand, but I've practiced. Every Shaker on To'Rahn does. I know how to wrap sand around a person's neck and cut off their air. I know how to stuff it down their throat until they suffocate. I am even strong enough that I ripped a practice dummy apart using sand. I don't know if I can do it on a real person.

For Norah, I will.

I cry out and Shake.

"STOP!" a voice screams. The quartz doorway disintegrates, and the Favored One himself walks into my cell.

"You!" I halt the sand knives but keep them poised, pointed toward him. A hostage could be very useful. I drop half of my knives and wrap sand around his arms, snaking up until it fits snugly around his neck. His eyes go huge.

The guard next to him, the Forger who removed the wall, reaches one hand forward. "Favored One?"

The two girls who were with him during the interrogation hurry into the cell, and the older one takes a step forward. I start to wrap another tendril of sand around her, but then she speaks.

"We're here to help."

I can barely hear her. I can only tell what she's saying because I read her lips.

"Please," she breathes. "Let him go." The younger girl steps forward. Takes the older one's hand.

The guard lifts a spear. "Release the Favored One. Now."

What do I do? *What do I do?*

I Shake, moving the Favored One closer to me. "Let me pass. Or I will strangle him." I tighten the sand around his throat.

The guard steps forward with a spear, looking uncertain.

The Favored One clears his throat. He turns his head to look at me. I keep my arms poised, ready to tighten the sand again if anyone moves.

"Zadock Penvaren," the Favored One says. "You are hereby released."

The guard's mouth drops open.

"By order of Atoille's Favored, this prisoner is set free." The

Favored One turns to me. "Please. We need your help. We need to save Norah."

I'm so shocked that I drop the sand.

The Favored One brushes off his clothes. He nods to the guard. "You are dismissed. I take the prisoner into my care."

The guard bows, a confused frown on his face, but he turns and marches away.

"What did you say?" Is this an elaborate trick? "We're going to save Norah? Where is she? Let's go!"

"She's on her way to To'Rahn," the girl says. "They're going to kill her as soon as Atoille rises."

I freeze. *What?*

"Three days?" I close my eyes and try to have hope. She's alive.

"My name is Imwraeth." The Favored One of Atoille extends his hand to me, a sparkling red gem in his palm. "I hear that you are the strongest Shaker of To'Rahn."

I take the moonstone and shove it into my pocket. Imwraeth keeps his hand extended. I take it, and he helps me up with surprising strength.

"Show me."

☾

I'm in shock.

Everything Imwraeth and Lylahn just told me is blowing me away.

But somehow, I believe them, because I'm hurrying through the streets of To'Morat beside them with a group of servants following us with supplies.

Norah, a Sustainer. My heart lifts with pride. She always wanted to be able to help people.

My legs are urging me to run—we have so little time to get to To'Rahn—but we settle for a quick walk so Imwraeth can keep up. I don't really understand Lylahn and Kaera's story, but they're driven to help, and that's all I care about for now. Lylahn jogs alongside us, holding Kaera's hand, and she keeps glancing at Imwraeth like she's worried about him, which is a little odd, everything considered.

The sandy streets are quiet, and the houses dark. It surprises me that To'Morat looks so much like To'Rahn. My whole life, I've been taught to fear and despise them. I always imagined their plateau to be, I don't know. Full of war barracks or something?

"So Norah is a Sustainer," I say, "and her sand gift can save us. Can make the world right."

Imwraeth nods. "As far as I understand it, yes."

"But she has to be killed for this power to be released." I swallow. If that is true...if people believe that... She will never be safe.

"Yes," Imwraeth says. "But we are going to stop it. There has to be another way." Imwraeth looks at Lylahn. "There will be no more killing. We'll figure this out."

Lylahn touches my arm as we walk. "I saw her, Zadock. She spoke of you. She thinks you're dead."

Oh, Norah. How she must be hurting. "Can we send a message to your armies, Imwraeth? Call off the attack and tell them to stop?"

Imwraeth gestures for us to turn a corner into a kind of plaza, and we follow. "I fear that my people would not listen to a message, even if we could be sure one got there in time. I must be there in person to call off the battle."

His face falls, and he looks like he's going to be sick. I can't imagine why since he must be used to telling people what to do. His army will have to listen to him.

We exit the plaza and pass guard towers looking over the edge of the plateau. Lined up along the brim are three measly boats.

"What?" I stop. "Where's the famous To'Morat fleet?"

Imwraeth looks at me. "Headed toward To'Rahn."

Right. Speck. There is so much at stake here. I don't feel adequate to deal with this.

Imwraeth chooses a boat a little bigger than the *Norah* and directs the tired servants to load supplies into the hold.

I pick up a box and start helping. Kaera watches the servants with interest. When I pass Lylahn, she reaches out a hand and touches my shoulder. I pause.

"I'm an Absorber," she says. "The Favored One is an Extractor, as is Kaera. You are our only Shaker."

"What?" I turn toward her and nearly drop the supplies I'm holding. "Can't Imwraeth order some of these servants to help us?" Oh, speck. This just keeps getting worse.

"None of them are Shakers." Imwraeth comes to us. A servant takes the box from my hands, and I let go. They finish the loading quickly, and they bow to Imwraeth and walk away. "There are a few Shakers left in the palace. Some that were left behind to guard me. But only the weakest were left, and I don't..." He frowns. "I don't trust them."

"Then we're doomed." My heart sinks. There's no way we can make this work. If I'm the only Shaker, how am I supposed to squeeze a seven-day journey into three? I turn away and run my fingers through my hair. Norah is going to die. Norah is going to die, and there's nothing I can do.

"Lylahn has an idea." Imwraeth looks to her.

"I can Absorb away your fatigue," she says. "Keep you going day and night, as hard as you can. It's the only choice we have."

"But will it be enough?" I ask. Even going day and night, I don't think I can make the journey in time.

Norah's face is in my mind. *You're an engineer, Zadock. That's part of who you are.*

I look around in frustration. What good is that now? My eyes fall on a tall pillar with strange markings. There's scaffolding around it, with tools and shards of quartz scattered around like there's a project going on.

I hurry forward and sort through the scraps. Lylahn and Imwraeth follow me. "Ok. I once had this idea to make a bucket and pulley go up and down by using Extracting to power it. If I can build something to push us forward in the sand, you could power it, Imwraeth, so we wouldn't have to just rely on me."

Yes! I find long, thin sheets of quartz. I'm not sure what they're for, but if I can attach them to each other, we may have a chance.

"Are any of those servants Forgers?" I ask.

Imwraeth nods. "Yes."

"We're going to need to call one back."

3 2

NORAH

I have to stop this.

Threh'hai. Faharic. They're plotting with the To'Morat. That might include everyone on the council.

Even Motah.

They're bargaining with my life. And now they're losing control.

I *have* to stop this.

I sit in a guarded tent and breathe in the musty, damp air. Rain patters on the tent flaps. The quartz ground that the To'Morat created is gritty with sand. I run my fingers along the surface while I think.

They haven't tied me up, and there's only a single guard outside the tent. I assume that they're not too worried about me escaping since we're on an island of quartz in a stormy desert.

I eat the meal that's thrust through the tent flap, though the food is tasteless. My mind is racing.

What am I going to do?

My village is in jeopardy. We cannot fight an assault like this. And people are trying to kill me—the To'Morat, and my own.

I close my eyes and exhale. Could I stop this? If what they say is true, if my death would cause a burst of life-giving power…

I want to talk to Motah. It's a risk. She could be against me. She could be the one negotiating my life away. But I need to know more.

I poke my head out of the tent flap. The rain is pouring, and my hair is immediately plastered to my face. There's a single guard there in red and black armor, frowning and staring out into the storm.

"I need to relieve myself," I say. "Where can I do that?"

The guard bends down and picks up a bucket. He thrusts it at me. "Here."

I frown and take the bucket back into the tent. Speck. That didn't work.

I wipe dripping hair out of my eyes and go to the back of the tent, where water is starting to pool under the flap.

Huh. I explore the edges of the tent. In most places, the fabric is pulled tight to the ground, tied down by quartz stakes Forged into the ground. But there's a puddle forming in one corner. I give the tent fabric there an experimental tug, and it lifts.

It's a tight fit, but I manage to get my head out. Rain slides down my forehead and into my eyes. My shoulders come next, then my stomach. Hips are a little snug, but I manage to squeeze through.

Well, that wasn't so bad.

Now what? I walk across the army camp, hugging my body and shivering. I weave through pitched tents, trying to stay out of sight. Where are all the guards? Inside because of the rain?

I hear a voice, and I duck around a tent corner, heart hammering. Then I realize it's Tysian. I glance around the tent and see that he's lifted himself up on a platform of sand, heedless of the rain. Someone next to him holds their hands high, the glow of Extracted sand emitting from them. Tysian's face is lit, a beacon in the darkness. A crowd of To'Morat warriors is gathered and listening to him.

Tysian's voice booms through the camp. "People of To'Morat, I salute you!"

A cheer arises, and fists are pumped into the air. More guards emerge from tents to listen. I hurry to the cover of the next tent, the rain masking my footsteps, getting closer to the edge of the quartz.

Tysian speaks again. "I am saddened to tell you that I have received word—our poor, dear Favored One's heart has finally failed him."

Murmurs travel through the crowd. I splash to the next tent, heart pounding, pressing myself against the wet fabric and praying to Atoille with everything I have that no one notices me. I shiver from the cold of the night, made worse by the rain. The stars are obscured by dark clouds, and Atoille is gone. It's so dark I can hardly see the next tent.

"We will mourn his loss," Tysian continues. "But for now, until Atoille chooses a new Favored One, leadership defaults to me, your Blood Rank One."

The crowd of warriors roar and punch fists and spears into the air. Shakers shoot jets of sand into the sky.

"I vow to lead this people to greatness!"

Another cheer arises, and I use the sound to hurry to the next tent, hoping that the darkness will work in my favor. I'm so close. The edge of the quartz structure is in sight.

"I vow to lead us to victory!" Tysian says. "The To'Rahn emissaries have gone. They refused to treat with us."

So Threh'hai and Faharic have left me. A lump forms in my throat.

"We will defeat the To'Rahn, and no one will stand in our way. We fight for resources we need to live, to feed our families, and for the glory of To'Morat!"

I break free of the rows of tents, confident that most of the warriors are behind me, enraptured by Tysian's words. I didn't like the Favored One, but I get the sinking feeling that he's been replaced by someone much worse.

There are a few skiffs tied down. Most of the large ships are moored to the pillar in the ocean of sand.

The pouring rain lightens to a drizzle. Dark thunder clouds are parting, starlight peeking through.

Tomorrow night, Atoille will rise. Tomorrow night is the day designated for my death. Tomorrow night, unless my people agree to be ruled by To'Morat, we will all be slaughtered.

My pulse hammers in my throat, and I try to push down the fear. I climb into one of the skiffs. It's small, but it should work to get me to To'Rahn.

But how?

I pound the wood, frustration choking me. I hate being so powerless. I. Hate. It.

I step back out and walk behind the boat. What am I going to do? Was my escape for nothing?

"Hey!" Footsteps. Running on the quartz.

I'm getting off this structure. Anything besides sitting and waiting to die.

I start to push the boat off the quartz cliff. I will jump in and fall, and I will get off this, or—

"Wait," says a feminine voice.

I turn. It's Riah, standing there with her spear in hand, helmet under one arm.

Riah leans down beside me and begins to push. I'm so shocked that I freeze.

"I'm here to help you," she says in a low voice. "I went to your tent, but you were already gone."

I hear more voices, speaking quickly and rising in volume. My absence has been noticed.

I just stand there, blinking. *What?*

"Look, I don't agree with what Tysian is doing. Atoille chose our Favored One for a reason, even if that reason is not apparent." Riah meets my eyes. "You are the tool Tysian is using. Without you, well, whatever he's planning will be harder. This is something I can do."

Relief floods my system, and tears prick the corners of my eyes.

After everything I've been through, this enormous gift is almost too much. "Thank you."

Together, we push the boat off the ledge and jump inside. I land with a thud on the wood, and for a second, we're free-falling. Then Riah catches us in a bed of sand, and we sink down into the desert. The quartz structure looms above us, blocking the light of the stars.

The rain stops, but we're both already soaking wet. The cold of the desert hits me like a slap. With one hand, Riah hands me a camehl-wool coat, and I'm so grateful the tears threaten to spill over again.

We land in the churning waves, and Riah looks around. "I can get you as far as To'Rahn, then I have to come back. I will do what I can to stop the attack."

"I don't know how to thank you."

Riah gives me a grim smile. "Let's start by making peace between our nations, yeah?"

I nod.

Riah swallows. "I have to admit I'm terrible at navigation. Out here, where everything looks the same, I have no idea which way to go."

I smile and check the sky, locate the planets and stars that Potah taught me to love. "I can help with that."

33

NORAH

I'm home.

It's been a lifetime.

I'm standing at the doorway of our tiny house, hesitant to enter. The sun is sinking in the sky on the evening of the last day.

Riah and I arrived at To'Rahn about mid-afternoon. After receiving some directions from me, Riah turned right around to go back to her people, saying that she would do what she could to halt the attack.

I spent an hour or so walking through To'Rahn, putting off what I have to do. I encountered only a few people. The market and plaza square were empty. I stopped by the grow walls—dried and bare. Things are worse than when I left. Much, much worse.

Most people I saw were on the outskirts of To'Rahn, Forgers and Shakers working together to build an enormous quartz wall. They've made it about halfway around To'Rahn now. To'Morat Forgers will eventually get it down, the speed depending on how skilled they are, but it might buy To'Rahn some time.

War is upon us. I failed. I couldn't stop it.

Tonight, Atoille will rise. Tonight, my sacrifice could change everything.

I turn away from the door and sit on our front doorstep. Sand gusts down the street.

I don't want to face her.

The last time I was here, Zadock was beside me. My eyes fill with tears.

I put my head in my hands and allow myself a moment to grieve. I have to warn the village, I have to help them prepare for an attack, and I have to find out what Motah knows so I can decide what to do.

I stand. I take a deep breath and raise one hand to knock. Just walking in feels strange.

The door opens, and it's Motah.

She gasps and brings one hand to her lips. There are dark circles under her eyes, and she looks as if she's lost weight. Her hair is thin and dull. She throws her arms around me and weeps onto my shoulder.

I'm so shocked that I freeze and let her hold me. But I don't hold her back.

"They said they went to find you... They said they never found anything... They said you were lost forever."

I take a step back. "Well, I'm here."

I move around her and enter the house. Our entryway is dim, and the floor is covered in sand, like always. There's a shriveled, brown, potted cactus in the corner. "Where's Shrey?"

She bounds around the corner. "Norah!" Shrey throws herself into my arms. Some of my sorrow melts away. I bend to her level and wrap my arms around her.

"I never got to tell you!" Shrey lowers her voice to a breath. "I love you, too."

My eyes fill with tears, but I hurry to wipe them away. "Thank you, Shrey."

I stand back up and face Motah. She's closed the door behind her, and she's watching me with large eyes.

"Did you know?" I ask.

Motah hesitates. Then she nods. "I knew." She turns to Shrey. "Go and set the table for dinner."

Shrey gives me one more grin before hurrying to the kitchen, yelling, "Norah's back!"

I stand and face Motah squarely. "You sent Zadock and me on a fool's errand." I don't hold the accusation and anger from my voice. "You knew there was nothing at the ocean of water. You lied." I remember Threh'hai's confused frown when I brought it up. "The council never sent us. They didn't even know we were going."

Motah's eyes fill with tears again, but she crosses her arms and squares her jaw. "Yes. I lied."

"Why?" All the hurt in my heart, all the anger, I direct at her. If we had stayed, maybe we could've done something to help. If we had stayed— "Zadock is dead!" The tears start to fall. I hate that she sees me crying. "Zadock is dead because of you!" My heart rips. I turn away. I feel so much hate in this instant that I think I could Sustain.

"Oh no, Norah—I'm so sorry. I didn't—"

I whirl back around. "You're sorry? You're *sorry*? That's it? Sorry won't bring him back!"

I push past her, back through the front door, and sit down on the sand. I sob and sob into my arms. I feel a hand on my back, and I jerk away. "Why? Why did you do it?"

Motah sits next to me. "I did it to save you."

I blink.

Motah stares into the swirling sands on the street before us. "Yes, I knew, Norah. You are a Sustainer. I've known it for nearly your entire life." She sighs and closes her eyes.

I don't speak. I can't speak.

Motah opens her eyes again. "When you were young but old enough that a sand gift should have manifested, I did some research. I wanted so badly to help you, to find out what was..."

"Wrong with me."

Motah swallows. "All right, yes. I was a worried parent. I wanted to know if something was wrong. As a council member, I have special access to all the sand gift records of the people of To'Rahn. So I kept searching until I found records so old they were crumbling, so old they had been long abandoned."

My fingernails dig into my palms. She knew about this since I was young. And still, she watched me struggle in school. Let me think that I was nothing.

"And then I found it," Motah says. "Records of the Sustainers of old. I knew that Sustaining had returned in you. I knew it by the way plants seemed to grow better when you were near."

I turn away, thinking of how I was always assigned to care for the grow walls and how much I hated it.

"But I also knew that Sustaining was different," Motah says, "and that we were missing something. Your power would never fully manifest. But we tried so hard, didn't we?" Motah reaches up to touch my cheek, but I turn away. "I worked for your entire life to make you hate me, Norah. Because I thought that your Sustaining might show. And I loathed every second of it."

I have to remind myself to inhale, exhale. Still, I don't look at her.

"On those records, I saw how the last Sustainers died. How they were killed." Motah lets out a ragged breath. "I knew that if others found out your secret, you would never be safe."

"But you told the council!" I burst out.

Her face falls, eyes sorrowful. "Yes. When I initially discovered Sustaining, I showed the council what I had found, hoping that together we could figure out how to make your gift work. But we never could. I *did not* tell them about a Sustainer's sacrifice. The rest of the council discovered it through their own research." She swallows. "Norah, I want you to know, I—I love—"

"Stop," I whisper. "Stop."

Motah looks away. "I wanted to keep you safe. I've always wanted that. The night of the Anointing, at an emergency council meeting, I discovered that others had found out what your death could do. I had to get you out, so I sent you and Zadock on a false errand. I was trying to buy some time, time to convince the council that there had to be a better way." She sighs. "I don't know if I did the right thing. Sending you away has brought everyone in To'Rahn to the brink of starvation."

"Why not just tell me? You let me suffer and think I was different, that there was something wrong with me. Why?"

"Because I know you," Motah says. Her face softens, and she smiles. "I know how much you want to help people, to save everyone. You don't need to give your life."

"So it's true?" Something stills and quiets inside me. "If I die, there will be a burst of energy that will heal the world and make food grow for a hundred years?"

Motah hesitates. "According to old texts, yes. But that's why there is so much wrong in the first place. Sustainers were killed until there weren't enough left. You cannot give your life, Norah."

I jerk to my feet in frustration. "Well then, what else can I do? I have tried and tried to use the sand. I just can't. What am I supposed to do?"

Motah stays seated, tilts her head to look up at me. "There's nothing, Norah. Sustaining is broken. You can't use the sand."

I can't use the sand.

I sit down again. My legs won't hold me up. "There's no hope then. The To'Morat will attack. They will kill us all."

"We will fight."

I close my eyes and take in a long breath, trying to still the tumbling emotions inside of me. "Isn't it worth it?" I whisper. "Isn't one life worth it to save everyone?"

"Norah."

I stand. I don't look at her.

Instead, I walk through the entryway, past the cactus plant. But then I stop and stare. It looks greener than it did before, the needles sharper. I pull off a few, even though it stings.

I walk into the kitchen, where Shrey is finishing setting the table. She gives me a big smile, and it's another jab in my heart.

I hold her close to me and hand her the needles. "For you."

She grabs them with joy on her face and runs off to our room to add them to her collection.

I watch her go, see her little blonde curls bounce on her back.

I know Motah will try to stop me if I go out the front, so I leave through the back door, quickly and quietly.

34

IMWRAETH

This. Is. Lunacy.

Even after three days of traveling like this, I still can't believe it actually works.

Zadock's idea is either totally insane, or it's going to be the new way everyone sand-sails.

We charge across the sand. The heat and wind whip me in the face. The sun is shining brightly above, so theoretically, we should be sleeping since the sands are calmer, but we haven't stopped once. Lylahn keeps one hand on Zadock's arm, Absorbing away his fatigue. He's still going strong at the rear of the boat, Shaking the sand to keep us moving.

I'm seated next to him. I have one hand on some kind of handle attached to the quartz propeller that Zadock directed the Forgers to make.

Thin sheets of quartz are stuck on top of a pole that juts upward to about the level of the sails, and they fan out from a central node and spin with the wind. It's my Extracted energy that gives them power and shoves us forward.

As long as I keep my hand on the pole and think of it as an

extension of my body, I can direct energy from the sand through me and into the propeller. Or so Zadock explained.

Lylahn alternates between Zadock and me, Absorbing away our fatigue. We've kept the boat going night and day with hardly any rest. But somehow, I feel amazing. Alive.

Councilor Therah creeps into my thoughts. I still can't believe that she truly wanted me dead, enough to attempt it three times. And she almost succeeded.

Therah was always the kind one, the grandmotherly figure knitting in the background. I never knew what was truly going through her mind. Even with my lie-detection ability, she kept this hidden from me.

I shiver, even though the hot sun is making sweat run down my back.

It still bothers me. The poison. The pillar's collapse. And then, finally, a knitting needle to the heart. Those were her plans, but the first two seem so different. They could've been passed off as accidents, less likely to get her implicated. And then she tries to stab me. But why? Was she getting desperate?

It's a mystery I'll never know.

Kaera smiles at me and puts a hand on the handle. With her other hand, she reaches for a handful of sand.

"Together?" she asks.

"Together."

However it works, we're making amazing progress. We might even make it in time.

☾

I SEE the quartz structure long before we arrive.

It's glaring in the sunlight, and I recognize it immediately. It's a classic To'Morat tactic. If we're not attacking right away, it's much more manageable to have a base to launch off. The Forgers will reverse it and turn it back into sand when they're ready to attack.

So this is a good sign. The attack hasn't happened.

It's the evening of the last day. Tonight, Atoille will rise.

Despite the Absorbing, Zadock slumps in his seat. Lylahn sits straight and tall, but there are dark circles under her eyes. The Extracting has given me extra energy, so I'm not really feeling it. But I know from experience that if I rely on Extracting too much and don't get some real sleep, I'll start to feel a little weird. Kaera is a decently strong Extractor, but she's had to stop and sleep a few times. But we did it. We made it in time.

I pull the rope to unfurl the To'Morat flag at the top of our mast so the warriors know we're a friendly boat, then sit back down and reach into our packs. "Let's stop and eat before we go up."

Zadock's head swivels toward me. "What? No. We're here. Let's get up there and save her."

"You can't help her if you drop over dead of exhaustion."

Zadock sighs but helps Lylahn pass out packets of food—dried sand lizard and strips of cactus flesh. Delicious.

The boat sways with the waves, and we eat in silence. I watch Lylahn take a sip of water. She lowers the waterskin and meets my eyes.

"Lylahn, I—" I break off and look away.

Zadock rips off a bite of lizard jerky, and his gaze darts between us.

Lylahn doesn't speak for a long moment. "I'm sorry, Imwraeth."

Truth.

It hurts, thinking of it all over again. The disappointment is cutting. "You lied because you had to."

She nods, her eyes scanning my face.

"How?" I ask. "I've never—I mean, I always—"

"I know," Lylahn says. Kaera sits next to her, gnawing on dried lizard.

Zadock frowns, confused, but he keeps glancing at the quartz structure, and I know he wants to get going.

"I know," Lylahn repeats. "Or, at least, there were rumors on

To'Shahera. That you could always, *always* tell when someone was lying. We knew that you took Absorbers prisoner. We assumed you needed healing, and you weren't getting it."

I swallow. "Yeah."

"Our older sisters—" Her voice falters. Kaera takes her hand, and Lylahn squeezes it back. "They made me lie to them every single day. It didn't matter about what. I lied and lied and lied. I hated it. It got to be where they didn't know when I was lying and when I wasn't. And still, I lied. Eventually, I could convince myself that lies were truth. I believed my lies." She meets my eyes. "It was because of my sisters. They saved me."

I sit back in the boat, holding my uneaten sand lizard. "Well. That explains that." I'm stunned. I've never been wrong. Never. And I'm crushed beyond belief. I was so sure I was going to be healed.

Another part of me is just glad she's alive.

Zadock sets down his waterskin and says, "Now?"

"Now."

Zadock raises his arms and takes the boat up, his determination clear on his face. All the exhaustion that showed earlier has vanished.

"Ok, so, you'll just tell your people to release her? And you'll call off your army?" Zadock asks, arms outstretched, lifting the boat upward. The guards at the top see the To'Morat sigil on the sails and hail us, waving their arms.

"Yes," I say. "Something like that."

Atoille's ashes, I feel sick. I've never done anything like this.

We reach the top of the plateau, and I step off the boat, my legs shaking.

"Favored One!" The two warriors glance at each other, mouths hanging open. Strange. It's not that odd that I attend my warriors on the day of battle.

I reach my hand behind me to help Lylahn down, and, after a moment, she accepts. My heart soars, swells with courage.

There will be no more killing.

Zadock steps off the boat and looks at me, fear in his eyes. "Please," he whispers.

I nod. Then I turn to my army.

The tents are stacked, row upon row, neat and trim. The main command tent, larger than the others and marked with the To'Morat sigil, is off to my left. That will be where Tysian is set up. They're probably keeping Norah nearby.

So far, everything's as I expected. Could I have been wrong about Tysian, too?

A few warriors walking between tents see me and halt, pointing. I frown but walk to the command tent, Lylahn, Kaera, and Zadock following behind.

The bored-looking guard standing in front of the tent snaps to attention. His jaw drops. "Favored One—you're—they said you were dead!"

My heart sinks. *Dead.* If Tysian has been telling people that I'm dead, I have to assume that he was in on the plot with Therah. He was counting on it. He's taken command from me.

I am suddenly overcome with indecision. What am I supposed to do about this? Should I find Lienos and ask for his help? Oh, right, he's in To'Morat. "I—I don't—"

"C'mon." Zadock passes me and pushes his way into the command tent.

Lylahn gives me a small smile, and I jolt. *She smiled.* "You can do this, Imwraeth." Kaera takes my hand and squeezes.

I close my eyes and breathe in deeply. Then I push back the tent flap.

General Tysian sits behind a desk—my desk—holding papers that show battle plans for attacking To'Rahn. He shifts his surprised gaze from Zadock, who's standing with hands swirling with sand, to me.

Tysian's eyes nearly bulge out of his head. Satisfaction makes me smile, but only for a moment.

How would Lienos handle this? I cross my arms and try to look nonchalant. "You've been spreading lies about me, Blood Rank One Tysian."

"Um. Ah, Favored One, I didn't know—"

"You'll be pleased to know that I am, in fact, alive, and now I am here to take command of my army." I'm shaking, and Lylahn puts one hand on my arm. "Where is the girl, Norah Saranyi? We are going to let her go, Tysian. There will be no attack on To'Rahn."

Tysian's eyes narrow. He schools his expression into calmness. "Is that so?"

"Where is she, Tysian?"

Sand swirls around Zadock's fists.

"She's not here," Tysian says, waving a hand. "The sacrifice is already on her way to To'Rahn."

Zadock lets out an angry cry.

Tysian rises to his feet. "I'm sorry, Favored One." His face takes on a look of pity.

I take a step back. Maybe coming here first was a mistake.

"I'm afraid your rule is over." Tysian throws his arms forward and lashes out with sand at an impossible speed. It wraps around my throat and clamps shut.

I gasp, clawing at my neck. Lylahn screams and scrabbles at the sand. Kaera thrusts her hands onto the sand at my neck and begins to Extract. There's a faint glow. If she can Extract enough, the sand will disappear. It's a good thought, but it won't be fast enough. Zadock turns toward me and lifts his arms. He's trying to wrest control of the sand away from Tysian.

My vision is clouding, my breath rasping, my heart zigzagging in my chest.

Tysian smiles. And the sand squeezes tighter.

35

ZADOCK

No *specking* way.

Imwraeth's own general whatever is trying to kill him?

And Norah is already on her way to To'Rahn. We have to leave. Now.

I Shake the sand, trying to grab it away from Tysian. I think back to all those practice sessions sparring with Felhar, how easy it was to wrest control of the sand away from him.

I pull.

And I *pull.*

Nothing happens. The sand around Imwraeth's neck doesn't even budge. Even Lylahn's and Kaera's efforts are doing nothing.

Sweat pools and drips down my neck. I keep yanking, keep trying to take the sand away from Tysian. It loosens just a bit from around Imwraeth's neck, but not enough for him to get a breath. His face is red, eyes rolling into the back of his head. Lylahn screams, clawing away at the sand.

I change tactics.

I release the sand around Imwraeth's neck and lift my arms, using the sand on the ground around me. I hurl it toward Tysian.

The sand flies into Tysian's face, cutting at his exposed skin. He gasps and, blessedly, loses control. The sand around Imwraeth's neck slides to the ground. Imwraeth falls to his knees, gasping. Lylahn kneels beside him.

"Help him!" Kaera cries.

Lylahn grabs a handful of sand and Absorbs, one hand on Imwraeth's neck.

Tysian turns toward me, his lips peeled back in a sneer. "I've heard of you," he says. "Zadock Penvaren. The strongest Shaker in all of To'Rahn." He smiles and looks into my eyes. "This will be interesting."

I swallow. Adrenaline pumps through my veins, and my heartbeat pounds in my ears. My body feels like it's on fire.

Yeah, I've done the training drills with my class. I've practiced combat moves and using the sand to kill. On dummies. I've never actually truly fought *against a person* before.

Ok. I don't have to kill him. I've just got to injure him, maybe, something to earn us enough time to get us out of here. We just have to get back to the boat and to To'Rahn as quickly as possible.

I hurl sand in Tysian's direction, another smokescreen of dust.

Tysian raises his arms and catches the sand, presses it back to me with ease. I step backward, not realizing how close I am to the fabric of the tent. I slip and fall.

"Gahhhh!" I writhe in the fabric that's engulfed me. Then I feel myself begin to rise, sand squeezing around my waist.

I throw my arms out to dissipate the sand around me, and it's too easy. Tysian was anticipating that. I fall to the ground and land in a roll of fabric.

Oof. That hurt.

I think of Norah and get back to my feet.

The fabric of the tent slides away, and I blink away the bright sun, looking in all directions at once. Where is Tysian?

The sand beneath my feet flies away, and I fall forward again.

Tysian stands to my left, a black shadow against the sun. I hurl a ball of sand toward him, and he catches it, ready to throw it away, but I push and push. As hard as I can. Sweat breaks out on my forehead as I stand and sink my feet into the ground, Shaking the sand fast to hold me in place.

The sand flies out of my control, and Tysian smiles.

Imwraeth climbs out of the collapsed tent, rubbing his newly healed throat. Lylahn and Kaera emerge behind him, watching me with solemn eyes.

This man is *strong*. I don't think—

Tysian hurls a knife of sand toward me. I dodge, but there's another. I leap out of the way. I don't trust myself to catch it.

A dozen different knives spring up around Tysian. He hurls them toward me. The edges glint in the sunlight, all of them sharp enough to cut, even without becoming quartz.

It's impossible to dodge them all, so I catch the sand and push back. The sand knives inch closer. *What do I do?* I release the knives and instead Shake the sand below me, jetting upward just as the knives dart forward. I rise on a platform of sand.

My chest heaves, my breath coming in gasps.

Tysian raises sand, one step at a time, walking higher on poles that lift to meet his feet. My jaw drops.

I bring sand up behind him and wrap it around his waist. I jerk, trying to fling him off balance. The edge of the quartz structure is near. If I could just—

Tysian jolts and starts to fall backward, but with a flick of his wrist, sand reaches up to support his back, and he rights himself. He looks at me and smiles. Then Tysian raises one arm and yanks my sand platform out from under me.

I scream, falling and flailing. I try to gather sand below me, but it shoots out of my control. I land hard on the quartz, and pain shoots up my spine. I cringe and groan, my head spinning. Tysian sweeps one arm, and sand grasps at my legs and pulls me backward.

I plummet off the edge of the platform, and my stomach drops. The edge of the quartz structure gets farther away as I fall faster and faster, down toward the ocean of sand. Tysian's sand forces me down, speeds my descent.

Norah. Needs. Me.

I Shake the sand below and bring it up to meet me, grunting as the forces of both catch me in the middle. I scream and press Tysian's sand to the side, at the same time pressing upward with sand from behind me. I grind out of Tysian's control and shoot back up toward the quartz.

Tysian looks down over the edge. "Excellent. I'm impressed. For someone from To'Rahn, you are doing very well."

I stand on the quartz before him on wobbling feet. My whole body aches, but I can still stand, so nothing is broken or seriously injured. I plant my feet in a warrior's stance and lift the sand.

"Imwraeth!" I cry. Tysian hurls sand spears, and I roll to the side. "We have to get out of here! Get everyone back to the boat!"

The Favored One looks at me with wide eyes. "We can't. I can't leave my people—"

Then sand swirls around me, lifting my feet off the ground. I'm not doing it. I throw out my arms, trying to Shake, but I spin in a circle. I'm out of control.

"Stop!" I hear Lylahn scream. "Stop this!"

The sand keeps spinning me. I can vaguely tell that I'm being lifted higher and higher, and then, it stops.

I fall. My stomach lurches, the world spinning. The quartz platform leaps in and out of my vision without any way to tell direction. Panicking, I grasp for sand but can't find any. I'm going to fall to my death.

At the last second, I sense some sand and bring it up to meet me. I jolt into it with a thud and then lower myself to the ground. My vision is still circling. I think I'm going to be sick. Tysian steps toward me through a tilting world.

I can't beat him.

"Imwraeth," I say. "We have to go!"

I stand and immediately fall again. Sand, wrapped around my

foot, pulls me downward. I hear another sand knife whistling through the air, and I flinch—

But then I look up to see the knife miss Imwraeth by a thread, the Favored One dodging just in time.

"To the boat!" I run, Lylahn dragging Imwraeth after me, Kaera hurrying at the rear.

Sand wraps around my feet, and I trip. I try to regain control, to take the sand back, but Tysian is too strong.

"Tysian!" a feminine voice calls out.

"Riah," Imwraeth says. His feet, along with Lylahn's and Kaera's, are also encased in sand.

"The Favored One is alive!" Riah cries and points, turning behind her and gesturing to other warriors. "He lives!"

Tysian freezes, one hand outstretched, holding us in place. He glances between the crowd of warriors and us.

Imwraeth's mouth works like he wants to say something. He takes a deep breath. "My people," he croaks. Imwraeth clears his throat and tries again. "Warriors—" His eyes take in the growing crowd, staring at him with cold eyes. He shrinks visibly.

"Why aren't they doing anything?" I say. "Why aren't they stopping this?"

Lylahn looks from Tysian back to the army. "They don't know who to follow. They're watching to see how the fight turns out."

No.

"Too long!" Tysian cries. He raises himself up on a platform of sand, but his grip on us doesn't lessen a bit. "Too long have we allowed To'Morat to be led by someone unfit for the task."

Imwraeth's head droops.

"No," I say. "No!"

Tysian shakes his head. "It seems as though the news I received was incorrect, that our poor Favored One's heart still beats, but for how long? The To'Morat cannot thrive under leadership such as this, in times such as these. To'Morat needs strength!"

My heart sinks as heads in the crowd nod. Riah shakes her head, and I see her mouth moving, but her voice is drowned out by Tysian's cries.

"We need someone fearless and dedicated to keeping our families alive!"

A few warriors pump fists in the air and shout.

"Imwraeth Jeriyah is not the man to lead us!" Tysian raises fists above his head.

The crowd roars. Riah clutches a spear, her legs falling into a fighting stance.

Imwraeth's head sinks down onto his chest.

"Say something!" I say. "Defend yourself!"

His head lifts, face solemn. He looks into the expressions of all those who are crying for a change in leadership. "My people." His voice is ragged. "I will—"

The crowd hushes and parts, and an older man with a long gray beard steps forward and holds up a hand. Even Tysian lowers himself.

Imwraeth's eyes bulge out of his head. "Lienos! How are you here? How did—?"

It's Imwraeth's councilor, the man who questioned me. A seed of hope lifts my heart. If Imwraeth isn't strong enough to stand up for himself, surely his councilor will be.

Lienos looks toward Imwraeth with a fond expression, hands clasped together in front of him. I think this is a good sign until I see Imwraeth wither.

"I took the remaining Shakers and Extractors on To'Morat," Lienos says. "Clever design, that propeller contraption. The servants, luckily, memorized the pattern and had it copied for me. With several Shakers and Extractors, I myself bearing much of the burden, I arrived only hours before you." Lienos looks at Imwraeth with a look of deep pity. "Imwraeth Jeriyah, you are a good man." His eyes meet the Favored One's. The crowd is silent. Lienos sighs and shakes his head. "But you are not fit to lead the To'Morat."

Imwraeth collapses to the ground, even though his feet are still held fast. He buries his face in his hands.

Lienos turns and addresses the gathered warriors. "Warriors of To'Morat, I, councilor to the Favored One, revoke my support of Imwraeth Jeriyah. Blood Rank One Tysian will lead us to greatness."

Warriors beat spears against shields and cheer. My heart plummets. This is bad. This is so, so bad.

"Atoille chose him!" Riah screams. She turns to the crowd, waving her arms and shouting, but her words are drowned out.

"The Favored One has failed us!" the people cry.

"We are starving."

"It's time for a change!"

The crowd pushes forward, and Tysian looks back at us. He smiles.

Oh no.

Tiny needles of sand rise into the air, thousands of them.

I wrench the sand grasping our feet from Tysian's grip, stumbling as I regain my footing. I raise my hands, bringing sand up around me. "Get close to me!" I yell.

Lylahn pulls Imwraeth forward, and I bring up a wall around us, making it as hard and impenetrable as I can.

The sand around us is jerked away, the dome slipping away in the wind. The needles of sand are poised to attack.

Wait. They're not sand. They're glimmering in the sunlight. Quartz.

A Forger is helping him.

I scream and try to bring the dome back up, but I can't grip it. The needles descend on us with a fierce whistle.

Riah screams as she throws sand around us, knocking the needles away.

I hear Tysian give a cry of disgust. "Riah! No!"

"Get out of here!" Riah cries. She throws up a wall of sand to knock Tysian down.

We run.

Sand grips at my feet, but I knock it away. Riah races on our heels, shooting arrows of sand backward and throwing up walls of sand that Tysian blows aside.

We leap into a boat, and I don't hesitate to push off. We fall, and I hear Kaera's screams. I Shake sand from the desert floor to catch us.

The boat crashes into the waves of sand. Riah and I both Shake, speeding us toward what I hope is the direction of To'Rahn.

I glance up and see Tysian watching us over the quartz edge.

"We're alive," I say. Honestly, there was a point when I wasn't expecting that.

Imwraeth sits very still on a bench, Lylahn beside him. Kaera has collapsed in the bottom of the boat, shaking with fear. Imwraeth stares straight ahead, eyes glazed over. He puts one hand in a bag of sand and Extracts. He looks at the sand with cold loathing, and then he sinks down, putting his head in his hands.

Lylahn looks unsure for a moment, but then she puts her hand on his back.

"I follow you, Favored One," Riah says beside me, arms working to speed us away. We're both breathing hard. "Tysian is wrong."

"We've got to get to To'Rahn," I say. "Fast. We can't let Norah be killed."

"Our warriors are attacking tonight," Riah says.

The sun is setting. Atoille will rise on the eastern horizon in a few hours.

Riah meets my eyes.

Together, we push.

36

———

NORAH

I've reached the edge of To'Rahn.

The plateau's sheer drop is mere inches from my feet. I look down over the precipice at the ocean of sand churning below me. The waves are already bigger, the sand particles at my feet beginning to hover. Atoille will return tonight, along with that extra tug from her gravity. The sky is purple and orange, the sunset glorious over the expanse of the ocean of sand.

Memories of Zadock and me sparring, talking, and looking at the stars punch me in the gut. I am hollow. I am empty. Nothing matters without him.

Soon I'll join him and Potah. I'll feel what they felt when they died, sucked away by the sands into oblivion.

I tell myself that I'm brave, strong. But that is a lie. I'm terrified. I'm shaking with it. I don't want to die. I don't want to know what it's like to be pulled under by thousands of pounds of crushing pressure, smothered and breathing in sand instead of air.

Zadock felt it. Potah felt it. I hope it's over quick.

My fists grip the handle of my practice spear. I grabbed it before I left. The spear that I worked so hard to learn how to use, that, in the end, did me no good. But it reminds me of my best friend, and I want to be holding it when I die.

He's gone because Motah sent us on a fool's errand.

He's gone because I was powerless to save him.

I clench my hands into fists and inch closer to the edge. I stand there for a long time, just looking down. The ocean of sand has given me so many moments of beauty and grace. It's been an escape from my troubles, a friend and a refuge.

It's also taken the two people who mattered most to me in the world. And now it will take me. I've leaped from the edge so many times, craving that feeling of flying, of being free. Zadock was always, *always* there to catch me.

Without him, I thought this jump would be easy. But it's harder than I thought.

The night darkens to black, and pinpricks of stars sparkle overhead. Atoille peeks over the eastern horizon.

There she is, the moon in all her brilliance. Even this tiny sliver showing on the rim of the desert is enormous, takes up half of the skyline. The skin on my arms rises in goosebumps as I look out over the gray wilderness.

It's beautiful. Beautiful and bleak.

The sand waves rise higher with Atoille in the sky. They crash and fall against the plateau, shooting up sprays of sand. Sand particles float and twirl around my heels.

If I have to die, I think this is the way to do it. Falling, flying free at last.

I close my eyes and think of Shrey. I wish I could explain this to her. She won't understand. She'll be heartbroken.

But she'll be alive.

I think of Zadock. I'll be with him soon.

I think of Potah. I hope he's watching. I hope he's proud of me.

I think of Motah. Anger grates in my heart. She lied to me, she beat me with her words, she manipulated me. I wish that I could part with her in a better way, but there's no way to fix this. It is what it is. And she will live.

To'Rahn will flourish. The To'Morat will see that things are better, and they'll call off the attack. Everyone will be ok.

I just have to step off.

"Ahhh, you're here, I see."

I jump at the voice and whip around.

Faharic Penvaren. His emerald sand cloak whips in the wind. He's looking sharp and neat and clean as always, with a smug smile on his face. My fingers grip the spear handle. "Traitor!"

He smiles. "I am not the traitor, Norah. I am trying to save To'Rahn."

"At the cost of your son?" I can't help it. I spit the words out. Fury boils up within me.

"Sometimes sacrifices have to be made for the good of all. You understand that, right?"

I blink so he doesn't see the tears. "Yes." The wind wails in my ears, and I don't know if he hears me.

Faharic nods. "So you know what you have to do. For the good of all."

I want to turn around, to leap from the edge on my own, but I am afraid to turn my back on this monster. "Yes," I say, louder. "I understand. I want to—to be alone."

Faharic takes another step toward me. "Of course you—" Sand snakes around his ankles and up his legs, holding him in place.

"DON'T TOUCH HER!"

What?

I freeze. That was... It couldn't be...

Zadock strides out of the darkness, trailed by the Favored One, Riah, another girl my age, and a little girl. Zadock looks exhausted, covered in grit and sweat.

But it's him! He's here!

"You're alive?" I breathe. Tears pour down my cheeks. I drop the spear and run to him. I throw my arms around him and sob into his neck. He smells so good, feels so warm. He puts his arms around me and holds me tight, and I wish this moment could never end.

Everything just got so much harder.

I back away. "You're alive."

Zadock takes one thumb across my cheek, wiping away the tears. "How?"

I see Faharic out of the corner of my eye, expression darkening in anger, his feet held in place by sand.

Zadock grins. "Well, I was almost smothered by an ocean of sand, battled, you know, a giant deathstalker scorpion, got captured by the To'Morat, and then came all the way back across the desert chasing after you." He presses his forehead against mine. "Wild girl."

"Zadock," Faharic shouts, "you will stop this at once. This—this is inappropriate. What of your Anointed partner?" Faharic takes a steadying breath. "Zadock, release me. And step away from Norah. She has something she must do for the good of all."

Zadock does step away from me, but he doesn't release his potah. The Favored One has dirt smudged on his face and dark circles under his eyes. Riah glances between Zadock and her leader.

"What is he doing here?" I jerk my head to Imwraeth Jeriyah. The last time I saw him, he was ordering me to my death.

Zadock squeezes my arm. "He's with us. He freed me to find you."

I catch motion out of the corner of my eye, and I glance to my left, over the edge of the plateau. I gasp, and everyone turns to look.

"The To'Morat," Zadock whispers.

They're here. Hundreds of ships descend upon To'Rahn, spraying waves in their wake. They rise from the sand and converge on the plateau. Guards from high up on the quartz wall give the warning cry.

The wall is still unfinished. I don't know how long it will last or how much good it will do.

A commotion erupts in the village not far away, lanterns lighting and soldiers crying out. We're not ready for this. Despite everything, we're not ready.

The Favored One raises his head. "I must go and try to stop this."

"I'll go with you." The girl squeezes his arm a little tighter. Riah nods.

"Wait!" Zadock fumbles with something in his pocket. "Lylahn, I need you to do something." He hands her a shining red gem.

I gasp. "That looks just like—"

Zadock grins. "I also picked up a little souvenir from the ocean of water." He turns back to the girl. "I think that, somehow, this is important. Take it, and, if you get a chance, put it into the statue of Atoille at To'Rahn's sparring arena."

Lylahn takes the gem. "I will." Lylahn nods to the Favored One, and she, Imwraeth, the little girl, and Riah turn and run.

Zadock turns back to Faharic. "Potah, listen—"

"Son, you will release me now. And then you will push Norah off the plateau."

Zadock takes a step back. "What?"

"Or you will allow me to do it." Faharic moves his arms, trying to Shake control of the sand at his feet away from Zadock. "Of course she's not going to do it herself. Why would anyone be that selfless?"

"I'm going to jump, Zadock."

He meets my eyes. "No. No. There's got to be another way. You can't. You can't."

I blink back tears again. This is so. Much. Harder.

I reach out and take his hand. "Goodbye."

Zadock shakes his head. "Norah, no—"

I take one hand and place it on his cheek. "Thank you," I say. "Thank you for being my—" I choke on the words. "My friend."

Zadock's control over the sand falters, and Faharic leaps free, sand swirling around him. Instead of trying to recapture his potah, Zadock wraps sand around my ankles and legs.

I gasp. "Zadock—you—you have to let me go. I have to do this."

In the distance, the sounds of battle rise on the wind, spears clashing and people screaming. A glance to my left shows me that the To'Morat are swarming the plateau. Their ships are suspended next to the edge, To'Morat soldiers streaming from gangways onto the dusty space of land before the village. Their Forgers are already disintegrating the wall, putting their hands on it and crumbling it to sand. Our Forgers are fighting back to keep the wall up, but the To'Morat are so strong. Their Shakers are using the sand to pull our people from the walls and fling them to the ocean of sand.

"Our people are dying, Zadock!" I cry in desperation. "You have to let me go. I'm the only one who can stop this!"

Faharic raises his hands, and the sand strains against me as he tries to take control, but even with everything Zadock must be feeling, his potah is still no match.

"Son, listen to me. Listen to your potah. Norah is right. She can save everyone."

Zadock holds his grip strong. He doesn't look at his potah.

"You are my son. You will do as I say. Just think, Zadock. A home. A family. All you've ever wanted. All yours." His eyes darken and narrow. "But only if you push. Norah. Off."

In that moment, I look at Faharic with so much hate that my heart twists and my stomach turns. How can he say that? How can he treat his son this way?

Out of the corner of my eye, I see a brown cactus plant shrivel and die. What?

Zadock takes another step backward, hurt filling his eyes. "Potah, I..." He squeezes his eyes closed. "I've always wanted to do as you say. I always wanted to be exactly who you wanted me to be."

When Zadock opens his eyes, there's determination there, and strength. "Whatever you do to me, whatever you say, it will be worth it if I can save Norah."

Tears spill onto my cheeks. He would sacrifice everything he's ever wanted for me. Zadock, my dearest friend, looks at me, a gentle smile on his face.

I know what he's feeling for me because the sand holding me falls apart.

I'm free. I turn and run, run with the wind in my ears and Zadock's cries begging me to stop. I leap over tendrils of sand that try to grab at my legs.

And then I jump.

The ocean of sand appears before my feet, ready to swallow me whole. Atoille is in the sky. We are at the turning point from the blackest night, the moment where a sliver of light begins to show. A sliver of hope.

I'm flying.

37

IMWRAETH

I dash through the streets of To'Rahn. Well, dash is a relative term. I walk as quickly as I can, Lylahn and Riah pacing themselves at my side. We hid Kaera in an empty home on the edge of To'Rahn, hopefully far away from where the battle will be. I put my hand in my bag of sand, Extracting energy and willing myself to go faster.

People are dying. People are dying, and this time I will stop it.

Fire rips apart the night sky. Screams tear through my ears. It's already beginning, the early ranks of warriors starting fires to add chaos to the battle. We don't even have to worry as much about burning resources as we did before. For one thing, there aren't many to burn. For another, Tysian knows that as soon as he kills Norah, none of it will matter.

Dust from the Shakers flies in my eyes, and already the heat of the fires warms my front, a sharp contrast to the icy chill at my back.

Faster, faster.

We turn a corner, and it's chaos, people screaming and running in all directions. Some race away from the fighting, carrying children and supplies. Many, some hefting spears and some cruising on sand, rush forward toward the battle.

What am I going to do? *How can I stop this?*

Someone bumps into me and hurries on. Lylahn reaches out a hand to make sure I'm steady, and my heart warms. I take a deep breath, full of smoke and ash. Courage.

We pass through an empty market plaza and go down another street, following the sound of the screams. We're nearing the eastern edge of To'Rahn, and the sounds of battle grow louder. We turn another corner, and the heat of the flames hits us in full force. Lylahn puts a hand up to shield her face. Fire eats at the cactus fiber homes, leaving charred quartz framework behind. More torches, guided by sand, fly over the low parts of the wall.

The quartz wall is crumbling in sections, and To'Rahn soldiers bunch up around the gaps, trying to keep my people from coming through. Shakers attempt to smother the fire with sand. The retahn shriek, and my warriors slash with spears and lash out with sand through holes in the wall. Forgers work, hands to the wall, on both sides, to bring it down or shore it up.

Shakers atop the wall hurl knives of sand, but the wall is disintegrating, and as many as stay atop the wall to fight are rushing down quartz steps, slipping and falling over each other in an effort to get down.

These people are not ready for war. They don't crave it. Not like mine do.

The fires spark and crackle. Battle cries roar. I'm frozen, watching. I'm on the To'Rahn side. How can I reach my people? How can I stop this? What am I supposed to do?

"I have to get over the wall!" I cry to Riah before I can think too much about it. She hesitates only a moment before swirling her hands to form a platform of sand and lifting me above the battle. I wobble but then find my balance and sail over the cluster of warriors hedging up the weaknesses. The To'Rahn glance upward, confused, but they let me pass over them.

It's my people I have to worry about.

The sand platform stops at a section of wall that is still intact, suspending me above my warriors. From here, I can see the battle more clearly. The To'Rahn are clustered in streets, trying to defend their homes. On the To'Morat side, lines of warriors stretch all the way back to the edge of the plateau. Many ride atop retahn, but most stand and wait for their turn to fight. The edges of the front lines push through sections of unfinished wall, cruising past areas where To'Rahn is weak and getting deeper into the village with torches and spears and waves of sand.

Atoille have mercy.

To'Morat warriors notice me and raise their hands, preparing sand to attack, but then recognition hits their features. I signal to Riah, and she lowers me about halfway down the other side of the wall to get closer to my people. I'm exposed, and I feel it, nerves churning in my stomach.

I take a deep breath. "My people—my warriors—please..."

Tysian lifts himself to meet me. His smile is bold and bright, a grin of triumph. I falter.

"You must—you must stop! I am calling off this attack!" I try to put power in my voice, try to muster every ounce of strength within me. "I'm the Favored One, Atoille chose me, and you must—"

Tysian flicks his wrist and wrenches the sand from under me, and I'm flying backward toward the wall. I brace for impact, but I pass through dust, and through sheer panic, I notice that To'Rahn's wall has fallen. It's only sand now. A hill of sand separates the horde of the To'Morat from a burning village.

"IMWRAETH!" I hear a cry, and I think it's Lylahn.

Sand begins to form beneath me, but then it's pulled away again. A war of sand rages between Riah and Tysian, but I know how this will end.

Strangely, the panic recedes. I did my best. I tried. I just watch the sand and sea of faces get closer and closer.

Tysian soars away across the village. Toward Norah.

Riah screams. A storm of sand all around me. And then I hit.

The pain collides with my body.

I blink, feeling groggy and numb. Smoke wafts across the night sky, and the clatter of battle rings in my ears. The pain is gone.

"You're lucky, Favored One. Very lucky," Riah says. Her arms are crossed, and she has a spear in hand, looking out over the battle that goes on in the streets on either side of us.

I turn my head and see Lylahn, and she gasps with relief. "We didn't know if we got to you in time. The To'Rahn helped me pull you to safety."

"You saved me," I whisper. I'm so relieved to be alive, so full of light and love that if I needed to Extract right now, I would probably be in trouble. I have never felt this.

I reach out and cup one hand around her face, stroke her cheek with one thumb. "Thank you, Lylahn."

She closes her eyes, and, slowly, puts her hand over mine. "When you fell..." She swallows and opens her eyes again. "Imwraeth, I want you to know that I—" Lylahn takes a deep breath. "I forgive you."

My heart swells with joy, joy like I have never felt. I thread my fingers through the hair at the base of her neck and pull her forehead down to meet mine.

Tears fill her eyes. "It still hurts. It was still wrong. But I choose to let it go."

"Thank you," I whisper. "Thank you, Lylahn."

"Favored One," Riah says. "You can't go back up there. Tysian is too strong. He will kill you this time."

I sit up and take in the raging battle around me. To'Rahn is being overrun. The meager force they have is being pushed back. "It appears that Tysian has left."

Riah frowns. "Then someone else might. The warriors are on a rampage now. I don't think anyone can stop them."

Lylahn looks at me with large eyes. *No more killing.*

"It doesn't matter, Riah." I stand on shaking legs. "I have to try."

38

ZADOCK

S he plummets off the plateau.

"NORAH!" I scream.

My potah gives a small, satisfied nod. No, no, no.

I race to the edge, and I can see her, falling, falling. Her arms are outstretched like she's a desert bird, plunging feet-first into the sands. She's holding her practice spear in one hand. I Shake, reaching out to grab her, but Potah rushes forward and shoves my sand away.

"No!" I scream. She's about to hit.

Rage lights a fire within me, and in a burst of strength, I shoot a barrel of sand into my potah with one hand and use the other to wrap a rope around Norah and hold fast. She jerks to a stop, waves of sand brushing her feet. I exhale a sigh of relief.

Potah shrieks a hideous sound of pure fury. I glance back in time to see him fly backward and land on the ground with a crack. He lies still. In spite of everything, I hope he's all right.

I bring Norah up. *Atoille, let her be ok.*

I lift her over the lip of the plateau, setting her on her feet next to me. She glares at me, her arms crossed.

"You're ok." I breathe in and out. I cannot feel love for her. I cannot.

"Zadock, you have to let me do this."

"No."

"Our people are dying. And I finally, finally have the power to protect everyone I love. Please." Tears spill down her cheeks. "Please, let me go."

I close my eyes. *No.* "I can't." The sand is already loosening from around her waist. Control is slipping away. "I can't lose you."

The sand holding Norah is dissipating, particles streaming off her. Norah brushes away what remains, and I can't stop it. With all my strength, I Shake, but I can't stop it. She turns to run.

"Norah!"

She freezes.

"Please," I whisper. "I...I love you."

Norah turns around. Tears shine in her eyes. She raises one hand and places it against my cheek, and then she slowly lifts her face to mine.

Our lips meet in a soft, perfect kiss. Then I'm wrapping my arms around her like I'll never let go and kissing her harder, faster. This is all I need. If this moment lasted forever, I would be the happiest man in the world.

My hand goes under her shirt to the soft skin of her back, and she lets out a little moan and grips me tighter. My other hand entwines through her hair, pressing her mouth deeper into mine.

"Well." A cruel, smooth voice breaks our eternity. "This is touching."

I part from Norah but keep one arm around her waist, holding her close.

Tysian smiles.

Dismay overwhelms me. No... Not him. Not now. Out of the corner of my eye, I see green, and I glance down at our feet. My mouth drops open in shock. Green, fresh plants have sprung up all around us, young and vibrant. *What?* Norah stares at the plants, her eyes huge.

Tysian shakes his head. "So touching. And yet, so weak."

My heart sinks because he's right. I love her.

I love her.

I raise my arm, but I can do nothing when Tysian pummels us with a storm of sand.

39

IMWRAETH

The To'Rahn are being slaughtered.

My warriors have driven them back, deeper into the city, and the fires are spreading. This is what the To'Morat do best. This is why we are known for our brutality.

The battle rages in the streets behind us. Riah holds her spear in one hand and readies sand in another, defending our position between two homes.

I've recovered somewhat, and I get to my feet. "Lylahn. You have to go do what Zadock said. Put the gem in the statue."

Lylahn hesitates. "I don't want to leave you."

Unsure if it's the right thing to do, I take her hand and meet her eyes. "To'Rahn is counting on you." I give her hand a squeeze, afraid to let go. "Be safe, Lylahn."

She gives me a determined nod and puts one hand in her pocket before rushing down a side street away from the battle. *Atoille, please keep her safe.*

"Riah, lift me up again."

"Are you sure, Favored One?" She raises her arms.

"Yes."

A platform of sand forms beneath me, and I rise, balancing as best I can. Again, Riah carries me over the To'Rahn and toward the fighting To'Morat. I'm not as high this time without a wall to scale. A few warriors glance up at me, but most have their attention on the fighting, the spears that are jabbing toward them and the sand flying around them.

The voices in my head are screaming.

You're weak.

Unfit to rule.

I open my mouth. "I—I—" I swallow. "Listen to me, warriors!" I try to shout. A few of the lines of warriors who aren't fighting look up. Some roll their eyes and look away, but many have startled, humbled expressions on their faces. I might be able to win them back.

Lie.

"My warriors! I, your Favored One, order you to stop this—"

I cut off, my mouth dangling open, as the crowd parts and a familiar stride walks toward me.

"Hello, Imwraeth." Lienos smiles.

40

NORAH

Zadock is losing.

Tysian has so much raw power that even if Zadock was at his strongest, he could not overcome this man.

My heart sinks as I watch them trade blows of sand, Zadock struggling to Shake but getting stronger. I grip my spear, wishing I could do something, anything. I look behind me at the plateau's edge. So close. Should I jump?

My eyes dart back to the battle. Zadock is fighting for his life. He throws up a wall of sand just in time to block dozens of sand knives. I can't leave like this. I can't leave him.

Faharic stirs off to my right, and I pray to Atoille to keep him unconscious for just a moment longer.

Zadock flings hardened balls of sand toward Tysian, so fast I can barely see them. Tysian moves his arms and raises himself on a platform, dodging easily. Zadock grits his teeth and sends up a cloud of dust to blind his opponent, but Tysian waves his hands, and it dissipates on the wind.

Tysian shakes his head, clicks his tongue. "Everything you do only delays the inevitable." Tysian glances toward me and with a flick of his wrist, sand wraps around my ankles and drags me backward toward the cliff.

I scream, scraping my hands against rock and sand, trying to grab hold.

Zadock cries out, lurching, one hand reaching out with sand to steady me and the other throwing up a wall of sand to block an attack from Tysian.

I stop sliding and scramble to my feet. I run, feet pounding across the desert, trying to get as far away from the edge of the plateau as I can. I am a liability there, but I will not leave Zadock. Not while he's in danger.

Because even if I jumped, I don't think Tysian would stop.

Tysian waves his hands, swirling them over and over until two identical whirlwinds of sand burst into being. One engulfs me, and I'm up, up in the air, spinning and flying, sand biting into my skin. I scream, and my mouth fills with sand.

Then the swirling stops, and I fall, the horizon bucking around me as I tumble through the air. A tendril of sand wraps around my ankle and I stop, hanging upside down. I think I'm going to be sick. I see the edge of the plateau. I'm hanging over the ocean of sand, the waves reaching up to greet me.

Zadock brings me up and back over the edge. I land on my feet, stumbling, clutching my stomach and my spear. I've got to get out of here. I've got to get help. I've got to—

Tysian raises his arms, and a thousand needles of sand lift into the air.

Atoille's ashes.

Frantically, Zadock reaches out for sand. A barrier forms around us, but then Zadock looks at me. The wall of sand isn't big enough, not enough—

The needles hurl forward.

"Zadock, no!" I cry.

His arms shove forward a wall of sand.

I cry out and beat against the sand, and a second later, it falls away.

Zadock is lying on the ground, his body torn to shreds.

"NOOOOO!" I scream and run to his side. His arms and face are marred by a hundred pinpricks drilled into his skin. Blood drips from his nose, his cheeks, his forehead, his beautiful messy hair. Red blossoms on his shirt in a hundred places.

"No. No. No. NO." I try to cover the bleeding, but there's so much.

Zadock opens his eyes. Smiles at me. Blood drips from his mouth. "Norah."

My eyes fill with tears, and a sob escapes my lips. "I love you." Not now. I can't lose him now. I will get Shrey. She will heal him. "Hold on."

Out of the corner of my eye, I see Tysian, his arms working, sand swirling around his body as he lifts himself up. "Your turn, Sustainer." He sneers.

I have to save Zadock. But I have to do something about Tysian first.

What can I do? I have a sand gift that I don't know how to use. I have a spear. I have my love for Zadock. Is it enough?

"Will you catch me?" I whisper.

Zadock frowns in confusion but nods.

I stand. I meet Tysian's eyes. I hold the spear at my side, and I shift into a fighting stance. It's just a practice spear. It can't do any damage. But Zadock's fingers swirl sand onto the tip, and it hardens into a deadly edge.

Tysian throws back his head and laughs. "You want to play that game, little girl? Fine. I'm not in any hurry." He steps off his platform and reaches out one hand to his side. A spear of sand forms in his grip.

I scream and charge forward. He cries out and rushes to meet me. Our spears clash in a flurry of blows, neither finding an opening. I strike for Tysian's side, but his spear blocks mine and dissipates. I'm surprised, and my momentum carries me forward, stumbling. Tysian reforms his spear and swings, trying to get a blow across my back, but I turn my fall into a roll and hurry back to my feet.

Tysian whistles. "Not bad, not bad."

I don't have time for this. But I can't leave Tysian alive with Zadock. Tysian jabs at my arm, but I block. The sand spear feels just as stable and hard as a real spear. For a moment, Tysian has the upper hand, and it's all I can do to parry his attacks. He's shockingly good for someone who has sand for a weapon.

He jabs through my defenses and nicks my left thigh. I cry out in pain, but the cut feels superficial. I can still move. Tysian grins.

With a scream, I lunge forward, going for Tysian's side again. He lets the spear dissipate a second time, but I'm ready. My balance is shot, but I let the fall take me, and I keep my spear going. I'm about to stab Tysian in the side—

But he shoots himself upward on a platform of sand. "Enough." Sand grabs me by the ankles and lifts me. I let out a cry, but I manage to keep a strong grip on my spear. And then I'm flung from the plateau.

I'm falling through the air, flying, spinning, clutching the spear to my chest so I don't lose it. Will Zadock catch me? Is he still alive?

I tumble toward the waves, but I feel at peace. My soul feels...whole.

I land on a platform of sand.

"Wait," I whisper. "Wait."

Zadock holds me there. He knows what I'm thinking. He always has.

Tysian looks over the edge to confirm that I'm gone.

I hurtle toward the sky, faster than Atoille's light, and I ram the spear into Tysian's gut.

His eyes bulge, and his mouth gapes. Tysian staggers forward, clutching the spear handle. Then he falls.

Down. Down. Down toward the waves of sand.

His body is sucked away in an instant.

I jump to the plateau and hurry to kneel beside Zadock. He coughs. He's lying in a pool of blood.

He smiles weakly. "Not bad, speck."

"You're going to be ok," I say. "I'll be right back, I'm going to—"

"No." Zadock grabs my hand. His face has turned deathly white. "Don't—don't leave. Not enough time. Please." He coughs again, choking on his own blood. "Stay."

I sob and lay my head on his chest. *No...*

Zadock is dying. And I'm powerless to stop it.

He closes his eyes.

41

IMWRAETH

Lienos. Lienos is here.

The words that were about to spew out of me sputter and die. The platform of sand that I'm on lowers to the ground in a pocket of calm behind To'Morat lines, and I'm not sure if it was Riah or Lienos who brought me down.

The sounds of battle rage in my ears. People screaming, dying. Warriors' cries as they slash and burn. The air smells like smoke and iron. Spears of sand and quartz fly from both sides, and trails of sand get in my hair and eyes. The To'Rahn defense is failing. To'Morat warriors who have held back push forward and join the fight.

A few warriors look my way but then glance away. Most are so engaged by the frenzy of battle they don't even bother. Retahn stamp and whinny, eager to rush forward into battle. The To'Rahn front lines are all that's protecting their children, hiding in homes deeper in the village. I have to do something. I have to stop this before more lives are lost.

"Stop—" I cry, but it comes out strangled. "Stop."

Lienos nods his head to me. "Favored One. Things are going excellently, as you can see."

Truth.

He gives me a wicked smile and crosses his arms as he surveys the battle's progress. "Well done."

Lie.

"I wish to—" I say. "I wish to address my people."

Lienos clicks his tongue and shakes his head. "No need for that, Favored One. I'll take it from here." Lienos turns and spreads his hands wide, his voice commanding and strong. "BURN, warriors of To'Morat! Push onward and let it burn!"

There's a great cry, and the warriors surge forward.

4 2

———

NORAH

"NO!" I sob. He's still. I've lost him. I throw back my head and scream to the wind. "NOOOOOO!"

Gently, I press my lips to his. "I love you." I lay my forehead on his bleeding chest. The blood has soaked into the ground and into the knees of my pants. And into the plants around me.

Plants.

Life.

Love.

It's love.

"I love you," I say, and I feel it. I let myself feel it in its full power. Love bursts in my heart, even though it hurts so, so much. "I love you!"

Plants, green and lush with life, spring up around my feet. I run my fingers through them, laughing, sorrow and joy warring within me. "I love you, Zadock Penvaren!"

His eyelids flicker open. Something is happening!

"Norah?"

My head whips around. Motah.

Just like that, my heart sinks, and anger fills my soul.

"Norah." Motah falls to her knees, and she cries into her hands. "You're here. You're safe."

I grit my teeth and turn away from her. Zadock's face looks pale, and his eyes are closed again.

"I love you," I whisper. A few plants sprout around me, and then nothing. "I LOVE YOU!" I scream. It's not working!

I turn on Motah. "Get out of here! This is your fault, all your fault!" Angry tears make trails in the dust and blood on my face. The heat of the fires is blowing on the wind, sparks and ash in the air.

Motah flinches with each blow. "You're right. I have made so many mistakes. I am truly sorry."

I clench my fists. I want to scream to the wind how much I hate her. What a nightmare from Atoille's Hell she has made my life.

And now, because she's here, my best friend—my love—is dying.

Motah sees the plants. "Norah...did these come from you? Did you do this?"

I nod.

Her eyes alight with realization. "It's love, isn't it? All these years, I was wrong. I was trying so hard to get your sand gift to show, but I was so wrong." A smile lights up her face. "I love you, Norah."

How long. How long I have wanted to hear those words from her lips. There is an ache in my heart, a deep, echoing hurt, that those words cannot begin to ease. It's too late.

"I love you, my daughter," Motah says.

I squeeze my eyes shut and turn away from her. No. No.

"How can you say that?" I ask, tears pouring down my cheeks. I turn back toward her, fury and hatred writhing within me. The plants at my feet go limp. "You don't mean it. My entire life, you have put me down, never listened to what I wanted, always tried to make me hate you." I clench my teeth. "You succeeded."

But something squirms within me. Something that wants to believe her.

Out of the corner of my eye, I see the girl—Lylahn?—running on the outskirts of the village, heading for the statue of Atoille. Something red glitters in her hand.

I don't know what will happen when she places the moonstone. Probably nothing.

Motah's face looks stricken. "You're right. You're right. And I am so, so sorry, Norah. I didn't know. I always thought I was doing the right thing." Her voice is barely a breath. "I love you. I have always loved you. Everything I did—it was because of love."

I turn away. I kneel beside Zadock's ashen body. "I don't believe you."

4 3

IMWRAETH

Lienos continues his cries, urging the warriors forward. My warriors ride or run, lifting spears or sand, pushing forward. There are still some To'Rahn warriors fighting, and their cries fill the air. Everyone seems to be ignoring me now.

My heart pounds as if it will burst. I reach my hand into my bag of sand and Extract.

"Ok." Deep breath. "Ok. You can do this."

Lie.

"They'll listen."

Lie.

"Just try. It will work."

Lie.

I drop to my knees as despair crushes my soul. "Why?" I whisper. "Why did you give me this defect?" Atoille gave me this—this wrongness that has held me back for all my life. Atoille gave me this weakness, and then she made me a leader. Why—

Atoille made me a leader.

Truth.

Atoille has faith and trust in me.

Truth.

Atoille knows that I am the leader my people need.

Truth!

I stand. I clench my fists at my side, and I step forward. I shout at the top of my lungs. "STOP!"

The warriors who can hear me stop running and look back in bewilderment.

"This is wrong!" I scream. "All of this killing, all of this burning, it. Must. STOP!"

Lienos turns toward me and glares. Some of the warriors ignore me and continue running, but some hesitate.

"Warriors." Lienos turns and spreads his hands again. "This is who we are. We will kill the To'Rahn, we will find the girl, we will bring salvation to our people!"

Riah crashes through the line of warriors and hurries to stand beside me. "I'm here, Favored One."

I nod to her, and she raises one arm to lift me up on a platform of sand.

"This fighting," I cry, "this killing. It has to stop." Many of my warriors listen, though there are too great a number running, creating chaos in the streets. It has to start with these, these ones that are willing to hear me.

"The To'Rahn, they are not our enemy. It is starvation. It is the curse upon these lands." I take a deep breath and yell. "We can continue to kill and take what is not ours, and then what? When the supplies run out, when there is no one left, will we turn on each other? Will we become beasts, tearing each other to pieces?"

"SILENCE!" Lienos screams. His face is red, shining in the firelight. "Imwraeth! You will stop this!"

"NO!" I cry and raise my fist. "I will NOT. BE. SILENT!"

The people below me cheer.

My heart lifts. "We will end this! We will work together to meet the challenges that face us. We will live together!"

The warriors who can hear me look at each other and nod.

"He is our Favored One!" Riah shouts.

The cry is taken up by my warriors. "He is our Favored One!"

"My people, my beloved warriors, help put out the flames. Show the To'Rahn that we want peace!"

To my utter shock, the people turn and listen.

44

NORAH

Motah kneels beside me, and I have this urge to shove her away. I want to be with Zadock, only Zadock.

Motah places two fingers on his neck. "He's alive, but barely."

He lives.

"I love you." I press my forehead into his. "I love you. Come back to me. I love you." Tears slip down my nose to land on his face.

I blink my eyes and notice that a few of the plants around Zadock look greener and larger, but he doesn't look any different.

"Can I save him?" I look frantically at Motah. "Do I have the power to save him?"

Her eyes are wide. "I'm not sure."

I let out a frustrated howl. "It's love, I know it is, so why isn't it working?" I grab at the sand, willing it into my body, trying to make it glow. "Why isn't it working? I love him!" I scream at the sky. "Why isn't that enough?"

A ruby-red light flashes from the direction of the sparring arena and the Atoille statue. Lylahn did it. She placed the moonstone.

I look at Zadock, expecting something, anything, but nothing happens.

No... All that. For nothing.

Motah lifts one hand, hesitates, then wraps her arm around my shoulders. I stiffen, but then I deflate, and I sob into her shoulder while she strokes my hair.

"I did this." Motah's voice quavers.

Something softens within me. I'm surprised when I find myself whispering back, "No."

"If I hadn't sent you—"

I sit up and look into her eyes. They are soft, so unlike the gaze I often held, pleading as a child. "No. Zadock made a choice. He—" My voice cracks. "He died to protect me." I run my fingers along the back of his hand. "He loves me."

Motah shakes her head. "It's love. I didn't know. This entire time. I didn't know."

I look at her again. Meet her eyes. I find that a part of me understands now. How a person would do anything they thought was right to save those they love.

Motah reaches into a pocket of her dress and pulls out my old doll. "I found this in Shrey's things. You probably don't remember this. How we used to play together?"

I stare from the doll to her and back again.

She fiddles with the hair. "Those memories are so precious to me, Norah. I thought for so long that I was doing the right thing, trying to get your sand gift to show." Motah meets my eyes. "I was wrong. I want you to know that I love you. I always loved you."

I am frozen, one hand still on Zadock's chest, feeling the rise and fall slowing.

Motah smiles through her tears. "Those were some of the happiest times of my life."

She remembers.

"Motah, I..." My voice comes out as a breath. "I forgive you."

The tears spill from her eyes. "Norah." She falls forward, and we embrace.

The world begins to glow.

45

IMWRAETH

My warriors rush forward, Shaking the sand to put out the flames, others shouting for their comrades to stop. It's taking time, for the battle has spread across many streets, but my people are listening. Hope glistens in my heart, a dewy, newborn feeling. Warriors from To'Rahn realize what's happening and stop attacking, turn their attention to the flames, and the effect spirals outward. Riah lowers me to the ground and gives me a huge smile.

A stunning white light fills the sky.

I close my eyes, and my vision goes red. What is happening? I can't open my eyes; the brightness is so white and blinding.

The light fades.

When I blink my eyes open, I see my comrades, my people, standing around me. The light of the sun shimmers over the desert, and the waves of sand go calm. Atoille is a sliver on the eastern horizon. I hope that Norah Saranyi is all right.

Lienos glares at me, his face a sandstorm of anger. He opens his mouth to speak.

I smile.

Daylight hits us in full, and now I see clearly. Plants. Fully grown plants cover the ground that used to be bare. Bristlebrushes full of ripe red fruit, squat trees with fat bushels of plantains, cacti with plump skin. There's almost no room to walk because there's so much life.

Lienos' jaw drops. "What?"

People around us point and whisper. The sounds of fighting cease. And then the shouts of joy begin.

"Norah," I whisper. My eyes fill with tears. "Go!" I call to my warriors. "Tell our brothers, the fighting is done!"

The people cheer and run, passing along the message, aiding the To'Rahn in putting out the last of the flames.

I reach out and touch one of the leaves, smooth and soft. I inhale, breathing in the fresh, clean scent of new growth.

She did it.

46

NORAH

Zadock opens his eyes.

I cry out in joy. The brilliant white light is fading now. The glow is being sucked into him. I will Zadock to take it, to breathe.

I grab his hands in my own, still covered in blood. "You're alive! You're alive." I sob, smiling. Relief, like a wave from the ocean of water, washes over me. I lay my forehead on his chest and laugh and cry. I didn't lose him. He's here. My love.

Motah places one hand on my shoulder. "Norah, you did it. You Sustained. You fixed everything."

The glow fades, and I sit up, taking in the light of the dawn. Plant life grows all around us, full green bushes bursting with berries. Tears fill my eyes, and I bring one hand to my mouth. *I did it.*

The white glow vanishes. Zadock pushes himself up onto his elbows, bleary-eyed.

"How do you feel?" I ask.

"Tired." He smiles. "But alive. There was a moment there when...I wasn't here."

I swallow, my throat dry. I take his hand and squeeze. "I'm glad you chose to stay with me."

Zadock envelops my hands in his. "It wasn't me, Nors. It was you. I don't know how you did it, but you brought me back. You saved me."

I smile. "Always." Zadock is alive. He's here. With me.

And I love him.

"Motah," I say. "This changes everything."

She nods. "Something will have to be done."

Zadock swirls the sand, spinning particles through the leaves of green plants. "Shaking feels different, too. Have you noticed, Katiyah Saiyu?"

Motah Shakes, lifting sand to swirl around her head, and she laughs. "You're right." She leaps onto a platform of sand, flying about our heads with a grin.

I laugh. I haven't seen this side of Motah in a long, long time.

"I love you, Norah!" And she flies, her Shaking as strong as ever. It's truly a miracle.

Zadock watches Motah. "Lylahn must've placed the moonstone. It changed something."

I nod. "It *fixed* something." I reach out and touch one of the plants nearby. I pick a purple berry and pop it into my mouth, feel it burst with sweetness. Then I put one into Zadock's. When his lips brush my fingertips, I feel a rush of pleasure. "We were meant to feel love. I know it."

Zadock's gaze locks with mine. "Norah." He takes one hand and cups it around my cheek. I close my eyes and just feel him. "I love you. I need you in my life."

My heart fills with joy at the same time it also echoes with loss. He's not mine. We healed the world together, and he's still not mine.

Motah lands her sand platform and kneels next to us, grinning. "The council is going to have to revise how we think about the Anointing."

NORAH

I sleep for an eternity.

Or at least it feels like it. My body is worn to the core. I've run myself to exhaustion.

It's so good to be back in my own sleeping pallet next to Shrey. I open my eyes, and there she is, her face inches from mine.

I smile. "Shrey."

She leaps on top of me and gives me an enormous hug. "You did it! You did it!"

I hold her close. I didn't think I was ever going to see her again. I breathe in her scent, cactus and earth, and a little something that is just her.

Shrey steps back, and I sit up, refreshed and rejuvenated, ready to take on the day.

"How long did I sleep?" I notice a quartz glass of water next to my bed and gulp it down.

Shrey shrugs. "Oh, just a day and a night."

Motah made me go to bed soon after the dawn when everything changed.

I Sustained. I fixed something that was broken. And the

moonstone is where it is meant to be. I want to go see it sometime today.

When I make my way to the kitchen, I see that the dining room table is piled high with fruits and vegetables. I gasp. "You picked all this?"

Shrey grins. "Motah and I thought you would be hungry."

We eat breakfast together, as much food as we want. It's delicious.

"Where's Motah?" I ask, shoving another fried plantain into my mouth. Is it possible that Sustained food tastes better?

Shrey picks up a berry. "She's talking with the council."

I wonder what they're discussing. I hope it's what I think it is.

After breakfast, I step outside, and my mood is dampened somewhat. The smell of smoke still clings to the air, and, though our home was unaffected, many close by were caught in the fires. Down the street our neighbors are already working to rebuild charred homes. It's strange to see so much plant life taking over among buildings that have burned.

Many bodies will be ceremoniously thrown to the sands.

Heaviness stills the joy in my heart. We won. We fixed things. But the price was steep.

I want to try Sustaining again. There's this fear inside me that it only worked once, that it won't work if I try it again.

To the right of our home, I notice a bushel of plantains. It looks like it's been mostly picked clean, and I think I have this plant to thank for my breakfast.

I kneel next to it. Pick up a handful of sand.

"Norah."

I jump and drop the sand, hurrying to my feet.

It's Saeri.

She stands in the street with her arms crossed, wearing a deep blue sand cloak. Her black hair curls about her shoulders, and her eyes glint like they're on fire.

I swallow my guilt.

Saeri steps forward, and then she rushes into my arms and embraces me. "You did it!"

I hug her back, shocked.

Saeri pushes back to look into my eyes. "I was worried about you."

I smile. "I was worried about *you*. Is your family ok?"

"Yes, we're all ok." Saeri pauses. "You disappeared. Nobody knew where you were. I hope you'll tell me everything."

"Of course."

Saeri bites her lip. "And Zadock...Zadock went with you."

I nod slowly.

"It took a few days here for people to notice that both of you were gone. Zadock's potah was pretty upset. He came around here several times, asking your motah where you'd both gone, but she wouldn't tell him."

My heart lifts at that. Motah, always protecting me.

Saeri glances down. "Norah, I—I know you love him. And with the moonstones..." She glances up at me. Swallows. "I want you two to be together."

I put a hand on her shoulder. "Oh, Saeri, I—"

"It's ok." She stops me. "Look, I like him, but it's not like I love him." She rolls her eyes. "For speck's sake, I want to choose. I want my destiny to be my own. If I don't want to be Anointed, I want to be able to have that choice. You know what I'm saying?" Saeri smiles. "I'll find someone who cares for me as much as he cares for you. I know I will."

I nod, grinning. "Thank you." I lean forward and hug her again, holding her tight. Atoille, it feels good. I can embrace my friend, show her how much I care about her, and not worry about the consequences.

Saeri pulls back. "Don't thank me yet. It's not completely up to us. The council could still say that the Anointings need to be honored."

"You're right," I say. "You're right." Still, the hope in my heart flutters. Motah is on the council. She will fight for me.

"I have to go," Saeri says. "My parents want me back to help rebuild To'Rahn. There's a lot of work to do. But I'll see you later, ok? You can tell me everything then."

I wave to her as she turns to leave.

I turn back to the plantain bushel, my love for my friend lifting my heart. And Zadock. Always Zadock.

I kneel next to the plant growing green with new life. I touch a leaf, run my fingers along the ridges. I grab a handful of sand and close my eyes.

Zadock. Motah. Shrey. Saeri. Potah. People I love.

I feel something happening, energy coursing through me, and I open my eyes. The sand in my hand is glowing. The energy buzzes within me, building, begging for a place to go. I direct it into the plant.

The leaves and stalk grow before my eyes. Plantain buds sprout and grow into full fruit in mere moments.

I gasp and laugh, pure joy and the thrill of what just happened coursing through me.

I did it. I used my sand gift.

own man. I will make my own choices." I allow my heart to soften. "But I will always be your son."

Potah smiles, and this time it's real. "Thank you. Son."

49

NORAH

I stop walking when I reach Threh'hai's cell.

He slumps on a hard bed, staring at his withered hands. His knobby cane is propped against the wall. He looks even older and more tired than before.

It's harder than I thought, seeing him. He's someone I have known since I was a little girl as a figure of authority, power, and justice in our community. Now he's locked away in jail.

For plotting with our enemies to kill me.

I'm only here for one reason. After we do this, Zadock's help is needed to continue rebuilding To'Rahn. Most sand-users are adjusting to the changes with their gifts, but Zadock took to it easily and, if it's possible, is even stronger than before.

"Threh'hai Saiyen," I say.

Threh'hai looks up. "Norah." He glances away. Is that shame on his face? "I'm glad that—that everything turned out all right in the end. I'm glad the people are being taken care of."

"As am I." Anger flickers inside me. At this man who so hurt me, who put me through so much. Who would have had me killed and, indirectly, almost had Zadock killed. He was doing what he thought he had to, but it was still wrong.

But then the anger dies. I don't want it.

Threh'hai stands on shaking feet. He grabs his cane and uses it to prop himself up. His eyes flit to mine then away again just as quickly.

"I just wanted you to know—" Deep breaths. "I forgive you."

Threh'hai's eyes widen. "Norah, I—"

"I know why you did what you did," I cut in. "That doesn't make it right. I should have had a choice. I would have chosen to die for this village."

Threh'hai lowers his head. "Yes. I see that now."

"That's all. I just wanted you to know." I turn and walk away, shaking. I am still angry. Still in shock at what happened and at what almost happened. I fell through the air, to the sand, with no one to catch me. I remember that feeling, that horrible panic gripping my throat, knowing that death was coming. I was a breath away.

And Zadock was that breath.

He waits for me outside the cell block, looking tired but happy. I take his hand.

We walk outside the building into the light of the sun. Plants crowd the pathway.

"That was the right thing to do," Zadock says.

"Was it?" I ask. "Neither of them deserved forgiveness."

Zadock turns to me and stops walking. "You don't need to hold on to their mistakes. You deserve to let it go."

I smile and squeeze his hand. A few streets over, I notice the Atoille statue stretching over rooftops. "Let's go see it, please?"

Zadock smiles. "Anything for you."

My heart flutters.

We walk down the sandy street. People I don't even know wave to me and cheer, and I wave back, blushing.

We reach the sparring arena and stand in the dusty circle where I felt so much misery for much of my life. We stop and stare up at the statue of Atoille.

There, in the second eye socket, is the red moonstone. It fits perfectly, like it was made to go there. It catches the light and glitters next to its partner stone. Different, yet similar. Distinct, yet belonging together.

"Want to get a better look?" Zadock asks with a grin.

I nod.

Then I gasp and throw my arms around him as the sand underneath us swirls and forms into a platform. We're lifted into the sky, Zadock and me together, flying on a disc of sand.

"Wow," I gasp, clinging to him. "That was—"

"Easy," Zadock cuts me off, laughing. "Shaking that sand was so easy." His arm around my waist squeezes tighter, pulling me to him, and I relish the feel of his body pressed against mine.

We're level with Atoille's face. I reach out and run my fingers over the smooth, faceted surface of the red stone. "Beautiful." I squeeze my arm around Zadock's side. "You did this. You fought a giant deathstalker—I still need to hear that story, by the way—and brought the moonstone back to its partner. You fixed the sand gifts." I turn to him, beaming, and bury my face in his neck.

Zadock wraps his arms around me. "I love you, Norah," he whispers. "I want you to be mine forever."

I pull back to look into his eyes. "I love you, Zadock Penvaren." I long to kiss him, but I don't. I can wait a little longer.

50

IMWRAETH

I stand near the rim of the To'Rahn plateau, watching my warriors pack our ships with boxes and boxes of supplies. To'Morat walk with To'Rahn, carrying crates and barrels full of fruits, vegetables, herbs, and grains. Newly appointed Blood Rank One Riah oversees the loading.

It's still odd to scan the plateau and see so many plants that there's hardly room to walk. It's breathtaking.

The flames were put out. The rift between our plateaus has begun to heal.

My Forgers and Shakers are working hard to help To'Rahn rebuild their city. It wasn't easy to convince all of my warriors, but in the end, without Tysian to bolster them and with Lienos flabbergasted, my warriors came back around to the traditional way of thinking. They follow their Favored One once more.

It buoys me up and warms my heart. This will bring about a new era, a new age for To'Morat. We will discover culture and beauty, something besides war that we can excel at. And I get to be the one who leads them to it.

It hurts to think of the cost, the lives lost on both sides. It took some debate from the To'Rahn's broken council before they agreed to let us help them rebuild. They didn't trust us, and rightly so. But things will change now.

Shakers helped clear away the dead on both sides, giving them a proper burial via the ocean of sand. The death count was high. Too high. But, with To'Morat and To'Rahn Absorbers working together, many of the fallen injured were saved. If the fighting hadn't stopped when it had, things would've been much, much worse.

And now there will be peace.

I breathe in the fresh, clean, sweet scent of a white flower. We don't have this type of bush on To'Morat. I pop one of the purple berries into my mouth and close my eyes. Sweet and tart. It's the best thing I've ever tasted.

As long as Norah can keep Sustaining, this life will continue to spread. Hopefully it can grow across an ocean of sand.

"Favored One."

I turn and see Councilor Lienos strolling through the brush, hands clasped behind his back, a stern expression on his face. "We must speak of what happened."

It's funny. That expression used to make me shrink and cower. I cock one eyebrow and smile, and it's all I can do not to laugh at his stunned face. "Yes, Councilor Lienos?"

He clears his throat. "Well. Let me be frank. We both know that you are better suited to ruling in image only. What you did was nothing short of disastrous. Yes, it ended well. However, I should have been the one to—"

"Councilor." How good it feels to cut him off. "Thank you for your service. Unfortunately, it will no longer be required."

Lienos' eyes go huge. "B-but I am loyal to you, Favored One. How do you think you are still alive?"

I stop.

"Favored One," Lienos begins, "I knew that there was a plot to kill you. That's why I poisoned your wine at the feast and Shook the pillar down on top of you at the warrior send-off. I was trying to—"

I turn back, mouth gaping in shock. "You? That was you?"

Wow. The first two murder attempts...weren't Therah?

Lienos crosses his arms. "Well. Yes. Since I didn't know for certain who was plotting, I wanted you to be on your guard. If I had told you someone was trying to kill you, would you have trusted me? Or would you have thought that I had some ulterior motive?"

I pause.

"I was trying to keep you alive." He rolls his eyes. "Of course I knew that poison and a fall would not kill an Extractor."

"It was you?" I'm still trying to wrap my brain around this.

"So you see, I am loyal." Lienos spreads his hands wide. "I did not betray you as Therah and Tysian did. I deserve to be at your side."

I turn to a pair of warriors walking back from unloading cargo. "Warriors, take Lienos and lock him in one of the ship's prison cells. He is stripped of his titles and will be tried for insubordination and attempted assassination once we reach To'Morat."

Lienos pales. "What? Favored One, be reasonable. Who will guide you? Who will help you lead To'Morat to greatness?" The two warriors grab him by his arms and drag him away. "You need me, Favored One! You must have a councilor—"

I smile. "I have found a new councilor. She's—"

"Imwraeth!" I hear a call from a familiar voice. The most beautiful voice in the world.

I turn and see Lylahn waving from across the plateau. Kaera stands next to her, giggling with Norah's little sister.

My face lights up at seeing Lylahn, her long brown hair blowing back freely behind her, a full smile on her face. I didn't know she would be done helping to heal the wounded so early.

"She's right here." I walk toward her as quickly as I can. My sandals slip in the sand, making it twice the work. My heart starts to pound and pump harder within my chest. I slow down and reach within my satchel of sand. A soft glow emits from it as I Extract.

Lylahn grins and runs to me.

I catch her in my arms and spin her around. She throws her head back, laughing. I set her down, but she keeps her hands resting on my arms, and I keep my hands around her waist. A deep yearning stirs within me, and I glance from her eyes to her perfect lips.

"I thought Norah was going to try to Sustain your heart."

"She did." The familiar disappointment pricks at me, but it's faded to a soft poke instead of a jab. "She tried everything, but Sustaining couldn't cure me, either. I'm stuck with this heart, and so is To'Morat."

Hesitantly, Lylahn places one hand on my cheek. I close my eyes and lean into her touch.

"I'm sorry, Imwraeth. I wish I could—"

"Shhh," I cut her off, my eyes still closed, savoring this moment. "It's all right."

"But you've had to deal with this for so long. Maybe I can try again."

I open my eyes and smile at her. We hear shouts of people, To'Morat and To'Rahn together, calling that the ships are ready to set sail across the ocean of sand. "No. You've done all you can. There's nothing to be done."

Her eyes lower, and the hand that's been stroking my cheek falls. I catch it and press a kiss to her palm, hoping I haven't stepped too far. She blushes and smiles.

"My whole life, I wanted to have a healthy heart," I say. "I wanted to be able to run. I wanted to be able to drop this bag. But most of all, I wanted to be the strong leader my people need." Our eyes meet. "I can do that with the heart I have."

Lylahn's smile widens. "Yes. You can." She moves her hands from my arms to my shoulders, putting us closer together.

I'm pretty bad at this stuff, but I think that's permission.

I pull her close until her body fits to mine. My heart leaps in the best way possible. And then tenderly, slowly, I kiss her.

Her lips are soft and delicate. She sets me on fire as she presses into me. We kiss again and again, ever so soft. And then a little stronger. Her hand moves to the back of my head, her fingers tangling in my hair.

Everything I've endured, all the pain and hurt and longing, I would go through again if it led me to this.

I pull away just enough to whisper. "You're perfect, Lylahn Velare."

She smiles. "I'm yours, Imwraeth Jeriyah."

I hold her tighter and kiss her again.

51

ZADOCK

I wave goodbye to Norah once we reach my home. Er, well, the enormous mansion that I think is still my home, even though Potah is in prison now.

I watch Norah walk away, her back straight, her head held high. I can't help but smile. She heads for the southern grow walls, walking through streets now bursting with bushes and people collecting their bounty.

The plants still need her care. They grow best when she is Sustaining, using the sand to promote life and growth. She's still figuring out how it works, but I can't help but be impressed with how naturally all this has come to her.

Nothing like that initial burst of power has happened again. Whatever made all the plants grow at once, whatever brought me back from the brink of death, Norah hasn't been able to replicate. We don't know why, but I don't know if anyone should have that kind of power at their fingertips.

With a sigh, I turn back to my home and open the door.

Chassi bustles into the front entryway, dusting off my clothes and hanging my sand cloak on a coat rack despite my protests.

I pass the front steps that lead up to the rooftop garden. I walk through the dining room and kitchen. It's empty, so empty.

I miss him.

I head up the stairs to my enormous room, with the bed I still drown in and the armoire I still can't fill. I walk across the rug and sink down onto the bed. It feels like an eternity since I was here.

I retrieve a letter on my desk. I smile. In big, bold lettering across the front, it reads, "Zadock Penvaren, welcome to the Guild of Engineers!" When the designers and builders of To'Rahn saw my propeller boat and I showed them the bucket I had designed, it was a unanimous vote to take me in as an apprentice. I'll start tomorrow, and equal measures of nerves and excitement swirl in my stomach.

I'm really doing it.

A soft knock sounds at the door, and I sit up. Chassi just barges in, so it must be—

"Hello, son," Motah says in her quiet way as she pushes open the door. She stands, hands clasped together, shifting her weight. No teacup in sight. "May I come in?"

I nod, and she closes the door behind her. She takes the chair at my desk and adjusts her skirts. Motah pauses for a while before speaking. "I know things have been hard for you," she says. "I know how much you looked up to him."

"Yes."

Motah fiddles with the trim of her shawl. "I wanted to explain some things to you. I have been distant." She pauses. "When you were born, I loved you. I loved you right away." Motah's eyes fill with tears.

My mouth opens. I'm so shocked I don't know what to say.

"Your potah, he knew. He could see how my Shaking was affected. He could see the way I looked at you." Bitterness creeps into her voice. "He made me give you to the Ki'Rhen to raise, despite how I cried and pleaded. Despite how much it hurt. I knew I could never handle that kind of pain again. That's why I started drinking rathil tea...to prevent me ever conceiving again."

I blink. "Motah, I—"

"I watched you," she continues. "I watched you grow up and loved you from afar. I knew you were mine. When Faharic wanted to take you back, it felt too good to be true. So I stayed distant." Motah reaches out, pauses, and then puts one hand on top of mine. "I just wanted you to know how proud I am of you, my son. I'm so proud that you are mine. And I love you."

I swallow back a lump in my throat. "Thank you, Motah." I reach out slowly and take her hand.

5 2

NORAH

It's been over a moon cycle since the attack.

I stand atop the Atoille platform in the ceremony hall. I look out over the audience seats, filled with the people of To'Rahn. Their faces are smiling, beaming at me. Me! Especially Motah and Shrey. I remember the intense hurt I felt the last time I was here for the Anointing ceremony. The pain feels so distant now.

I turn back and meet the eyes of my beloved, Zadock Penvaren.

We're dressed in our white ceremonial Anointing robes, standing across from each other. The hall goes silent. Ki'Rhen Dalayn grins from ear to ear. She Shakes the sand, easily lifting the pitcher of Anointing water and setting it in place.

I smile at Saeri, and she winks at me from where she sits in the front row. Her happiness for me looks genuine.

Along with Motah, her potah was one of the most persuasive of the council members to argue for change, that people should be allowed to marry for love now that the sand gifts are so different. He even went as far as saying that the recent partnerships should be called off, that changes should be allowed to be made, that we should get to choose.

I can't help but think that Saeri was the driving force behind that, and I'm proud to have a friend like her. She liked Zadock, but I know she cares about me.

Zadock squeezes my hand and beams. His sandy hair is as messy as ever, and I love him for it. My heart is so full of joy I think it might burst.

Ki'Rhen Dalayn pours two drops of water onto our clasped hands. "Zadock Penvaren and Norah Saranyi, you are Anointed, to be partnered for life. The community of To'Rahn welcomes you into its arms."

Tenderly, Zadock unties the band from around my left arm and reties it onto my right. I do the same for him. Out of the corner of my eye, I see Motah, her face lit with a smile and tears in her eyes.

I look back into Zadock's eyes, and my heart soars. I can't believe it. I am partnered with my best friend, my whole heart. I didn't know a person could be so happy.

Zadock takes my hand and guides me from the platform. The crowd erupts in cheers.

"Well, my love," Zadock says, slipping an arm about my waist. "We've got somewhere to be."

☾

ZADOCK and I step to the edge of the plateau, hand in hand, looking out over the rolling waves of sand.

We've had word by sand gull from Imwraeth. The people are doing well under his rule with Lylahn by his side. Shreyen has already exchanged several letters with Kaera. Imwraeth's people are so grateful to him that they even had his name Forged into a pillar that is sacred to them. Zadock and I are thrilled for him, and especially for peace.

Though the harvest on To'Morat is improved, it's not enough. The people still need more food.

They need a Sustainer.

I close my eyes and place my hands into the sand at my feet near the rim of the plateau. It's so easy now. All I have to do is think of Zadock.

When I Sustain, it's like all the connections in the world are at my fingertips, and I can push them any way I like. I sense the roots of the plants beneath the soil, and I can urge them to grow. The clouds and sun and wind are within reach, and I can move them toward their destined path. The base of the plateau calls to me from deep underground, and I can shore it up to stay strong.

There's so much to explore with this new gift, and so many needs to be met. It's hard work, but every time I Sustain, I am filled with life and joy.

I dust the sand from my hands and stand. Before me, my new ship, commissioned and given to me by the council, is being loaded up for a journey. It's a large ship, beautiful, shining in the sunlight. She's got *Norah II* engraved on her side and a giant propeller attached to her stern. She's perfect.

Zadock and I and a small team have been commissioned by the council to travel the sands. We will help other plateaus rebuild and recover. We will make the world right.

I climb up the boarding plank and stand on the deck next to Zadock. "I wish that Potah were here for this."

"He would be so proud of you, Nors." Zadock slips an arm around my waist. "A month ago I swore I would never get on one of these again."

I smile. He dips me down low, and I cry out in laughter, but it's soon muffled by his tender kiss.

"Awwwww!" Shrey sighs and I look up in time to see her clasp her hands to the side. "Precious! I knew you were meant for each other. I just knew it."

Motah walks up behind Shrey. "We came to say goodbye."

I look at Motah.

And I smile.

There is no hurt. There is no anger. This past month has been perfect. We cooked together in the kitchen and laughed. We got out my old doll and played with Shrey. Peace has filled my home and the holes in my heart.

I run back down the loading plank and stoop to embrace Shrey. "I'm going to miss you."

"I love you, Norah!" Shrey bursts out. "Motah says I'm allowed to say that now."

I laugh and laugh. "I love you too."

Her face goes very serious, and she holds out her hand. Cactus needles.

"I've been collecting more. For good luck."

I put them in my pocket, then pat it to make sure it's closed. I'll have to put them somewhere else later so I don't get poked. "For good luck."

Zadock laughs behind me, chatting with one of the workers loading up supplies. I glance behind me and smile, sure that this moment could not get any more perfect.

Motah stands beside me. "You know, the famine started when your potah died. I've been thinking that that wasn't a coincidence. He loved you." She turns and meets my eyes. "That love must've made your gift work, even if just a little. When he was gone…I didn't fill that void." Motah hangs her head. "Norah, I'm—"

I grasp her hand, and she looks up. "Motah. You did what you thought was right. You just didn't know, none of us did. It's already forgiven." I give her hand a squeeze.

Motah smiles back, and her eyes fill with tears. "I'm so proud of you, my precious daughter." She wraps her arms around me, and I hug her back. "I love you, Norah."

☾

"Here we go!" I shout. The boat plummets off the edge of the plateau, and Zadock works with four other Shakers to catch the *Norah II* in a wave of sand. We set out across the desert.

The wind gusts and blows the hair out of my face, and I'm laughing and dancing across the deck. I don't think I've ever been so happy.

The boat lurches on a wave, and I fall into Zadock's arms. The *Norah II* is bigger than the original. She's got to be to carry so much cargo, and she requires Shakers and Extractors to steer her. They are working at the stern now, moving us across the waves. Zadock can take a break and be with me.

I smile and lean back into him. Zadock wraps his arms around me, and we stare out across the sand. It's beautiful, endless and orange, the waves spraying against the hull. A full Atoille hangs on the eastern horizon, and the stars are just beginning to glitter in the sky.

Zadock rests his chin on top of my head. The smell of him, the feel of him, is all around me, and I think I could stay like this forever. I close my eyes and just breathe.

"You, my wild girl, are perfect," Zadock says.

I turn around. His eyes meet mine, deep blue and sparkling like the starlit sky. He smiles. My heart leaps with joy.

Zadock Penvaren, my best friend turned love, is mine. He's really mine.

"Sometimes I still can't believe it's true," I say. "We're Anointed. It really happened."

Zadock smiles. "We're Anointed. You know what that means?"

"What?" I grin.

Zadock leans forward slightly and his grip around me tightens. "I get to do this as much as I want."

Our lips meet in a soft, perfect kiss. I move my hands up his back to bury my fingers in his hair. Our kisses become stronger, more urgent. My stomach flutters pleasantly, and I smile beneath his lips. I could care less that others may be watching. Let them. I've waited my entire life for this moment.

Everything. He is everything to me.

"I love you, Zadock Penvaren," I say. "Always."

EPILOGUE: NORAH

Two weeks later

We reached To'Morat quickly, thanks to Zadock's new propeller invention. A seven-day journey took us three. Ships are adopting it all throughout the desert. I can't help but feel a swell of pride every time I think of him, of all he's accomplished and the good he's doing.

I look over at him as I stand at the edge of the To'Morat plateau. The wind ruffles my short hair, which is growing long now. I need a cut soon. Zadock's showing some other To'Morat engineers how to build the propeller, and his design is getting more sophisticated. I smile.

I still can't believe it. We've been Anointed for two weeks, and I still get a little thrill every time I look at him. I'm his. He's mine. We'll get married in a few years to seal the Anointing, as is traditional. We'll have children together. We'll be allowed to love them. Maybe some of those children will even be Sustainers, and our world can continue to heal. I blush a little at the thought of having Zadock's children, and my stomach whirls, but not in an altogether bad way.

"Norah!" Lylahn calls. Imwraeth's hand is in hers. I'm happy for them, too, especially once I learned how much they both did to save To'Rahn. They hurry toward me, Lylahn smiling from ear to ear and Imwraeth's face red from the exertion. I tried to heal his heart. I don't know if Sustaining is even capable of healing like Absorbing is. I brought Zadock back from the brink of death in that initial burst of energy, but I haven't been able to replicate anything like that yet.

Imwraeth doesn't seem too worried about it, though. He puts a hand in the satchel of sand he carries, and a soft glow emits.

"Norah, you're needed," Imwraeth says. "I'll show you where our grow walls are. They're improving but could still use your attention. To'Morat has a lot of mouths to feed."

I meet his eyes, and, though he seems happy to be with Lylahn, I can see deep regret in them. An urgency to heal his plateau and his people. I know he's sorry for everything To'Morat has done. Imwraeth has been pushing me hard the past two days we've been here, leading me to grow walls and crop lands, pressing me to develop my gift even further. Sometimes the power comes effortlessly. Other times, it's like wading through wet sand, and I'm not sure why. Maybe I just need more practice.

I know why Imwraeth pushes me so hard. He wants more resources to help rebuild the plateaus that he ordered to be destroyed. I think he hopes to reestablish To'Shahera, where Lylahn is from, but I don't know if either of them should revisit that graveyard. But I keep my mouth shut. It's not like I'm an expert on relationships or anything.

"All right, I'll be right there. Just let me finish up here." I turn back to the plants I've been working on.

I feel life around me more and more, especially as I hone my sand gift. Sometimes I can sense the weather, and I know when rain or a sandstorm is going to come. But last week there was a sandstorm that no one predicted, and the plateaus still seem to be eroding too quickly. I have a lot more to learn and no one to teach me. It's frustrating, but I am hopeful. Things are already getting better.

There are bushels of bristlebrush fruits growing here with their spiny shells. In the initial burst of power that happened about a month and a half ago now, these bushes popped up, but they need more help to grow further. The fruits' growth is slowing, according to the To'Morat people. My presence helps with everything, but Sustaining directly can speed along the process even more.

The plan is to work our way through each of the plateaus. We'll keep traveling, Sustaining, and moving on, never staying in one place for too long. It's a dream come true for me. And the *Norah II* is speedy, thanks to Zadock, and a real ship. She's beautiful.

I put one hand on the bristlebrush leaves, careful to avoid the red fruit and the spines. I grab a handful of sand and Sustain. Love. It's easy now. I only have to look at Zadock.

The sand in my hand glows, and, like Extracting or Absorbing, it begins to dissipate, dissolved into energy. I can feel that energy coursing through me, filling me with joy.

I watch in wonder as the plant grows before my eyes. The leaves become larger, the green color deepens, and the fruits grow in size. I have to adjust my hand so I don't get poked, though Shrey would love it if I brought home a collection of spines and needles for her. By the time I've burned through the sand in my hand, the plant has grown about a foot taller, and the fruits are ready to be picked. Good. Sustaining is working well at this moment.

"Wow," Imwraeth says. His hand is still in Lylahn's.

"It's incredible, what you can do," Lylahn says. "I've never seen anything like it."

I smile at them, blushing a little. I'm not used to this kind of attention, to being recognized for a skill. I move on to the next plant.

Out of the corner of my eye, I see Zadock's face turn pale. He was talking to the engineers, but he goes silent. Their eyes, as one, look toward the sands.

I turn around and stand. What is happening?

It's a ship?

The biggest ship I've ever seen crashes through the waves. The design is unfamiliar to me. It's sleek and sharp, narrow in a way that's impractical for traveling across the desert. It's beautiful, built with shining black wood. The sides are inscribed with markings in a language I don't know, and the bottom and sides are crusted with rocks. Ridged rocks stuck to the sides of the boat?

The sails of the strange black ship are tan, with more of the odd markings written across the canvas, and they're big enough to block out the sun.

Where did this ship come from?

"What is that?" Imwraeth breathes.

Zadock comes to stand next to me. He puts a hand on my arm, his touch warm and comforting. "Who are these people? Norah, have you ever seen a ship like that?"

"No." I shake my head. "Never."

"Wherever they're from," Lylahn says, "it's not a plateau we know."

Imwraeth frowns and studies the ship. People around us stop what they're doing and gather in close. To'Morat warriors are already readying sand. It swirls through their fingertips.

No. Not more war.

"Maybe they're friendly," I say.

The ship rises to the level of the plateau, and I see the man standing at the helm. He has long black hair, down past his shoulders, whipping in the wind. His eyes are cold. There's something odd about them. My stomach sinks. The ship edges closer to the plateau, still floating on sand, and I can see his frozen stare. His eyes are white. Pure white. He has no pupils.

I gasp and bring a hand to my mouth.

He is lean and hard, with large black boots and leather clothes that match the color of his ship. A group of men and women dressed similarly congregate behind him, weapons strapped across their chests. Their eyes are all the same. White. Their skin is pale, unnaturally so. Blue veins swirl underneath the surface.

"He looks like he eats deathstalkers for breakfast," Zadock says.

I force out a laugh but dread wells up in my stomach. Who are these people, and why are they here?

The man's gaze roves over everyone gathered. He looks at me and stops. His eyes fixate on me. A chill snakes up and down my spine, even with the hot sun beating down. I try to meet that stare, but Atoille, it's hard. Everything within me is crawling right now, my body filling with adrenaline, preparing to run.

Imwraeth steps forward, and the man tears his gaze from me. "Welcome to To'Morat. I am Imwraeth Jeriyah, the Favored One of Atoille and leader of To'Morat. I'm afraid we do not recognize your sails. Where are you from? We would love to offer you all the hospitality To'Morat has to offer."

"He's brave," Zadock whispers to me. "I would not want them to stay on To'Rahn."

All I can do is nod. I can't tear my eyes away from this scene, can't shake the feeling that this is bad, bad, bad.

And that somehow, this has something to do with me.

"What may I call you?" Imwraeth asks when the man says nothing.

The man's voice comes out low and deep, in a strange accent I've never heard before. "My name is Agriad Zul. We come for her." He points at me.

My stomach sinks at the same time Zadock's grip squeezes my arm. "No!" he cries.

Imwraeth makes a placating gesture in Zadock's direction. Lylahn glances from the newcomers and back to Imwraeth.

"This woman is a visitor here and under my protection." Imwraeth gives a slight shake of his head. "I cannot allow you to take her."

The man seems to process this. People behind him on the ship murmur to each other. The ship floats suspended in sand on the edge of the plateau. They place their hands on their weapons.

This could get ugly fast.

Imwraeth whispers to Lylahn. "Go, get back up." She nods to him and turns to leave.

Lylahn takes one step away from the strange meeting, and I hear a zing. Zadock's hand darts out with sand, stopping something from hitting Lylahn.

It's a sharp piece of quartz, the length of my finger. A dart. My eyes go wide, and I glance back at the ship. One of the women behind Agriad lowers a blow gun from her lips.

So fast.

My breathing starts to come quicker. I don't have a spear on me. I only have Sustaining.

Lylahn freezes in place and inches her head back around. Zadock lets the dart fall.

Imwraeth turns on the newcomers, fire burning in his eyes. "You will not hurt my people, or I will be forced to take drastic actions."

Lylahn doesn't move. Imwraeth puts one hand on her arm.

Agriad sneers. "We have nothing to fear from you." More people behind him rise. All of them put blowguns to their mouths.

Zadock readies himself, sand swirling through his fingertips. Other warriors around us do the same. Extractors brandish spears.

Imwraeth holds up a hand. Everything is still. My heart thunders in my ribs.

"Norah, go," Zadock whispers. "Run. I will protect you."

"I'm not leaving you."

"Give us the girl," Agriad says, "and we'll be gone. You will never see us again." He speaks slowly, enunciating each word. He still leans against his ship in a casual, calculating pose. "We will go back across the ocean of water to where we came."

Zadock and I look at each other.

"The ocean of water?" I whisper.

"There is no way," Zadock says quietly. "No. They must be lying."

"Give us the girl," Agriad repeats.

"Not happening," Zadock says. "I will die before you take her."

"So be it." Agriad raises one arm. The blowers inhale.

"Wait!" Imwraeth cries.

For a space of a breath, the newcomers pause. Agriad holds.

"Why?" Imwraeth asks. "Why do you want her? Isn't there another arrangement we can reach?"

Agriad's face twists in anger. His eyes bleed from white to black. Pure black.

I take a step back, my breath catching.

"She did this." Agriad points behind him. His followers lower their blow guns, but only slightly. Their eyes change, too, from white to black. They part, making way for something.

"What is that?" Zadock whispers.

One of them steps forward, carrying a body. It's a girl, a young woman. Brown hair, a little longer than mine. Her eyes are vacant, staring forward, empty. Empty and white.

"What in Atoille's Hell?" Imwraeth breathes. Lylahn gasps, her hand flying to her mouth.

Horror. Horror engulfs me. My knees go weak, and I think I might fall. Zadock grips my arm.

The body.

It's me.

AUTHOR'S NOTE

Thank you so much for going on this journey with me! Hugs all around!

I hope you enjoyed Oceans of Sand. Let me know what you thought. I would love to connect with you on my website, https://www.jessicaflory.com/. You can sign up for my newsletter there and be the first to know about all my books, giveaways, book signings, and more. You can also join me on Facebook, Twitter, Instagram, or TikTok with the handle jessicafloryauthor.

It would mean so much to me if you'd leave a review of Oceans of Sand on Amazon, Goodreads, or any other social media outlets you use. It doesn't have to be eloquent or long; even a simple review does so much to help an author out!

Thank you again. I think you're specking great.

ACKNOWLEDGMENTS

So much goes into a book, and I have so many people to thank for making Oceans of Sand a reality. It's a dream come true that you are holding this book in your hands right now.

First off, thank you to my incredible husband, Devin. You are the love of my life and my biggest support and cheerleader. Thank you for watching the kids so I could pound through the ending and deadlines. Thank you, not least of all, for that surprise ticket to LTUE where I pitched this book to Immortal Works and got my contract! This dream is coming true because of your unwavering support and love.

SO MANY thanks to Lindsay Flanagan, the best editor I could ever ask for. You made Oceans of Sand sparkle, took it from good to great. Thank you for your tireless work and support... and for putting up with my overuse of ellipses.

GINORMOUS thank you to the best writing group ever, the Hot Mess Critique Group. Tracy Daley, Valerie Doll, Patrice Hale, Heidi Rogers, Jordan Wright, David Munk, and Tamara Bailey, Oceans of Sand would not be the same without you. (For starters, Kaera would not exist and Zadock's life would've been a lot easier. Patrice, sole credit for the giant deathstalker goes to you.) Thank you for cheering me on throughout the years, crying and laughing with me on Marco Polo, get-togethers at Aubergine, and your friendship. Some of you I have never met in person, and I still consider you among my best friends. Thank you.

Thank you to Ruth Mitchell for hour long discussions on marketing. They were immensely helpful.

Thank you to Holli Andersen, Jason King, and the whole team at Immortal Works. I feel so lucky to have been able to work with all of you.

Thank you to Janette Rallison for support, guidance, and marketing know-how. You are an incredible author, and I appreciate you so much for showing me the ropes!

Thank you to Brandon Sanderson. Not only are you my writing hero and the author I hope one day to be (ok, I'll stop fan-girling), but you are also an incredible writing teacher and just a great guy overall. Thanks for helping out us newer authors and for writing books that keep me up way too late.

Brian Hailes, you are a boss. Thank you for the most gorgeous cover art I have ever seen. It takes my breath away every time I look at it. I can't thank you enough for bringing my vision to life. There are no words.

Spencer Quinn, thank you for your marketing expertise and answering my non-stop questions. You are a business warrior.

Thank you to Traci and Cory Jensen, the best parents in this or any other world. I love you. I appreciate you so much. You read my first stories (sorry about that), and made me believe that I could do anything. Thank you.

Last, thank you to my angels—Sam, Grant, Owen, and Gwen. Sammy, if you had a sand gift it would totally be Forging. The things you build and create always astound me. Grant, you would be my Absorber. You've got a healer's heart. Owen, your gift would hands-down be Extracting, though you've already got plenty of energy. And Gwen, you would be a Shaker, but you don't need sand to wrap me around your finger. Devin, my wonderful husband, you get to be the Sustainer of the family, because even when these kids suck the life out of me you are there to pump it back in.

I love you, little stinkers. Thank you for being mine.

ABOUT THE AUTHOR

Jessica Flory has a bachelor's degree in Molecular Biology from BYU, Provo, and she uses that science background to dream up cool settings and magic systems. Jessica has been a proud member of the Hot Mess Writers Critique Group since 2013.

Jessica is a mom of three crazy boys and one girl, a fitness instructor, and an avid baker. When she's not writing, she can be found chasing her kids, making a mess in the kitchen, or reading with her husband. Connect with her at jessicaflory.com.

This has been an
Immortal Production